Find Me

SHELLEY K. WALL

author of *Text Me*

CRIMSON
ROMANCE

F+W Media, Inc.

Published by
Crimson Romance
an imprint of F+W Media, Inc.
10151 Carver Road, Suite 200
Blue Ash, OH 45242. U.S.A.
www.crimsonromance.com

ISBN 10: 1-4405-8399-4
ISBN 13: 978-1-4405-8399-5
eISBN 10: 1-4405-8400-1
eISBN 13: 978-1-4405-8400-8

Chapter One

Amanda Gillespie wasn't about to let the bile in her stomach keep her from showing up at the damn outdoor adventure club meeting. It was just nerves. She could do this. *Had* to do this, since she'd stupidly, irresponsibly taken her friend Darlene's bet that she wouldn't. Now five hundred bucks hung in the balance.

She smoothed her skirt and shoved through the door of the beautiful eighty-story Darshwin Tower, wishing she'd gone home to change clothes after work. But that would have made her late to the meeting, and there was no way in hell Darlene was going to give her peace if that happened.

Darlene Fitch was a bulldog both in reputation and stature. Though small, her mind was a flytrap of details that made her one of the best criminal attorneys in the state of Texas. Amanda strived to be half as good. Darlene had a ten-year start on her, so maybe in time she'd get there. The woman was also faultlessly protective of her friends—not in a motherly way, but in an in-your-face, don't-fuck-with-my-friend way.

Why Darlene had turned Amanda into a pet project was a mystery.

"You're such a workaholic pansy. Just enjoy yourself—have fun for a change," Darlene had tossed at her after they'd finished eating lunch over legal briefs a week earlier.

"I am *not*. I have fun."

"Really? Prove it. When's the last time you did anything that didn't have a roof and an air conditioner involved? Or traded those heels for a pair of sneakers, for that matter?"

Amanda sighed. "Okay, so maybe I prefer to be clean and... and I have allergies."

Darlene rolled her eyes. "Oh, brother. To what? A good time? Amanda Gillespie, we're going to get your blood pumping if it kills us. Or maybe just you. I'm too young to die. Besides, how are you ever going to date someone who doesn't have their nose in legal briefs if you don't leave the office?"

"Maybe I like briefs."

Darlene giggled. "I like briefs too—or boxers—or nothing at all. They're all good. Listen, we all know you can kick ass as a lawyer but can you do it outside in the fresh air? I highly doubt it. I think you're a born and bred book-addicted *nerd.*"

That was the challenge that took her over the top. Competitiveness was bred deep in the Gillespie family and challenges of any sort rarely went unanswered. That was what happened when you grew up in a household with two older brothers. Everything was a contest. Amanda took the bait, and agreed to Darlene's bet proposal: Whoever did better on two out of the three challenges would win. Now she was regretting it.

Amanda clip-clopped on high heels toward the elevator bank and her cell phone rang. She glanced at the display, then snapped it to her ear. "What? You're checking up on me? I'm at the elevator, Give me five minutes."

Darlene laughed. "Cluck, cluck, cluck, cluck …"

Is she really insinuating I'm chicken? "Oh, stop. I'll be there before you can find your next client."

Sure, it was a jab to mention Darlene's ambulance chasing but the woman actually admitted to perusing the daily paper for victims. Er, clients. Amanda strung the strap of her briefcase over her shoulder and sandwiched the phone above it between her ear and the shoulder pad of her suit. With her other hand, she unknotted her scarf, slipped two buttons of her silk shirt open, and let out a sigh. "You could have picked something a little closer to the office, you know. I had to practically jog in these damned heels. I think I have a blister."

"You should carry loafers like I do. Hurry up. The instructor is tall, tanned, and tight-ass free, something we rarely meet…uh, oh. I think he heard me. Gotta go."

Amanda grinned as the phone went silent. For a woman with a stellar legal career, Darlene despised attorneys—a.k.a. tight-asses—and had a strict rule about dating them. The irony of her choosing not to date someone of her own species apparently escaped her brilliant brain. But, based on the few single attorneys Amanda knew, Darlene wasn't all wrong.

Amanda punched the elevator button and stepped into the first one that opened. Five hundred bucks was a lot of money, and she planned to win. Neither of the women was athletic, but Amanda was pretty sure she could handle herself well enough to best her friend. Betting she could beat Darlene in a couple of outdoor activities seemed an easy win.

· · ·

For Jackson Holstenar, the elevator was a fundamental part of life. It was how he traveled to the gym on the top floor of the building, to his friend Carter's office, to his father's office, to his own office. Though his berth could hardly be called an office. His choice. His father wanted him upstairs with the bigwigs, but Jackson preferred to pay his dues like all the other new staff.

He waited for the doors to open. Carter had wanted to talk about his new project before the weekend adventure seekers group. Ever since Jackson had accidently gotten Carter fired, he felt guilty and listened patiently to Carter's work stories. The firing had been unintentional—Jackson had mouthed off at a project manager because he and their friend Roger wanted to set them up. She hadn't liked the comments and blew a gasket before complaining to Carter's management team. Carter had taken the heat because

Jackson's dad just ignored the complaint. Carter's new job seemed to fit better, so it wasn't a complete loss.

Jackson's phone signaled a text message from Carter. *Let's just talk after the group meeting. I'm already there.*

Ding.

The doors slipped open. He smelled oranges. *That* brought back memories. He glanced over at the tall blonde with her hair sleeked into a gold barrette. Was he hallucinating? It had been eighteen months since he'd seen Amanda Gillespie. He stuck an arm out as the doors started closing, then stepped into the elevator. No, it was her.

Could he really have missed her annoying perfume?

"Amanda?"

The woman in the peach twill suit stopped fumbling with her bag and popped her head up, her sea-blue eyes widening like portholes on a Caribbean cruise ship.

"Oh my God. Jackson! What are you doing here?"

His throat threatened to choke back his words and he swallowed. "I'm meeting a friend in a few minutes upstairs. What about you?"

Amanda slicked a hand over her hair. "Me too. Sort of. I'm a little late actually. Work. You know."

Was that supposed to mean he knew how harried her new job was? He didn't. Not anymore. Not since she'd quit working at his dad's office and sneaked out without even saying goodbye.

He still felt the sting. "Work. Of course."

Jackson focused on the lit elevator panel and the soft sounds as they moved higher. The seconds it took to rise to his floor seemed like hours. A thousand questions fogged his brain but he wouldn't ask any of them. Nope. She'd run out without telling a soul because that was what she wanted. No explanation. No apology. And no indication of where she'd be in the future. She ran *away.* From their work relationship and their friendship. Hell—she'd fallen off the planet.

Jackson sure as hell wasn't going to ask why. Not now. When the doors opened, he motioned for her to lead and followed her down the hall—to the same door he sought. Should he turn around and leave? Admittedly, seeing her brought mixed emotions—shitty and relieved ones. Did he really want to deal with that? He couldn't abandon Carter. They'd been friends forever and hadn't seen each other in a while.

"You're going here too?" Amanda frowned. Apparently she wasn't all that excited about seeing him either.

He nodded. "I had no idea you were into this kind of thing." The only athletic thing he'd seen her do was jog and that was only one time when she'd been trying to catch a bus. Still, based on the muscle tone in her legs, she didn't spend all her time on a sofa

"I'm not. My friend Darlene bet me five hundred bucks that I couldn't do at least two of the three challenges better than she did. Apparently I don't have an adventurous bone in my body. But since neither of us has done anything like this, I figured my size would give me an advantage. I'm five inches taller and have not only the height advantage but longer legs."

Inside the room, voices tumbled excitedly over the wild beat of some sort of retro music. Jackson couldn't place the band but he felt the energy.

"Hey! There you are." Carter rushed forward and circled an arm over Jackson's shoulder, then scooped Amanda in as well. What the hell?

Carter kissed her on the cheek and Jackson could tell he'd had a beer before showing up, maybe two. He was relaxed. Loose. Not his normal tight-wound demeanor. "So, this is your new girlfriend, Jax? Wow. She's gorgeous."

Amanda pulled free and frowned. "Um, hell no, I'm not with *him*. I'm with *them*." She pointed across the room where two women beckoned for her to join. "Good luck with that new girlfriend, *Jax*." Amanda's tight business skirt snapped as she clipped away.

Carter coughed. "Wow, should have known you'd never score a chick like that. What was I thinking? So, where is the new love?"

Jackson shrugged. "Gone. We stopped dating a couple weeks ago. She wanted serious and I wanted anything but. So, what d'ya think about this shindig?" The two men strode to the nearest chairs and plopped down. It felt good to sit and stretch a bit.

The instructor, who called himself a *coordinator*, introduced the other organizers and outlined their first three outings. All three were mild for Jackson's taste: a hike through the canyon near Fredericksburg, zip lining above the trees near the lake, and a mud run obstacle course. Easy-peasy.

Jackson was tired and figured he'd listened attentively enough so he searched the room. For Amanda.

"Introduce me."

"What?" Jackson returned his thoughts to Carter and the group surrounding him.

"Introduce me to that girl you came in with. You obviously know her."

"She came up the elevator with me."

"Yeah, saw that…but you know her, right?"

"Sort of. She used to work with me. She left a year and a half ago."

"Good, then you'll make a great wing man. Let's go." Carter yanked Jackson's sleeve and slid from his chair.

Jackson cringed. "You really don't want to know this one, Carter. She's…high maintenance."

Carter punched Jackson's arm. "She can't be all bad if she showed up for this club. You're the one who said I should get out there and meet someone. Besides, I had a great week. I'm on a roll. This might be good."

Yeah, but roll somewhere else, man. Not toward her. Jackson pushed out of his cushy comfortable chair. Perfect. He was introducing his best friend to the one girl who was off limits—for him, and everyone else. She kept everyone in the "friendship" category, which was where she'd shoved him years ago when they were classmates.

As they strode toward the women, Amanda met his gaze. Jackson held onto her eyes like they were liquid gold. How should he do this? Her friend swiveled to look over her shoulder and gasped. "Well, aren't you a tall thing? You look like you could shimmy through that obstacle course like nobody's business and come out slathered with mud in all the right places."

Jackson blinked. Her friend was giving him the once-over. "And I bet you'd make mud-wrestling an art form. This is Carter Coben." He waved a hand at his best friend who completely honed in on Amanda. "And I'm Jackson." He offered a hand to the shorter woman.

"Darlene. And this is Amanda." The two were as opposite as night and day and appeared significantly different in age as well. Amanda had to be significantly younger. How'd they ever become friends? "We're attorneys over at—"

Oh, of course. Darlene the Bulldog. He'd seen her ads. "I recognize you now, though you should sue your marketing group. Those ads don't do you justice."

Darlene giggled and put a hand to her throat. Jackson let the smile on his face go dead as Carter wedged between them and sat next to Amanda. Carter put a hand on his leg and flexed his bicep, his signature move. Jackson rolled his eyes.

"You ladies like to do these things a lot?" Carter asked.

Carter had made one small error in his move: He'd left a comfortable amount of personal space between himself and Amanda. Jackson flopped down between them and threw his arms behind their chairs. "Don't kid yourself, Carter. Amanda here won't even step in a rain puddle, let alone do a mud run. And I'd bet the only thing she's climbed or hiked lately is the Galleria Mall when there's a shoe sale. Right, Mandy?"

Jackson noticed her pink cheeks and the flash of fire that swept through her baby-blues. She clucked and tapped a palm to his face. "Oh, Jax. It's so nice to see you throwing your typical childish bullshit insults again. Don't you think you're a little old for that?"

Darlene's mouth dropped. "You guys know each other?"

Amanda huffed. "No."

It came in unison with Jackson's "Yes." He grinned.

"Figures," Darlene said. "I'm always late to the party."

Amanda sighed. "Jackson's an attorney, too. We worked together very briefly."

Jackson cocked his head sideways. "Yes, *briefly*. Why is that, Amanda? Why so briefly?"

The crowd had begun to disperse as people signed up for whatever events they chose then gathered belongings and left. Amanda stood and thumbed at the lists, ignoring his jab. "Gotta go, gentlemen. I have money to win and work to get back to. Nice meeting you, Carter." She waved, then cast a hate glare Jackson's way before striding off. Her friend Darlene followed after tossing him a quick wink.

Carter frowned. "That went well. You could have at least tried to be civil long enough to give me a shot."

Jackson shrugged and pointed at the wall of paper with scribbled names. "You don't need my help. This one's a no-brainer. Go look at what she's signed up for and put your name on the same list."

Revelation crossed his features. "Think I will."

Once Carter left, Jackson followed his own advice and added his name to the lists as well. No sense in letting Carter get kicked around without his wing man.

...

The following Sunday afternoon, Jackson stood by his Jeep, sipping cold coffee and watching Amanda's tight shorts rise up her ass while she lifted gear from the back of an SUV. Great way to start the day. He leaned against the hood, crossed his legs, and took another sip. "Need some help with that?"

She lowered the box onto the ground and glared at him. *Hmmm. Nice to see you too.* She tossed her hair back and returned to digging through the trunk.

Jackson tossed the paper cup in the trash bin beside his car, then strode her way. "Guess you didn't hear me. Do you—"

"I heard you. I just didn't answer. If I needed help, I'd ask for it. Okay?"

Carter shoved in front, scooped the box from the dirt, and pulled a bag from her hands. "What kind of guy lets a woman carry heavy boxes while he's empty handed? Come on, the group's already starting toward the trailhead. Are you planning to take all of this on the hike?"

Amanda opened her mouth to protest, then stopped. She gave Carter one of those dazzling smiles and Jackson cringed. He remembered how many times she'd used that look with him. It had caught his breath on occasion but he shrugged it off as hormones—or maybe just hadn't understood. Carter stopped for a second. Yep, that look went straight to the man parts and his friend wasn't immune, damn him. It wasn't jealousy seething through Jackson's skin. Amanda was like a sister. Okay, she *had* kissed him a little too passionately one night in law school when they were both drunk. *That* had stunned him, coming from her. Still, she deserved better and he'd managed to keep the losers away before. But Carter? He wasn't a loser. So why the hell did the fact that it was Carter bother him more? "That's sweet of you. No, I just wanted to put the drinks in the coolers for the after-party.

John, the organizer, said we could drop them off at the starting point. Do you mind carrying them that far?"

Carter winked and threw the box onto his shoulder. "Piece of cake. You look amazing, by the way."

Amanda slammed her trunk closed and dropped a hand into the pocket of her tight cargo shorts. She shot Carter another megawatt smile. "Thanks. I wasn't really sure what was appropriate for this kind of thing."

Jackson felt his face flush. Seriously? She was flirting?

Steam started to rise from his already sweating forehead. Couldn't she see what an idiot/asshole Carter was? Surely Jackson wasn't the only person to notice his complete lack of personality. Sure, they were best friends but friends know each other's faults best.

Amanda tucked a hand into Carter's arm and walked alongside as he toted her things.

At the trail head, the organizer handed out maps to everyone, then told them to be back at five. "The sun goes down at six so if we don't have a full headcount at five fifteen, we'll send out a search party." The man laughed, then waved his hands like Moses sending his flock into the ship, two by two. Carter dropped into step by Amanda and her friend. It was a dumb move since the path wasn't wide enough. Then Jackson had a thought.

He and Carter had competed in almost everything since they were kids. Technically it started right after Carter's sister died but he never brought up specific dates. Carter was strong and built like a college quarterback. He worked hard to stay fit and hated that Jackson's natural athleticism often beat out his own work ethic. Jackson sidled up to his friend. "Have you looked at the map yet?"

Carter glinted into the sun above Jackson's head. "No, why?"

Jackson unfolded the paper. "There are four trails. Each one is different and they're classified by difficulty. Let's take this one here and first one to the summit buys the other a beer."

Carter glanced at the map. "You do realize that the drinks in the cooler are free and they have beer, water, and juices? Technically, we're not buying anything."

Jackson slapped Carter on the back. "Such a smart ass. Okay, then first one up to the summit and back wins. That means the first to reach that cooler full of drinks."

Carter's eyes flickered with interest. "What do I win?"

"Assuming you actually make it down first, you win…I don't know. What about …"

Amanda twisted the cap off a water bottle with a click. "Skinny dipping in the river behind those trees while the rest of us cook and clean up."

Gulp. Jackson leaned into her ear and whispered, "Would that be with or without you?"

Her hair whipped his cheek as she stepped into a power walk. She glanced over her shoulder. "Without. This isn't a team event. See you in my dust, Jax."

Hmm. That idea backfired. Beating Carter would be easy; the guy never bested him at anything. Beating Amanda, though? He could do it but she might hate him even more.

Four more steps and she vanished into the trees. The image of Amanda skinny dipping stopped him dead for a couple of seconds. Long enough for Carter to dart past and disappear behind her. Oh, hell no. If anyone was going to be in that ice-cold, fish-infested water with—or just watching—Amanda, it wasn't going to be Carter.

Jackson took off at a trot. It took him about five minutes to catch Carter. He yanked him by the neck and shoved him into the trees before focusing on the back pockets of Amanda's shorts. Thank God she hadn't seen his strong-arming. Carter rustled out of the undergrowth. "Hey, asshole. You're dead meat."

Jackson picked up his pace. Amanda was about fifteen yards ahead. Unfortunately, the path tilted upward. Her calves tightened and bulged as she stair-stepped up and over rocks. Jackson followed suit. Long legs were a distinct advantage when it came to rugged terrain. Within minutes, he was behind Amanda. He glanced upward at the rocks and pine needles, seeking a solid footing so he could make his move. He dug into the pebbled dirt with his toes and lunged forward.

A vise grip clamped around his ankle and killed his forward movement. What the hell? Jackson teetered and fell to a knee. Below him Carter cursed and held tight to his other leg. Jackson kicked. "Let go before we both roll down the hill."

"Nope. You're going down."

"Like hell." Jackson kicked again. The movement caused him to lose his footing. He hit the dirt like a sack of potatoes, mashing his face into the side of the rock-covered hill, and his left cheek banged against a hard stone. Shit, that stung. His eyes watered.

Carter let out an evil laugh and dug a hiking boot into his back as he stepped over him to catch Amanda.

"Son of a bitch." Jackson felt his eye. The skin below was puffing up into a healthy bruise. He ran a hand over his spine. "I think I slipped a disk, you fat-ass."

Carter climbed up the hill. "Jax, you're a pussy."

A pussy? Yeah, right. That came from the guy who has yet to beat me in a sport other than pool. Jackson pushed off the ground and lunged forward. It took four long steps to reach Carter. Jackson dove on Carter's back, wrapping him up in an old-fashioned football tackle. Both men went down with a thud, cavorting in a barrel roll.

"Hey!" They jolted around at the sound of Amanda's voice. She speared a finger at them—or just behind. "Look, you Neanderthals."

Jackson felt a cool breeze of air. He glanced over his shoulder. *Holy shit.* He was two inches from rolling off the path's edge, right into the tree tops ten feet below. Maybe not certain death but definitely serious injury-bound. "Oh, thanks."

Carter fisted Jackson's shirt and rolled his body to safety. Crawling to a knee, he gave a final shove to Jackson's chest and stood. "Grow up."

Jackson wanted to throw a retort but knew it would be equally juvenile to respond. He simply rose and dusted himself of debris while Carter joined Amanda, both leaving him standing like a ten-year-old caught playing in the mud before church. He wondered briefly where her friend Darlene had gone. Had she seen their wrestling match also?

Feeling chastised, he stood still and enjoyed the sun and scenery a moment before following. They crested the hill a few minutes later and took a different route to the bottom. Jackson pulled the map from his pocket, searching for a way to bypass them and win the challenge.

If he took the second trail to the left, he'd gain a quarter mile over the others. It looked steeper and he'd have to ford the water in the creek to beat them. *Wait.* The creek. Where Amanda *or* Carter would be skinny-dipping and soaking their tired legs if they won. He decided not to try to win the challenge after all. He grinned and hoped his timing would be impeccable.

The trees were shrouded in near-darkness when he finally reached an outcropping of rocks that smelled of damp moss and leaves. Eureka. Water spilled over the stones into a pool less than five feet below, then moved lazily down the river. The top of a head glistened, shiny and wet. From between the stones it was impossible to identify whether Carter or Amanda had won the bet but his money was on Carter. He seriously doubted anyone could outrun the former track star and health nut. Except himself, of course.

Jackson shucked his shorts and shirt, peeled off skivvies and shoes, and launched into a cannonball. He grabbed his knees, unworried about the water depth. They'd swam here as kids. It was safe. "Incoming!" His voice echoed off trees and hillside—along with the corresponding high-pitched scream.

Of Amanda's naked friend, Darlene. Shit.

Don't look, asshole. What an idiot idea.

When Jackson rose to the surface, he blinked twice and focused on the bank as he scrambled toward anonymity. Above he saw three sets of legs, two male and one female. Carter, the club organizer whose name escaped him, and Amanda.

"What the fuck, Jackson?" Carter frowned.

Darlene glided to the far side of the stream, then plunged behind an outcropping of granite that rose to make a great sunbathing ledge or hiding spot. She laughed. "Look, cowboy, as much as I like your company, give me a warning next time, okay? I'll skinny-dip with you any day but you scared the shit out of me."

Amanda plopped her hands on hips, chewing a wad of gum. Her eyes volleyed between Jackson and Darlene. Without a word, she threw her gaze toward the treetops and stomped away.

Chapter Two

A month later, Jackson still burned when he thought of that night. Carter had taken advantage of Jackson's screw-up. He'd thrown the charm on with Amanda and never left her side, the bastard. For the first time in his life, Jackson wanted to beat the shit out of the guy. It didn't matter that Carter was the only person who'd given a crap about him as a kid. Nor did it matter that they'd always been a bit competitive. This was more than that.

Or was it?

It wasn't like he'd ever dated Amanda. In truth, they'd been together a lot but never in any sort of romantic way. It wasn't until things got really crazy at work that he had even given a single thought to taking their friendship down that path. If she hadn't packed it up and ran for the hills a year ago, he probably would have asked her out. Most likely they'd have dated a short while and then moved on. End of story. He'd have put it behind him and still have his brains intact.

Now you're thumbing Carter's number every few days and listening in agony while he details their budding relationship. Shit. Like he wanted to hear *that.*

Carter's voice on the phone yanked Jackson back to reality. "It's been a little over a month."

"Wow, that's a record for you."

"I know. Think we should celebrate, or would that be a little too creepy?"

Jackson fumed but kept his voice calm. "Probably creepy. Wait at least another month or two. Changing the subject here—congrats on your project. I heard the board approved for you to take the lead on this one. I'll be in on it too as far as the partnership is concerned." Jackson had lobbied for the companies to do the deal together because he thought it'd be fun to work with his buddy. That was before Carter and Amanda got involved. Now he wished he'd left it alone. Real-estate developers were a dime a dozen and someone else would have snapped up the chance.

"Thanks, man. We're celebrating Friday after work. Want to join us? We're going to the Top Shelf Bar."

Did he really want to endure seeing more of her—with him? No.

"Sure, what time?"

•••

Jackson Holstenar had a knack for making rumpled shirts and khakis look like an Armani suit. Putting the straw of her drink to her lips, she watched him approach while she peered over Carter's shoulder. Two other women followed his steps with their eyes as well. No surprise there; he'd always managed to draw a fan club.

Returning her focus to Carter, she pasted on a smile. "Carter, want another drink? I'm going for a refill."

Carter dropped a kiss to her cheek. "Sure, I have a tab open so just add on. Everything okay? You seem a little distant."

She nodded. "Fine. Just a big day. Some contract issues with a client." *And I want to avoid Jackson before he gets any closer.*

Jackson's eyes locked on hers for a second. Was he pissed? She could swear there was anger in the depths of his pupils. She tapped Carter on the cheek, then turned and headed for the bar.

Why did Jackson get to her? They were friends. Just friends. She'd watched him date more than a handful of women. Correction: bimbos. Why did a man with a good brain go for that type? It made no sense at all. Or maybe it did. He was smart, talented. That was the catch. Perhaps it was a relief for him not to deal with the constant debates and depth of conversation that they'd had together. He liked the stress-free adoration of clingy and noncommittal bar hoppers. Like the one who'd boldly attached herself to him while Amanda waited for the drink order. That hadn't taken long.

She turned back to the bar and snagged an olive from the bartender's stash when he wasn't looking. Seconds later, the drinks she ordered arrived and she carried them to the booth where Carter and Jackson had moved to.

Great. Jackson's new pick-up girl was in the booth.

Carter stood and waited for Amanda to slip onto the vinyl cushions right next to pick-up girl, who introduced herself as Tammy.

Amanda sucked on her straw. "So, Carter, where'd you and Jackson meet each other?"

Carter's focus was on the television over the bar as ESPN highlights displayed with the trailers scrolling across underneath. "We grew up together. He moved into a house down the street when I was a kid. I lost touch with him when we graduated. We went separate ways to college. When I landed here afterward, I called him up and we started hanging out again. Why do you ask?"

She shrugged. "No reason. I just wondered."

Carter put a hand on her neck and rubbed his fingers along the pulse point, which felt great because she was incredibly taut from work stress. "He's a good guy. Right, Jax?"

Jax raised his glass in agreement but said nothing. The daggers in his eyes were quite impressively explanatory. He hated her.

Carter continued to knead the tension from her shoulders. "Tough day today?"

Amanda closed her eyes and let herself revel in the feel of his fingers on her neck. Tough? Hmm. A multimillion-dollar deal nearly failed because one of the partners didn't like their percentage of ownership. The boss's wife stormed in and ranted because he had disappeared from the office—and apparently their house the night before. And Amanda was sitting in a booth with Carter while he rubbed her neck—and all she could think about was his asshole friend and the girl beside him. "Yeah."

When Carter's hands no longer kneaded her neck, Amanda reluctantly slid her eyes open. She waited for the room to come back into focus. Bam. *Why the hell is Jackson staring at me?*

"That was great, Carter. You have amazing hands. I see a couple of friends from work over in the corner. Mind if I say hello?"

"No problem. Go ahead." He stood and Amanda extricated herself from the booth and maneuvered through the bar. It was a good excuse to escape the man-cave atmosphere that had become stifling when Jackson arrived. The last thing she needed was work talk with people she spent most of her day around, but Darlene was different. She had somehow mastered the work/life balance thing.

"Is the hottie you're with the same guy I played outdoor-bathtub around last month?" Darlene asked.

Hmm. Honesty might be a bad idea. Would Darlene be embarrassed they'd both seen her bare ass? "Which one?"

Darlene did one of her annoying laughs that ended with a snort. Amanda had been around her long enough to find it a little endearing, like a period on a sentence. "Good point. They're both hotties. I'd cross the street to talk to 'em. Which one are ya banging?"

"Um, I'm *dating* Carter, the one on the end, but we're not—"

"Great, then you won't mind if I talk to Tall and Lanky, would ya?" They both glanced at the booth where Jackson and Carter were glued to the television over the bar. The party girl next to Jackson was intently thrusting her fingers between the buttons of his shirt, attempting to wrangle his focus her way.

Amanda smiled. "He looks a little preoccupied at the moment."

"Yeah, but guys like him find that kind of trailer trash bothersome. She'll be gone in five, four, three, two…see, what'd I tell ya?"

Across the room, Jackson untangled the woman's hand from his shirt and shoved his way from the booth. He strode to the bar, empty glass in hand, and ordered a drink, then dropped to a bar stool and continued to watch the game.

Darlene adjusted her navy business suit over her shoulders. While not the tallest person, she still had a nice look that men noticed. Or at least the guy at the table behind them had when she smoothed the tight skirt down her ass. Darlene grabbed Amanda's forearm and pulled her toward the bar. "Introduce me, blondie."

"You already met him, you don't need me for—Jackson, you remember Darlene, one of our partners?"

Jackson peered over a shoulder with a beer bottle to his lips. "You look a little different in clothes."

Darlene's face went crimson. Was she searching for an exit? Two seconds passed, then she extended a manicured hand. 'So you have a law degree, too? What's your specialty?"

Jackson slid to face them on his stool, his lanky legs almost touching Amanda's knee. "Yeah. Amanda didn't tell you? We went to school together, studied together for the bar. Spent a lot of late nights over law journals, beer, and chips. Then when she graduated, we both ended up at my dad's firm. Me, because I had no choice. Her, because I told her to apply if she couldn't find anything else. Jobs were tough for new grads. We worked together on a couple of contract things. Didn't we, Mandy?"

Darlene crooked a brow. "Mandy? He calls you that? So you and Jackson—?"

Amanda huffed. "No, Jackson and I didn't…weren't…Don't call me Mandy, Jax. You know I hate nicknames."

"Like Jax. Right. Yeah, you're too big-time for that, aren't you? You with your designer suits and silk shirts."

"Blouses."

"Does it matter?" He stood abruptly, beer in hand, and his fingers nearly grazed the silk he'd insulted. Amanda sucked in a breath. She should step back and give him room, but—God, he smelled good. She'd missed that.

Darlene shrugged. "I can see you two have things to talk about. Nice to meet you, Jackson. I guess I'll see you again soon."

Amanda retreated a step, ready to follow Darlene.

"There you go again. Running away without a word. No goodbye, no 'kiss my ass,' not even a 'have a nice life.' Just rip a guy's heart out and dance off to your next victim. Do me a favor and don't be quite as harsh with Carter. He's been through a lot and doesn't need your shit." Jackson lifted his beer to his lips and drew in another sip. They were spatting like a couple of high schoolers.

"I wasn't running, and I didn't rip anyone's heart out. That's ridiculous. I doubt anyone missed me at all." Okay, maybe she had run but it wasn't like she'd had a choice at the time. Her supervisor had made it very clear she wasn't wanted and would be terminated if she stayed. No hearts involved—not even close.

"You think not?" Jackson swallowed the last of his beer, thunked the bottle on the bar, and strolled back toward Carter.

What the hell did that mean? He missed her? No way, they'd only been friends in college and coworkers for a brief moment. Nothing else. They'd laughed and had a few drinks after work but not once had they ever—

Okay, maybe once. Her thoughts went back to the day she'd passed the bar exam. The memory still brought warmth to her girly parts. They'd only kissed out of celebration and as much as she'd enjoyed it, it never happened again. Not once in the months they worked together. While she'd thought it amazing and slightly life-altering, obviously his perception was different—something he didn't want to repeat.

Carter beckoned her to join him, and Amanda worked herself back into the booth between the two gorgeous men, making every woman in the place envious. All she wanted to do was run but she managed to drink another drink and keep up with the small talk for almost two hours.

When she yawned, Carter ran a hand across her shoulders. Oddly, it was warm, nice, and void of the reaction that made her stomach tighten. The type of reaction that just came from Jackson's hand falling against her thigh. *Oh no.*

"Carter, mind if I take off for the night? I have a deposition early tomorrow and need a little prep time." She gave her best try at puppy dog eyes, hoping he wouldn't get mad that she needed to ditch.

"Really? It can't wait?"

"It can but I'll just have to stay up super late and I was—"

Carter held up a hand. "Okay, okay. Go ahead. I don't want you to pull an all-nighter because of me. I'll walk you out."

Amanda put a hand to his chest and clutched his shirt, then pulled his mouth to hers for a short kiss. "No need. Have fun with the guys. I'll be fine. Oh, and congratulations on getting to take the lead on your project. You deserve it."

She slung her purse over a shoulder and left the bar, thankful to get away from the crowd, noise, and fake smiles. The landing around the elevator was deathly silent. Periodic dings and lights signaled a long wait before one of the door sets would open. She swayed from foot to foot, ticking off a mental list of things she needed to research and use as discussion points in the deposition tomorrow.

Ding.

The doors opened and she joined the two men already in the elevator. Another person charged in behind just before the doors closed. She pulled a notepad from her purse and jotted down the list she'd ruminated over so she could tackle it when she arrived home.

"Is Carter on that list?"

Huh? Was she going to be haunted by that voice again? She jerked her gaze from her list to—Jackson. He was the person who had rushed into the elevator at the last minute. "Are you following me?"

"You're still making lists."

"Okay, you caught me. I like to write things down. Big deal."

Ding.

The doors opened and one of the men with them exited.

"Show me." Jackson reached for her purse.

Seriously? No way. "A woman's purse is sacred, you don't…hey!"

He wrenched the strap from her arm and parted the snap to peer within. She wanted to slap the grin from his ruddy cheeks.

Ding.

The doors opened and the other man with them took a step forward, held a hand to the door, then stopped. "Are you okay, ma'am? Do you need help?"

That was nice. The stranger wanted to protect her—or at least her purse—from Jackson. Did she need help? No—she could handle Jackson in her sleep. Uh oh. The image that flitted across her legal brain was totally inappropriate.

"I'm fine, but thanks for asking."

The man still didn't exit, and the buzzer started to hum. "He's not bothering you?"

Should she answer that honestly? Amanda hesitated. "No, he's just being his normal pain-in-the-ass big brother self. We're fine."

The man shot a look between them, then stepped away. Okay, no one would believe they were related, but how else was she supposed to explain Jackson's annoying hovering?

Amanda stomped a foot and reached for the bag. "Knock it off. Give me my purse."

Jackson lifted it higher. "Make me."

"Make you? What are we, ten? This isn't the school playground, Jax, and I'm not the little cheerleader you want to coax out of her pleated skirt. I don't play kiddie games anymore. *Give. Me. My. Purse.*" He had always liked to tease. It drove her crazy.

The whoosh of his cologne enveloped her as he stepped forward, his chest almost touching hers. *Oh God.* Was he really taunting her? Daring her to wrestle him to the ground just to get her bag? Well, fine. Two could play that game. Only she could play a lot dirtier now. *I'll show you exactly what you missed when you sent me packing—you and your big-shot family.*

Amanda twisted his shirt between her fingers and yanked. Thud. Their chests melded and she put her mouth against his and gave him a kiss. The kiss-to-end-all-games. He couldn't escape the death-grip on his shirt so she adjusted her mouth and flitted her tongue across the crease of his. *That'll teach you to mess with me.*

Clink. Her purse hit the floor of the elevator as Jackson raised his hands and slid them around her neck. Amanda tried to back up but he palmed the sides of her head and held firm. His breath toasted her cheeks as he spoke. "Okay, I won't play kiddie games either. Just remember you started it."

Jackson put his mouth solidly against hers and rained kisses across her lips, her cheeks, and then down her neck. Mmmm. Wow. He pressed his entire length against her and she fell backward. Thank God the wall was there or she would have been horizontal in a second. She loosened her grip on his shirt and strung her fingers into his hair.

Ding.

The doors slid open.

Chapter Three

I saw her first. The words waltzed through Jackson's head. So juvenile. Carter would probably want to kill him. How would he explain?

Amanda's fingers massaged his scalp as she responded to the kiss. God, she was amazing. They'd kissed once a long time ago and he remembered it as nice, but this? This wasn't nice; it was fricking angry. Savage. And sexy as hell.

He lowered a hand to her waist and pulled tight. There wasn't an inch of air between them, yet he wanted to close the gap. The gap that had been shoved in his heart a year and a half earlier when she disappeared.

The elevator doors slid closed and he punched the red stop button. He wasn't going to deal with her disappearing act again. Nope, time to lay his cards on the table.

"Is it paranoid to think I'm being punished for something?" He waited while she slowly opened her eyes. He liked the haze that proved the kiss hadn't turned out as intended.

"You can't dig in a woman's purse and—"

"This has nothing to do with your purse and you know it. You're angry with me for something. Since we haven't seen each other in two years, I'm lost here."

"It hasn't been two years, and does it matter? I'm dating Carter and according to him, you're dating half the city."

Thanks, Carter. Make me sound like a whore-chaser.

Jackson pressed his forehead to hers. "I'm not officially dating anyone. You're dating him but you just kissed the shit out of me. I'd say you're not all that vested in my friend and I don't know whether to celebrate or clobber you."

The alarm on the elevator blared and Jackson hit the button again. The doors slid open. He doubted he would ever consider an elevator boring again after this encounter. He could still feel the warmth of her leg as she'd wrapped it around his thigh.

Amanda was holy-hell hot and kissed like no one he'd ever known—and she was dating his best friend.

Shit.

She scooped her purse from the floor and stepped away. "Well, Jackson, one thing about you, you never were very good at reading people. You haven't got a clue who I'm vested in—and that kiss? It was just a means to an end."

She slung her purse over her shoulder, patted the tooled leather, and grinned. "See?"

That was all about the damn purse? Her ass swayed nicely when she walked away, the clip-clop of her heels echoing on the tile floor. Like a hammer to his heart.

The doors began to close and he jutted out a hand, then slipped from the elevator to head toward the door. The expanse of the lobby was meant to impress. With pelting rain outside the thirty-foot glass windows and gleaming steel structural beams at regular intervals, it was simply austere. Cold.

Amanda stood under the door awning. Jackson strode toward the security desk and grabbed an umbrella from below the counter, then joined her. Outside, he inhaled the smell of rain on concrete. It was oddly comforting.

He pulled Amanda underneath the umbrella. "Come on, I'll walk you to your car. As much as you admire that purse, I doubt it'll keep you dry in this downpour. Where'd you park?"

She pointed down the block and drips fell to her wrist as her hand extended beyond their tiny tent of dryness. "The garage on the next block, but I can walk. I'll just wait until it lets up."

Jackson grabbed her bag, tossed it over his shoulder, and scooped her closer. "You'll be soaked if you do. Don't be ridiculous. I'm not letting you walk that far in this. It's wet and dark. Let's go." Without waiting for an answer, he dragged her along.

Water splatted below her heels. Hmm. Her feet would get soaked anyway, judging by the shoes. Open toed, strapped across her ankle. The umbrella kept all but their legs dry, which was better than nothing. Amanda didn't protest and after walking twenty steps or so, he felt her tremble.

"You're cold."

She nodded. "A little."

Jackson pulled her tighter and rubbed along her arm. Her suit jacket was almost as thin as her silk shirt. It was damp to boot and clinging to every inch of her. It took willpower not to stare at the way the moist cloth under the jacket clung to the curve of her breasts and accentuated the roundness. Yes, she was definitely cold. He rubbed faster.

His phone summoned from the depth of his pocket. He ignored it for two reasons: one being it was too wet to extract it, and the other being that both his hands were preoccupied.

"D-d-do you n-n-need to get that?"

"Later. Besides, I only have two hands."

"W-w-want me to get it for you?"

Wouldn't that be interesting? "You're offering to dig in my pocket for me? I like the sound of that." As if agreeing, his phone blurted again. "Go for it."

Amanda peered up, her nose nearly touching his cheek. "Um, never mind."

Jackson snickered. They plodded across the abandoned street, their feet burrowing through puddles. When they reached the other side they turned together toward the garage and moved in unison to the entrance. Once inside, he reluctantly removed his arm from her side and closed the umbrella. He shook the water out.

"Thanks for the help." She continued toward a stairwell.

"I'll walk you the rest of the way. Which level?"

"No need, it's right above us."

It was late, dark, and wet. A movement in the corner of the garage caught his attention. No surprise. The homeless had to seek refuge from the rain. Where better than an open garage? "Shut up, Amanda. I'm walking you. Take the elevator." He steered her toward the doors and pressed the button. The doors opened instantly. Before she could protest, he shoved her inside.

His cell phone summoned again and he pulled it from his damp pants and noted the number. Work. He hit the call button and blurted his name.

His father. "Where are you?"

In an elevator with a gorgeous, wet blonde, thinking about getting her out of these damp clothes, Dad. "Downtown. What's up?"

"We need to talk about this new deal you're working on. I think there might be a problem with our client."

"Can it wait until tomorrow?" The elevator dinged, the doors slid open, and they exited. He followed as Amanda clipped toward a dark blue Ford Explorer. He still had a hard time with her car choice; he'd always expected something more predictable or perhaps classy.

On the phone, his father huffed. "I'd rather not. We're having dinner at the Italian place by the office. Why don't you stop by here on your way out? You're not too busy for that, are you?"

At the moment, he wasn't sure. "Okay, Dad. I'll be there in ten minutes." Jackson wondered if the "we" in his father's invitation included his mother or someone else.

Amanda's head swiveled. "That's your dad?"

Jackson nodded and listened to the voice on the other side. His father spoke. "You're with someone."

Not really. "Sort of."

"Who?"

"Carter's girlfriend."

"Oh, you're with Carter? He has a girlfriend? Bring them with you. I haven't seen him in a while."

"It's just her. I walked her to her car."

Two seconds passed before the voice on the phone responded. "Then bring her. I'd like to meet her."

Amanda dug her keys from her purse. The jingle of metal in her hand accompanied the patter of rain outside the garage.

Jackson put his hand over the mouthpiece. "He wants to meet you."

She stopped with the keys in hand and raised a brow. "Does he know I used to work there? That I worked for David?"

He shook his head. Of course not. At the moment all he knew was she was with *Carter*. Her name hadn't even been mentioned. Ironic that his dad was as interested in Carter's life as his own. Actually, his father was likely *more* interested in Carter.

An evil twitch at the corner of Amanda's mouth made him second-guess the offer. Especially when it spread into a grin. "Sure. Why not? I'd love to meet the pompous old fart."

Uh oh. That didn't sound good. No matter his own opinion, insulting his parents didn't set well. "Don't you have work to do?"

She dropped her keys back in her purse. "It can wait. Where to?"

He shivered. What was she plotting? Suddenly the thought of dinner made his stomach lurch. The pompous old fart comment made him nervous. Was that why she'd left? His dad?

Amanda gestured for him to lead the way.

No, his dad never ventured to the cubicle areas where they'd worked. Not his style. Besides, his father would have mentioned on the phone if they'd met. He would have recognized her name. Wouldn't he?

Jackson put his mouth back to the phone. "We'll be there in about five minutes. We're just a block away." He hit the end button.

Amanda flung her hair back and water dripped from the ends. "Are we walking or driving?"

"If it weren't for the rain, I'd say walk, but…can we take your car? Mine's back at the building lot."

"Sure, but you drive. I need to dry off a little and you know where we're going."

Amanda tossed him the keys and clip-clopped around to the passenger seat. Ten minutes later they strode up to a table covered in black linen and adorned with an appetizer plate of cheese, olives, and bread.

Jackson's father was an older version of himself. In looks only. They weren't at all alike in personality. Where his father was stern and boring, Jackson prided himself on being relaxed and fun. Nose to the grindstone for Dad. Nose to the wind for Jackson. His mother wasn't much better than Dad. Her crisp business suit at such a late hour hinted she'd also worked late. It was such a contrast to the hidden agendas they managed. Jackson never understood how they could continue working together all these years, especially knowing the only depth to their relationship was in the company's balance sheet. Sad.

Amanda's hair hung in tendrils around her face, curling into her neck. It was—incredible. So was the flash in her eyes that signified something he hadn't seen before. Jackson swallowed and started to do introductions.

"Amanda, meet—"

"Amazing." Amanda slapped a hand on the table. "You don't *look* like an arrogant, pompous ass."

"What?" Jackson's stomach burned. Where did *that* come from? His father's fork screeched to a stop and the olive in his mouth swan-dived onto his plate, then bounced to the floor.

"I beg your pardon." His mother's eyes flared. One thing he'd always loved about Mom was her protective side. Anyone who pounced on her family had a surprise coming regardless of the distance between husband and wife. Amanda had just pounced and Jackson had no idea why.

"Oh, I don't need an introduction, Jax. I'm Amanda. You're Robert and Lynn Holstenar." Amanda thrust a hand out, waited a nanosecond for them to shake hers, which they did reluctantly, then she dropped into the chair beside his dad. Both his parents were speechless. He wanted to laugh. When was the last time they'd been shocked into silence?

Amanda thrust her limp hair back and smiled. "So, how's the food in this place? Good, huh? Hmm. Wow, what a menu…and look, Jax, it's all in Italian. Isn't that adorable?"

"The waiter can—" He stopped when she raised a finger and tsked twice.

"What's the matter, sweetie, you don't think this podunk little farm girl can read a menu? Just like you didn't think I could be a lawyer, let alone a good one?"

Jackson doubted she'd ever set foot on a farm. The waiter arrived and took in the three astonished faces and Amanda's smug one. He hesitated for a second. Jackson was sure he wanted to go back to the kitchen. "Everything okay here? Any questions about the menu?"

Amanda laughed, and launched into a flurry of Italian. What the hell? Jackson had no idea what she said, but the waiter patted her arm and laughed, then trudged away. Jackson's parents sat with their mouths agape. She spoke Italian? Why hadn't he known that? And what the hell had she said to make the waiter wink?

Dad cleared his throat. "So you're an attorney and speak Italian, or maybe multiple languages? You obviously know more about us than we know about you…other than that you're dating Carter."

Amanda slapped a hand to the table and everyone within ten feet jolted. "That's right. I'm dating Carter. Why is that, Jax?"

He was clueless. "What does that mean?"

Her face was calm in a scary-as-hell way and she plucked an olive from the tray that the waiter dropped in front of her. She waved it, then shrugged. "Nothing. Not a thing. I mean, Carter's great, right? Smart, nice, handsome. Who wouldn't want to date him?

He's obviously a high achiever, just like me. Look at all he's done so far." She popped the olive in her mouth and grabbed another.

Jackson grimaced. He suddenly had an urge to knock Carter off his pedestal. "He hasn't really done all that much. He got fired."

Amanda tapped the cold olive against his nose. It felt like a wet frog. "Heard about that one. Thanks to you. You're so cute when you're jealous of his success. You're *such* a great friend. Does he know you let him go down for your potty-mouth comments?"

"Jackson, what's she talking about?" His mother reached a fork to the tray and stabbed some cheese, then gracefully slipped it into her mouth.

"Nothing, Mom. She's just—drunk. We were—"

"I am not."

Wow, he'd never seen her like this, not that he'd seen her all that much in the past couple of years.

Dad pasted on a smile. "Oh, look, here's our food. Whatever did you order?" Three waiters arrived with trays and began placing dishes around the table.

Amanda giggled. "It's not on the menu. I come here once in a while with clients. The chef makes this wonderful fish and pasta dish but it's by request only because it requires a pretty healthy tuna steak. He normally doesn't carry a lot of seafood."

Another surprise. What else did she have up her sleeve? Or, bigger question, what reason did she have for all the craziness?

"So, how long have you and Carter been—an item?" His mother took a sip of wine while waiting for a response.

"An item? Well, Jackson introduced us a little over a month ago. Wasn't that sweet of him? Just so brotherly like." She scrunched her shoulders and eyes in a mocking isn't-that-cute way.

Brotherly? Does she normally exchange saliva with her siblings? Jackson tucked a finger into the collar of his shirt and stretched the material. Geez, it was hot in the restaurant.

"What are you doing, Amanda?" he finally asked.

Chapter Four

The chef peeked out from the kitchen and waved. Amanda lifted her fingers and wiggled them in return. "Me? I'm just having a nice dinner. You invited me. I have no idea why you did but, hey, here I am. So, what's this about?"

Robert adjusted himself in his chair and Amanda wanted to snort but she didn't. She liked that he seemed just a tiny bit edgy. Thank God Jackson was nothing like his father, other than his looks. "We just thought it would be nice to talk to you. About Carter. He's been through—"

"A lot, yes, I know. Jackson said that. Good lord, you'd think the guy was twelve, not thirty. Why do you feel this incessant need to be in his business? We're just going out. I'm not planning to get knocked up and force him to marry me." Amanda plucked a piece of bread from the basket, ripped it in half, and stuffed a piece in her mouth. With her cheek bulging, she grabbed her wine glass. His parents stared.

Amanda wanted to giggle when the cheese that Lynn Holstenar was chewing fell in her lap. His family had a serious problem with dropping food. Oh my God, this was a hoot. She'd show them. How often does a person get the chance to confront the very people who sent her packing because *she* wasn't good enough to work for them? And now they wanted to tell her she wasn't good enough for Carter either? Ha. Fat chance.

Frankly she didn't care.

Jackson's mother coughed. "Well, that's certainly good to know. We're not trying to get in anyone's business, Amanda, dear. It's just that Jackson and Carter grew up together and well, we were there when his sister died."

Holy shit. Did she really just say that? All Amanda's remaining bravado hit the brakes with a brain-scorching screech. The giddiness evaporated. "His sister died?"

Lynn nodded. "You didn't know? Yes, she died when she was a teenager. She drowned trying to save one of her friends who couldn't swim. It was awful. Carter never quite got past it. He's never been able to trust anyone since, nor has he made any effort to build long-term relationships. In fact, you're probably the first girlfriend we've heard about."

The bread Amanda swallowed stuck in her throat and she took a lengthy drink of water. Carter had never mentioned a sister. In truth, he barely talked about family at all. Wasn't that an odd indicator of just how well they knew each other? "That's terrible. I'm so sorry."

Her eyes started to burn and she blinked to keep the wetness at bay. This was why she couldn't study criminal law. She prided herself on keeping her emotions controlled but she had limits. Jackson reached under the table and patted her knee. His big fingers felt warm through the skirt. "It's okay. You had no way of knowing. He doesn't talk about what happened."

Suddenly the desire to get even with the entire Holstenar family for forcing her to leave a job she loved didn't sound too enticing. All she could think about was the nice guy she'd just walked away from when he was celebrating his big work achievement. What a horrible thing to do. Of course, it paled compared to seeing a family member drown. "Was he there when she died?"

"No. It happened while he was at school. He was a teenager."

"Oh. Wow. No wonder he's so—distant."

"You have no idea. He's a hundred percent better now than he was a few years ago." Jackson's voice was strained. His parents' faces took on a sympathetic veil of kindness.

Amanda wanted to comfort him. It didn't make sense that she'd feel sympathy for the friend, rather than Carter. "You guys were really close?"

Lynn lowered her wine glass to the table. Wariness crossed her features. Amanda expected Lynn wasn't sure of her sincerity.

Who could blame her? "Until then, they were like brothers. Best friends. The town pretty much knew wherever one went, the other was close behind. Carley's death was so hard on Carter, we nearly lost him. Jackson helped, though. He kept hounding and pushing until Carter finally stepped back into life. We were so proud of the way he supported him—all of them, really."

Amanda blinked. How many were there? "All of them? How big a family does he have?"

Jackson sighed. "You've dated for weeks and he's never told you any of this? What the hell do you talk about?"

Good point. Not much, if she was honest. They merely "hung out" together, spending half their time in the same room but doing separate things. Like texting or talking on the phone. She often read her emails and responded. "We haven't really talked all that much. It's been more—"

Jackson's hand flew over her mouth, stopping the words. "I don't want to know."

Robert held a glass up for the waiter to fill. Glancing from Amanda to Jackson, he smiled for the first time since she'd arrived. "You should help her, son. You know him better than anyone. Give her a little advice. What makes him tick? How does she get past his shield? We all know what a great kid—"

Jackson snorted. "He's not a kid, Dad. He's thirty years old. Besides, Amanda doesn't need help with men. She's got that covered."

"Right. We all know what a great man he is but he's not going to show that to someone easily. Amanda would be good for our boy."

Jackson chewed on his food. "You realize you're saying that about a woman who just called you a pompous ass, right?"

Amanda's face was hot and she assumed the color matched the red napkins on the table. He was right. She'd said that and more but that was *before* she knew how much they cared. About Carter.

Robert turned to level his gaze with hers. "I'm sure she has her reasons."

Jackson blew out a windstorm of air. "I'd sure like to know what they hell they are, wouldn't you?" His eyes darted from one parent to the other, seeking agreement. Neither answered.

Amanda punched Jackson's arm, imitating the way David had acted the day she carried her boxes of belongings out of the building for the final time. She reiterated the words overheard from David to Jackson that day: "Oh, come on. They don't need to be bothered with trivial personality conflicts, right?" The words still made her stomach yearn for an antacid tablet.

The prior words from David, which had been passed down from Mr. Holstenar himself, were worse though: "Look, Amanda, Robert feels your attorney capabilities for the company are overshadowed by your lust for his son. He doesn't think you have the right perspective."

Seriously? She had tried to call them the next day and clarify exactly what her perspective on their business model involved but she was told they couldn't be bothered as they were in meetings.

She'd walked in with the intention of finally airing her opinion—telling them what she thought of their preconceived judgment of her abilities and pompous idea that she'd *ever* lust after Jackson. Unfortunately, they ruined it with their empathy for Carter. It was impressive they worried so much they were willing to tolerate her rudeness. She felt six inches tall. The rest of the dinner was spent listening to Jackson and his parents reminisce about the two men's history. Wow, you'd think Carter was a saint by what they were saying.

Later, his parents gave her an awkward handshake and left. After they paid for the dinner. Make that one-inch tall.

In the parking lot outside the restaurant, Amanda waited for Jackson to unlock the car. "Why do you think Carter's never mentioned any of this? I mean, am I really such a cold person that he can't tell me something so important? Did he think I wouldn't understand? Am I really that horrible?"

"Of course not. Men aren't that complicated, Mandy. If he wanted you to know, he'd tell you. It's not something he wants to talk about, so he doesn't."

"Okay, but if you really are *dating* someone, shouldn't they tell you personal things about themselves? I've never even met his parents."

"Parent. His dad died a few years ago."

Amanda's heart twisted. "See?"

Inside the car, Jackson turned to her. His hand rested over the back of her seat and the warmth of his fingers hinted at rubbing her neck as Carter had done earlier. Why would that thought flit through her mind at a time like this?

"He doesn't tell you those things because that would be *intimate*. For him to tell you, he'd have to feel close to you. You aren't giving him any reason. Face it, you're not an easy person to get close with. Hell, when were you planning to tell *me* you spoke Italian? Does he know? And what the hell did you say to that waiter to make him wink at you?" Jackson moved his hand from behind Amanda and started the car.

Was that true? She'd always felt like she was easy to know but not an emotional shirt-sleever, a term her father used. Being able to hide emotions and wrestle them into control at important moments was a key component of her success. Attorneys didn't cry or burst into emotional rants. Not ever. Okay, she hadn't really mastered that calmness with her family but at work, she was fine. No one knew what a bungled mess her insides were beyond the workplace.

"I told him I wanted to give my future wicked stepparents the best meal of their life so pour on the charm and bring me a stiff drink." She held up a hand when his eyes bugged. "I know, I know. It was a lie but hey, he got a laugh out of it. Look, just because I don't cry or throw tantrums doesn't mean I'm standoffish. I can be intimate." Had he forgotten the kiss in the elevator? She wished she could.

Jackson swerved the car to the curb and killed the engine. The sound of rain pounding on the roof echoed between them. Amanda waited. He turned to face her.

"I don't really know what problem you have with my parents but I'll assume it was work-related. You can tell me or not, your choice, but when it comes to Carter—that's easy. Men are pretty simple. They like women who make them feel needed and wanted. Face it, Amanda, you have your life completely under control. You don't need anything or anyone."

He was wrong there—she definitely had an unfulfilled need. "I thought all men wanted was to get laid."

He snickered. "Well, that's true, but if we're gonna hang around we have to know that you want us there."

"And that you'll get laid." She wasn't an idiot. She'd seen Jackson with a few girls in college. Enough to know his motivation was purely physical.

He shrugged. "Every healthy relationship has its physical parts. I guarantee you, there's only three steps to getting and keeping Carter. Or any man, to be honest. None of them has to be in any particular order, they just have to be 'in the mix' at some point. First, you have to make him feel needed. Second, you have to feed his ego. Third, give him sex, the more the better."

Amanda rolled her eyes. "It's really only a one-step process, isn't it? Give him sex."

Jackson grinned and held up his hands. "Well, a guy can last a bit with a girl in a purely physical relationship. We're not complicated, and that'd work for a while, but long term, we need a little more."

"Yeah, right."

"We do, seriously. So, tell you what I'll do. Tomorrow, you and I will go do a little 'man training.' Meet me at the Starbucks by his office and we'll see what we can do to help you catch and keep my friend."

"What makes you think I can't do that on my own? I can be all those things without coaching. In fact, I *am* all those things. What about the kiss earlier? Surely it wasn't *that* forgettable?" God, she wanted another one. She tried not to share into his eyes. Right now.

Jackson leaned into her, his mouth inches away, and grinned. "I forget nothing, babe, and that kiss was a great start. Needs a little more work but definitely a good way to get his motor running. Provided you follow through."

What? "Follow through? What was wrong with it? You seemed pretty involved at the time."

He focused on her mouth and for a second Amanda thought he'd lean in for another taste. "Nothing was wrong and for the record, I *was* involved. Kinda hard not to be when you go all octopus on me…but I'm not the guy you're trying to snag here."

He wasn't? Oh, of course. Carter. Amanda tore her gaze from his face and shoved out of the car. She didn't care if the rain drenched her; she needed a little distance. She rounded to the driver's door and waited for him to join her. Which he did. He stepped right into her, pressing the full length of his lanky body against hers, then leaning down to put his lips to her ear. His voice tickled, sending shots of warmth down her neck. "I'll see you at ten tomorrow morning. Should I get you one of those lattes you like?"

Oh, God. Kill me now. She nodded. She didn't need his help but damned if her body didn't want more of his touch.

Chapter Five

The following morning Jackson stepped out of the shower and wiped the steam from the bathroom mirror. The small room smelled of fresh soap. He reached in the cabinet for a razor, then frowned at his reflection. The situation with Amanda was hysterical if he thought about it much. He was going to give her advice, pointers—training, so to speak—on how to take Carter from casual dating to full-fledged relationship. It was funny because he'd never really managed to maintain a relationship for long himself, and Carter wasn't her type at all.

Amanda needed someone serious about his future. Driven. Willing to work long hours for his career and able to squeeze in time with a woman around a hectic business life. Amanda had made no bones about wanting to be a good attorney and build a reputation. Any man who dated her had to respect that. The man should respect her intelligence as much or more than the fact that she was the kind of woman that people couldn't ignore. Beautiful and sexy in a simple, don't-give-a-shit way, yet always pristinely dressed.

Wait.

Jackson fumbled and dropped his razor in the sink. He cursed, retrieved it, and started shaving. Hell, who was he kidding? Carter was perfect—they were identical. Two peas in a pod. Two workaholics with no social life whatsoever.

Shit. Carter was *exactly* her type. Why did that piss him off?

Amanda needed someone like herself. Jackson's Dad had seen it the minute he introduced her. Dad had a way of manipulating people that only lifetime attorneys could manage. It was his best talent and the most annoying trait in a parent. When Jackson was younger, he rebelled and fought the "coercion techniques" that his father used to corral him away from inappropriate or embarrassing behavior. Jackson learned quickly that if he listened without responding, a debate could never occur. Once the lecture was over, he simply chose to do what he wanted.

That worked because all of his friends were close by and would cover for him and he did the same. It didn't take long to see that most of these "friends" were destined to never leave home and very likely some would have a long fight with either drugs or trouble. Jackson tried to distance himself but when you spent all your time growing up with kids, you just didn't always see the warning signs until you were so far past the starting point there was no going back.

When his parents decided to move to the country, it made him furious. No kid liked to uproot and leave all his friends behind. Looking back, it was the smartest thing they'd done. His mom hadn't really wanted to make the move and over time the strain between his parents took a toll. He'd come home to some hellacious fights. To avoid all the drama, he often would crawl out his bedroom window and take his bike for a ride. The first few weeks, he spent a lot of time sitting on the dock at Carter's house pondering how screwed up his life was. Of course, at that time, he didn't know it was Carter's house.

The night Carter showed up on the dock and scared the hell out of him had been a particularly bad fight night for his parents. One of the ones that made him fear for the future.

"Whatcha doing there, kid? Don't you know this is private property?" It was mid-July and Carter wore a torn T-shirt that looked like it hadn't been white in months. His shorts looked like they'd been equally worn-in, something that made Jackson like him instantly.

That night Jackson knew his face was streaked from crying but he sucked in a breath and chose his best smart-ass voice. "Uh, no, I don't see any fricking signs anywhere." Yes, he'd used the biggest curse word he knew and felt damn proud of himself.

Carter pointed at the road. "We have a fence. People don't put fences around things that don't belong to them."

Jackson had snot running down his face. He also had tears but if he swiped wide across his face, he knew he could get all of it and maybe the kid wouldn't notice. As Carter stepped closer Jackson ran his fingers across one cheek, then under the nose, and back.

"Yeah, well, *most* people have fences to keep animals and stuff in, *not* to keep kids out. Besides, it's not like I'm hurting anything. I'm just sitting here. You got a problem with that, I'll leave."

Carter squinted with one eye and stilled. He shifted from foot to foot in only a way that a boy not comfortable with emotional situations can. "I don't got a problem. Sit all you want. *I'm* gonna try noodling. You ever done that? It's where you dig down into the mud and try to pull a catfish out. I saw something on this show where these guys were doing that in a river and they got this huge one." Carter held his hands wide to signify size.

Thus began their friendship. They spent almost an hour digging in the mud finding nothing but more mud, catching frogs, and then hosing off behind Carter's barn. It was the best time he'd had in months. From then on, they were inseparable. Until Carley died.

Jackson wiped the fog from the mirror again and shrugged.

Amanda deserved Carter and vice versa.

Chapter Six

Amanda loved Saturdays, especially Saturday mornings. It was the one time she let herself be lazy. She rose from bed at a very late eight in the morning, threw on sweats and a baggy shirt, then ate toast and drank tea while reading the news on her tablet.

Nine forty-five. She'd already scrubbed the counters in the kitchen and bathroom *plus* washed every stitch of laundry in the hamper. She should leave right this minute if she wanted to be on time with Jackson.

No, she wasn't going.

She didn't need his help to get a date, nor to get a *relationship*. She snorted and plodded barefoot to the bathroom. Staring at her makeup-free face in the mirror, she grabbed a brush and attacked her wild hair. Okay, maybe she wasn't exactly gorgeous at the moment but who cared? She was comfortable.

Smart.

Men loved a smart, accomplished woman. Right? She leaned into the mirror and examined the bags under her eyes. Smart and tired-looking.

Thirty minutes later, Amanda strode into the coffee shop in the same sweats and shirt with her oldest pair of sneakers on her feet. She'd tied her hair in a retro side ponytail and brushed her teeth. If Jackson wanted to school her, she'd make it a challenge, and show him her worst self. Her Saturday self.

Jackson shoved a steaming paper cup filled with tannish froth toward her and snickered. "You look charming. Just get out of bed?"

She reached for a packet of sweetener and shook it twice, then started to tear it open. He grabbed her hand and shook his head. "Already did that. One sweetener and a shake of cinnamon. You're good to go."

He remembered how I liked to drink a latte? What did that mean? "Thanks—for the drink, not the charming comment. For your information, I've been up and cleaning all morning. It's Saturday. My lazy, comfy day. These are my comfy clothes. What's wrong with 'em?"

She was ready for a fight if he wanted to insult. *Just go there, Jackson. Make me lose my temper.*

He took a lazy eye-stroll down her face and body, then back up to her eyes. He stuck his coffee stir stick in his mouth and rattled his head side to side. "Nothing's wrong. Comfy's good. I like comfy, but you can be comfy and still be a woman. If you've been cleaning all morning, I'd hardly call you lazy."

A small burn started in her brain. "I *am* a woman regardless of what I wear. In fact, I am a woman even if I wear nothing. Clothes don't—"

Jackson jerked the stick from his mouth and pointed her way. "Now *that's* the kind of comfy a man likes. Naked. In fact, it's probably on every guy's mind at least three times in the first few hours he meets a woman. What does she look like naked and how do I get her that way?"

Amanda wanted to spit the burning liquid from her mouth; instead she swallowed and felt the burn all the way to her stomach. "Oh my God."

"Hey, it's the truth. Here, let me try something." Jackson's hand snaked toward her and he slowly undid the top button of her shirt, then yanked the cloth to the side. When the shirt fell off her shoulder a cool breeze from the fan above drifted over her skin. "Well, *that's* an okay start."

"What?"

He pointed at her shoulder. "You're not wearing a bra. Of course, who would know in that oversized blanket of a shirt? Wear it like that, off the shoulder. Show a little skin. Men like a bare shoulder. It's sexy."

Oh brother. Actually she was wearing a bra but she wasn't planning to correct the image. "I'm not really trying to be sexy at the moment, Jax. Hence the word 'comfy.'"

He leaned in and lowered his voice. "Wrong answer, honey. You should *always* be trying for sexy even if there's not a man within two hundred miles."

Amanda sipped another drink. "Don't call me honey and that's the stupidest thing I've ever heard. You want me to get out of the shower every day and put on my slinkiest gear on the off chance that Carter might just show up? What's wrong with the way I look, anyway? Guys like smart women. Smart *is* sexy."

"Smart is smart. Look, I don't know why but most guys fantasize that the woman in the business suit is wearing a thong underneath. You want to be comfy, fine. There's no reason you can't. Still, that shoulder right there"—Jackson's fingers tickled as he ran them softly across her collar bone—"that makes me want to see the rest of the package. See how the fabric drapes across the top of your breast, showing just enough cleavage to entice? That's…great. Carter'd love that."

She rolled her eyes. "Seems to me a guy hopes there's a thong under pretty much anything a woman wears, even if it's old sweats or fishing waders."

His face slowly turned wicked as he grinned. "Bingo. Now *that's* an image. Are you wearing one now? No, don't tell me. One of those black lace things that's see-through in front and rides lightly across the hips, right? Or maybe a VS sport-like thing in florescent pink? Now that puts great thoughts in a guy's head."

She slapped his arm. "Yeah, I'll bet it does. I just wonder which head is having those thoughts."

The grin on his face was annoying—and sexy. "The only one that matters, babe. The one you need to get on your side if you want to build a relationship with Carter. Or any guy, for that matter."

"Don't call me babe, either. You're disgusting, Jackson. Remind me, why were we ever friends all those months? I can't really see anything about you that is remotely more interesting than an orangutan."

"I'm just a guy, Amanda, like every other walking male on the planet. We're all disgusting. While you're talking about friendships, remember I'm also *the* guy who's been friends with the one you're trying to nail for years. You want my help or not?"

Amanda opened her mouth to speak but hesitated. Was his help worth all this wasted effort? Um, not sure. Something about the latest comments and the direction he was headed sounded like they were teetering toward a very dangerous path. "For the record, I'm not trying to *nail* Carter. There's a big difference between wanting to date someone and whatever that means. Why the two of you are friends completely escapes me. You're not at all alike."

Jackson stood and motioned for her to lead the way out of the shop. Did she really want his advice? She needed a second or two to evaluate the situation but he wouldn't give one. "We're all alike. Get up, woman. We're burning daylight and I have things to do later. Let's get moving." He snapped his fingers twice and Amanda obediently moved.

Once in the street, she was curious. "Where are we going?"

"Tell me, when are you seeing him next?"

"We're going dancing tonight." She was looking forward to it; she loved to dance. Carter had reluctantly agreed, mainly because there was a live band. He'd heard them before and enjoyed the performance.

Jackson stopped in his tracks. The stir stick he'd chewed on for the past fifteen minutes hit the ground. "Carter dances?"

Amanda shrugged. She had no idea. "I guess."

The smack of his hands clapping shocked her. "Well, okay then. Dancing. Perfect. What are you planning to wear? Please tell me not one of those fancy lawyer suits."

Of course not; she'd never wear work clothes to a bar. They'd end up smelling like smoke. "I thought maybe jeans and a shirt. I have this great pink—"

"Stop right there. No jeans. A skirt or dress, something that shows a lot of skin."

Her thoughts flew to the blue satin number she'd bought in New Orleans. She'd seen it in a window on her last business trip for the contract with her client who owned a bakery business. It was spaghetti-strapped and dipped low in front while hanging loosely over her hips. The open back that gaped nearly to the curve of her ass was gorgeous. She'd never worn it because it made her self-conscious. "No problem, but it might be cold. Oh, and by the way, I *am* wearing a bra. It's a bandeau thing."

"What the hell is that? Makes me think of one of those red handkerchiefs men used to wear to work when my Dad was kid."

Amanda searched the street for pedestrians, of which there were none. It covered more than a sports bra so she didn't see much harm in a preview. She flipped the shirt up and down briefly. Jackson's eyes rounded, then narrowed.

He cleared his throat. "Not exactly the sexiest thing but hell, it made my day. Braless would be better, of course."

She growled and stomped away. "Caveman."

Jackson had the nerve to laugh. "Guilty."

Chapter Seven

Jackson trailed after Amanda, enjoying the moment. Yes, he was coaching her to seduce his best friend when he'd rather it were him, but the banter was fun. Beggars couldn't be choosers. Thinking back over their time at school, then work, they'd never talked this way. He'd always been on his best behavior, trying to impress.

The freedom to say whatever came to mind was cleansing. Especially when he could say it in regard to Carter and not worry she'd take the words badly. So, they were going dancing—loud music, lots of booze, their bodies plastered against each other. Swaying. Grinding. Shit. He hated Carter.

Jackson picked up the pace and grabbed her hand. "Come on, let's work on your rhythm."

"My rhythm is fine."

He imagined that was true. Still, she'd just given him an idea. When they reached the spot where his Jeep was parallel parked in front of an empty building, he pressed the unlock button.

"Hop in and we'll see about that." He opened the passenger door and waited.

Amanda eyed him warily. "Where are you taking me? I thought this was going to be a quick and easy thing."

Jackson sighed. "Just get in, Mandy. I'm taking you to one of Carter's favorite places and we'll talk about that rhythm thing. Trust me, okay? Besides, didn't you say your friend wanted you to be more adventurous?" Should he mention it was also his place to unwind?

"Now, you're really scaring me." Despite her hesitation, he was relieved she stepped into his vehicle. He rounded the hood and seated himself, turned on the radio, flipped it to country music, and headed for the freeway.

"How far is this place?" Amanda's hair flapped in the wind. She curled a foot up and slipped it under her butt.

"About thirty minutes. Just sit and enjoy the music and company."

She fingered the garter belt tied around his air conditioner vent and frowned. Should he tell her it was from a friend's wedding? Everyone scattered and left him to catch the damn thing and while all his friends teased, he considered it a gift. She frowned. "I'll enjoy the music—jury's still out on the company, though."

"Thanks."

Amanda dropped her foot to the floor, leaned back in her seat, and closed her eyes. It took a little longer than thirty minutes but when he pulled the Jeep down the gravel road, he could hear the slight huffing of Amanda's breath over the music. She was snoring.

They hit a tree root and the Jeep bounced her awake. "Where are we?"

"Almost there."

Jackson rounded the last pile of stumps and pulled to a stop.

"Almost where?" Amanda blinked and rubbed her eyes. Damn, she was cute. He chose not to answer—no need to spoil things before she gave it a shot.

"Hop out, we'll walk from here." Jackson pointed toward a path that led through a few trees. Morning light filtered through and winked for them to hurry. He wished they'd left an hour earlier.

While Amanda extricated herself from the passenger seat and smoothed her hair, he pulled his gear from the back. A tackle box, two fishing poles, and his portable stereo.

Amanda turned and her eyes widened. "Fishing? Carter's favorite spot is a fishing hole?"

Jackson nodded and grinned. "It's not really a hole, it's a river bed, but yes."

She dropped hands to hips. "And how exactly is that supposed to help with this dancing date-slash-rhythm thing?"

He held up the portable stereo. "I brought music." By the way she looked around, he half expected her to call for help. She glanced past him as if seeking another ride.

"Very funny, Jax. Take me home."

"Not yet. We only have about another hour before it gets too hot. Besides, think of me as Yoda or your spiritual coach. Just go with it and see what happens. I think you'll like this." Jackson squinted at the sun, which had risen higher than he hoped. He'd already waited longer than he wanted but she was worth the time. He looked at the fabric slipping from her shoulder and her clean face, void of makeup. Hell, she was worth waiting even longer if he needed to but the sun probably wouldn't agree.

"Too hot? What the heck does all this have to do with me, Carter, or dancing?"

"Can you just relax for a little while? It's Saturday, the weather's nice, and you don't have to be anywhere for hours. Follow me."

He tromped along the path, glad that he'd dropped the keys in his pocket. Otherwise, she'd likely drive away and leave him stranded.

An hour later, he admired her Shrimpini Pink toenails as they hung over the edge of the bass boat. He knew that was the correct color because she'd told him as much. As far as he was concerned, it was pink. Her legs, smooth and bronzed, made a damn good decal for the boat. Floating along with their lines in the water and the music softly humming, Jackson felt content for the first time in years. His dad's health, the company's financial troubles, his workload stress—all were a distant image too small to trouble over.

The music and the waves lapping against the boat hull were the only sounds.

He'd prefer quiet but knew she'd never go for dead silence. She swatted a fly from her face and leaned her head backward and upside down to meet his gaze. "This is peaceful. No wonder he enjoys it so much. It's kind of therapeutic."

Thank God she had acquiesced and gotten in the boat. It was a long shot, but it worked. He would have been happy just to fish from the bank but she saw the cover and yanked it off, then had to try.

"See? Yoda delivers his first lesson." He set the trolling motor to keep them even with the current.

"Okay, Master. I'm enjoying the boat ride and the fishing seems like it's just an excuse to laze in the water but I don't see what this has to do with my rhythm."

"That's just it. Your rhythm doesn't matter—just be yourself. Enjoy the moment. Like right now…you have your shoes off and your head tilted back to soak in the sun. That fishing pole is settled in and waiting for the right moment to bless you with whatever is yours. You can't lose."

"A fish is my blessing? Couldn't I have something better, like a winning lottery ticket, or a pot of gold popping up from the water?"

She leaned over and peered into the gentle froth of ripples and he felt his heart take a nosedive. She was perfection and didn't have a clue.

"Amanda, look around us. The water. The fish. The music. Blend it all together. There's a perfect rhythm in all of it. You just have to want what you have."

The top of her pole dipped but she was focused on him, which ordinarily would be great. She squinted. "Are you trying to give me one of those profound speeches my mother always went for because if you are—"

"Look."

"Oh God, you're not going to tell me to stand up in the boat and balance in one of those crazy stork-like poses that the karate kid did, are you?"

He wanted to laugh but if she didn't get her ass in gear she was going to lose it. "You have a fish, Amanda. Pick up the damn pole."

"Oh, shit." She fell into the hull of the boat and grappled for the pole. Zzzzzzz. The line tightened and threatened to break. "What do I do?"

He gave the trolling motor a slight jig. "Reel it in slowly. If it starts to pull too hard the line will break. Just take your time. That's the thing about fishing. If you take it slow, you'll eventually wear the damn thing out and it'll be yours."

She did exactly that and when the fish finally flopped its weary fins in the water beside the boat, she sighed. "Now what?"

"We let it go."

She darted eyes up. "Seriously? I worked my ass off so that you could cut it loose? What the hell for?"

He grinned. "Because otherwise he'll die. What good is that? We're not planning to eat it or mount it on the wall."

"Says who? That's my first catch."

"It's not big enough for a trophy. In my family, if you're gonna eat it you have to *clean it*. You know, cut it open and scoop out the guts, then cut into filets. Frankly I can't see you elbows deep in fish guts. Besides, don't you want to let him have his own moment?" He pulled out his fish de-hooker.

"It's a fish."

With a single movement he set the little bugger free. "Yeah, but even fish have family and want to belong. I bet if he could talk, he'd probably say the only reason he was going for your bait was because he wanted to brag about it when he got home. He probably has a little school of baby fish somewhere that needs feeding. You know what they say, family is everything."

She rolled her eyes. "Oh, pulleeeze."

Okay, that was a stretch, and probably the dumbest thing he'd ever said. The look on her face said she thought so as well.

"Who are you and what happened to the guy I knew in college?"

They caught two more fish, one larger and one smaller, then headed back to the city. Amanda didn't ask about rhythm or Carter, nor complain about fish bait or flies. All in all, he was pleased with himself for showing her a small piece of his world. Admittedly he'd represented it as Carter's world but they'd both enjoyed this place many times.

Once he'd packed the car and bounced them back to the main road, she started humming to the radio.

"You suck as a matchmaker, Jax."

That was true, not that he cared. "Maybe so but don't tell me you didn't enjoy that because you'd be lying."

"I can enjoy just about anything if I force myself."

He knew better. "So you want me to believe you forced yourself to kick your shoes off and tilt your head back. Your toes tapped to the music unwillingly and your mind was totally focused on work—or Carter."

She stared straight out the window, ignoring him as he willed her to turn his way. Her breath made a tiny oval on the window. "That's right."

They rode in silence until he was a block from the coffee shop where they'd started the day. He found a parking spot street-side and maneuvered the Jeep between a pickup and a minivan. He turned his stereo to club music and stepped out of the vehicle. Rounding to her side, he pulled open the door and held out a hand.

"Show me your stuff."

She stared. "What stuff?"

"He's taking you dancing, right? Let's see you dance."

She glanced up and down the sidewalk, obviously hoping no one would see them.

He flipped his wrist and beckoned her to take his hand. "Come on. Music's playing, we're all by ourselves, this concrete works as a dance floor. Get your ass out here."

"I'm not going to dance right here on the side of a street in downtown. That's dumb."

"Come on, show me your stuff, kiddo."

Amanda huffed. "Don't call me—"

"Kiddo. Got it. Let's dance."

Amanda's neck bulged as she swallowed. "Here? Now?"

"Of course. There's no one around. It's not like you're going to be seen. Dancing is a great way to reel a guy in—or turn him off, depending on what you do. If you're good, it can lead straight to the bedroom."

"Puleeze."

"What? Too honest for you? Come on, this is a great song. Let's move." He yanked her against him. A huge mistake because her shirt was thin and so soft he wanted to squeeze the cloth between his fingers—or rip it off. Crap.

Amanda started to move her hips, slowly. He was helpless to do anything but hold her and stare. Then she thrust an arm out, grazing his jaw with her fist. The next thing he knew she was riding him and punching the air like a female Ali. What the hell? "No. No, no. Stop that. Come on. You're a damn attorney, for Christ's sake. Attorneys don't thrust their hands like a boxer and hump men on the dance floor."

Amanda's eyes popped—not exactly her best look. She dropped a hand to her hip and moved her head left then right. "Oh, so *now* I get to be an attorney? Since when was there a classification for dancing that had anything to do with one's profession? I thought good dancing was simply…good dancing."

"You call that good? I call it trashy. No one really does that twerk thing anymore, do they? I mean it'd be great if you were just looking to get laid, but if you plan to keep him around for a while and build a relationship, that's probably not what he's expecting. Knowing Carter, it'll embarrass him. Hell, it would embarrass me and that's almost impossible."

She was pissed. Her face flushed and there was a slight tick at the corner of her mouth, so slight he wouldn't have noticed if he didn't have her against him. He could almost imagine lightning bolts coming out of her eyes. Amanda stilled and the music took on the feeling of pending doom. "For your information, that wasn't twerking. Besides, it's pretty hypocritical of you to call my dancing trashy or to comment about getting laid. I remember enough about you in college and work to know you're the king of short-term things—as in, so short it doesn't exist." Amanda lifted the fist from her hip and pinched her fingers together to signify size.

He wanted to laugh but was afraid she'd belt him. "You're really gonna do the small-penis thing? Seriously? How would you know?" He grabbed her hand and placed it on his shoulder, then began swaying to the music. "Two steps to the right, one to the left. That's all you need to do. Enough to show you have rhythm but not so much that he can't talk to you. You're trying to build a connection, not an erection. What exactly do you remember about college, Mandy, because all I remember is studying my ass off all the time. With you—and we both know that went nowhere."

"You should have just installed a revolving door on your room. There were too many girls coming and going to count. As I recall, the trashier the better. None that lasted though, so I don't really consider you a good resource for relationship advice."

Jackson dipped her backward, then lifted her until their noses almost touched. "You sound jealous. What's wrong, you didn't get enough when younger so you're mad at me because I did?"

To be honest, he hadn't really noticed whether she dated or not. Back then he was just having fun. Studying with Amanda had been a necessity to get him through law school. It wasn't until they neared the end of the year that he noticed—everything about her.

He felt her shaking in his arms then the most unexpected noise came from her throat. She *growled* and stomped her foot. "That's it. We're done. I don't need your help. Carter can go jump off a cliff if what he's looking for is anything at all like, like, *you.*"

She yanked free and started for the door. He'd gone too far. Maybe it wasn't about her being jealous. Maybe the truth was staring him in the face. *He* was the jealous one. "Wait, don't go. I'm sorry…I was just messing with you. Let's just finish the dance, okay? I'll be quiet."

The music slowed and he pulled her in. She fought, a halfhearted attempt to put distance between them, before relaxing against his chest. An overwhelming feeling hit him the moment her cheek's warmth seeped through his shirt. An odd yet comforting serenity that equaled the contented warmth of their fishing trip. This felt right. He closed his eyes and lowered his head to bury his nose in the softness of her hair. God, she smelled good. *That* he remembered.

He had no idea when the music stopped and a commercial replaced the beat. When he finally pulled his head sleepily from hers, dread hit him hard. Why in hell was he fixing Amanda up with Carter? *You're so amazing, Amanda.*

"Thanks. That was nice coming from you."

Huh? Wait, he'd actually said that out loud? Holy crap. How do you follow up something like that?

"So, why'd you run away last year?"

Chapter Eight

Amanda wasn't prepared for his question. He'd asked it before, but she'd been in a fighting mood then. Now? How could he ask such a thing? It was like rubbing salt into an open wound. He *knew* why she'd left. Hell, he'd recommended it, according to David. Nope, she wasn't up for a fight at the moment. Not when his arms were around her and she struggled to hold herself together. "Awww, big-bad-man-whore Jackson, you missed me. Now *that's* amazing. It wasn't like I had a choice to leave, you know. Was I the one who got away?"

She patted his cheek in her most patronizing way.

Jackson's cell phone jolted into action in his pocket. Amanda giggled. They were so close the vibration against her mid-section tickled. "Actually, yes." He let it ring again before dropping his hand from her waist and answering the device.

Actually, yes, what? He missed her? She was the one who'd eluded his man-talent? Or was he saying there really *had* been a choice? Was that the best answer she'd get? She shook her head and reached for her purse.

"I'm busy. I'll call you back," Jackson blurted before clicking his phone off and striding to her side. "I think you're good to go on the dancing part but let's talk a little on the way back about Carter. Or us, or what happened that made you bolt out of the office like a bat out of hell."

"There is no us, Jax. Don't you have a phone call you need to make?"

• • •

Jackson didn't give a flying flip about work at the moment, nor did he care about Carter and helping Amanda snag him. He cared about one thing and only one thing—he just couldn't get his arms around what it was.

Watching her stomp off in a tizzy wasn't it. So he strode after like he'd done half a dozen times in the last couple of days. Maybe all he hoped for was an explanation. Why *had* she left?

With the worn-out sneakers, Amanda could clip along much faster than in the heels she sported last night. He picked up his pace and gained some ground. Just before the street corner, she whirled and thrust a finger in his face. "This is *not* one of your stupid games, Jax. He's a nice person. He treats me like a queen, not like a back-alley hooker, which is probably more your style. I don't know why I bothered to come here this morning. There's nothing you can tell or show me."

"Treats you like a queen, huh? How so?"

"We go out for nice dinners, we spend time together, we… we…chat back and forth during the day when we don't see each other for a while."

"How often is that? Seeing each other, I mean." He was curious.

"I don't know. A couple times a week, maybe. Does it matter? The point here is…Carter isn't always staring at my boobs, or the skin on my shoulder, or my ass. He's not that kind of guy." A car whizzed by and they both gazed after it until it rounded a corner on the next block.

"Amanda, I hate to burst your bubble, but *every* guy is that kind of guy. Carter included. If he hasn't thought about getting you into bed at least half a dozen times when you're together, then he's planning a way to dump you."

She pursed her lips and the act sent a pain straight through him. Visions of the elevator kiss fogged his brain. She growled and threw her hands in the air then turned away. The rubber of her shoe soles squeaked on the concrete. She rotated back to him and crossed her arms. "Okay, let me get this straight so we can end this little tutoring session you think I desperately need. You want me to dress as sexy and provocative as possible, dance with my chest pressed against him but don't get too into it as that's over the top, make him think I *need* him somehow, and…oh, let's not forget… have sex with him. But if the list is too long, I can just go straight to the last part. Is that right?"

Whoa, wait a minute. "I didn't say have sex with him."

"Oh yes, you did. Men are simple, right? They have only a few basic needs and that's one of them."

"Yeah, but…isn't it a little soon?"

Amanda rolled her eyes. "You say that like you think we haven't already."

"Uh, I, have you?" Hell. He did *not* want to hear that.

"For your information, I am not the complete loser with guys that you seem to think. Carter and I get along great. In fact, I'm pretty damn good at a few things which I'm not talking about with you—things he seems to find very, very interesting."

"Oh, really? Let's hear about them." That sounded like she was sidestepping the question.

His phone chirped into action again but he ignored it. When it continued to ring, he pulled it from his pocket and switched it to silent mode.

"I *said* I wasn't talking about them with you. Someone really wants to talk to you, Jackson. You should probably take that."

"Not now. Come on, Amanda. Spill." For some stupid, self-serving reason he needed to know what she saw in his friend. Or for that matter, what he saw in her. Sure, they were alike but how boring was that? Jackson thought for a minute. Who was he kidding? What he really needed to know was if she'd slept with him. "Tell me, does he like to grab your ass when you kiss? Slip you the tongue? Or maybe he's not an ass-man, maybe—"

"Shut. Up. You're such a Neanderthal. Give me a break. We're not like that. He loves my…my intelligence. And my drive. He likes that we can sit together for hours and work without needing to talk."

Jackson snickered. "Seriously? You guys spend hours together doing…nothing? And you *like* that? Jesus, Amanda, that is *not* good. Uh-uh. No way. He should be so involved that he's thinking about getting in your pants or at least getting you out of them. And you should be on the same track with him. You can sit in a room with a damn cat or a bird. You don't need a man for that."

Amanda dropped her hands to her sides and fisted them. "You know what? We're done here. Your advice sucks, Jackson. Getting Carter in or out of his pants isn't the issue for me. Having someone I can count on, that's what matters. Someone who has my back when I need him and shows up when things get rough. Someone who doesn't hide behind family loyalties and elitist…crap." She twirled fingers in a tornado-like motion and he wondered what kind of "crap" she referred to in the gesture. "I want someone who I don't have to go looking for when I need a support system, someone who will find me instead. Why? Because for some stupid, silly woman-reason, I want to *matter* to him. Do you want to know why I disappeared? Why I didn't talk to you the day I left or answer your calls? You want to know what was wrong?"

Her voice was starting to squeak and Jackson dreaded whatever came next, even though he needed to hear her reasons. He'd spent countless nights wondering what the hell had happened. "Yeah."

Amanda stepped toward him and thrust a finger to his chest. "It was you, Jax. I left because of you. Because you wanted me gone. I could handle your parents and that stupid wimp of a boss, David. I just couldn't understand why *you'd* turn on me like that."

What the fuck was that supposed to mean? Turn on her? He hadn't turned on her. He wasn't even sure why'd she'd ran off— which she'd just chosen to do once more. He stared as she broke into a sprint. In less than five, four, three, two, one seconds she was gone. Again.

Badeep deep. Hell, now whoever called was texting? Their timing sucked. He dragged his phone from his pocket and looked at the display. Holy hell.

Mom: *Your father is in the hospital. Pick up the phone.*

Chapter Nine

A stroke.

What shitty luck. Just when a man got to the top of the ladder, the peak of his game, so to speak, Mother Nature decided to throw him a curveball. Jackson's father had spittle flowing down the side of his face as he stared out the window. His clouded eyes held little emotion and barely registered the movements around him. Jackson's emotions, however, were spinning like a kite in a tornado. Did a person lose their thoughts and feelings after something like this? Or just their memories and motor skills? Was his father really there? Who could tell?

God had just swiped his hand across the chessboard of Dad's life and cleared the game. An optimist would say it was a chance for a do-over. Of course, such optimist would have to completely ignore the fact that he might have lost all memory of the past *and* needed to relearn a great deal of motor skills. For the CEO of a family-held company, that would certainly affect his decision-making skills. It was time for a new strategy. Jackson seriously doubted this particular scenario was in the cards when Dad had talked to him about moving out of the cubicle and taking his "rightful" spot with the company.

Only his mother could phrase it in a way that drove the stake in place without sugar-coating. "I guess now you'll have to stop playing around and get serious at work."

Stop playing around? Was that what he'd been doing when he spent six years in college making straight As, passing the bar exam, and taking a job in legal like every other intern? Was it really playing around to want people to take his efforts seriously and respect him for his work and not his name?

"I didn't know I was, Mom. Besides, you know as well as I do that David has more experience and can run the company. Hell, *you* are more qualified than either of us. You should take the helm."

"That would have been nice, wouldn't it? Your father had other ideas. He's written into the company charter that you would take over certain duties if he's unable to fulfill them. I had a role some time ago but that was removed when—well, when his focus shifted." He tried hard to ignore the glittered wetness of her eyes. *Focus shifted. Is that what they call an affair these days?*

It wasn't the first time either. Why had his mom tolerated it all these years? "Mom, why'd you let him run over you? All those years…all those…'shifts in focus.' Didn't it bother you?"

The curtain closed on her lapse in control. She raised her shoulders and looked out the window over Dad's seemingly comatose body. Did he hear them? Did he understand? Jackson couldn't care less. The man he called Dad had been a pillar in the community, an enthusiastic and successful businessman, a half-decent father—and the worst husband on the planet. Ironically, he'd hidden it well from the public and his mother had never said a word.

"Don't pass judgment on something you don't fully understand, Jackson."

"I understand enough to know he treated you like crap in private and pretended to idolize you in public."

"Watch your words, young man. He's still your father. Not to mention he's sitting right here in front of you."

"Mom …"

Lynn Holstenar held up a hand. "Enough. What happens between your father and me is not your business. What happens with the company is all that matters at this point. Well, that, and getting Robert back to normal."

"What exactly would that be?"

Normal. Jackson didn't want his Dad's "normal" self. He wanted something more, or perhaps less. The company *wasn't* all that mattered in Jackson's eyes. It was the only thing that *didn't* have importance at the moment. If his father never returned to them, never came out of this shell, what would be the most important thing he left them?

A company worth a small fortune? A legacy?

Jackson turned his hands over, trying to come to terms with what his father actually stood for. There was a lot of pride in his work ethic. He'd built the company from the ground up, and they'd had more than a few lean years in Jackson's childhood. Unfortunately, as time passed, all Jackson could remember was all the times his father was gone while Mom held their family together.

She'd been there when he broke his arm and had to be rushed to the hospital. His father was in L.A. at the time. When Jackson graduated from college, she arrived an hour early to snag a spot in the front row, then stood and cheered when he traipsed across the stage. She was alone and embarrassed, but she was *there*. Dad was negotiating a contract in Thailand. Robert had shown up when he graduated from law school, only to spend much of the ceremony and after party pacing behind the crowd and talking on his cell phone.

Still, he'd been present. Not perfect but there and Jackson knew there were a lot of people in the world who'd never had a dad at all.

At seventeen, Jackson had spent more time at Carter's than home. He'd had a multitude of reasons—Carter needed him and Jackson's house was depressingly quiet. His mother had been at the office almost as much as his dad so Jackson often was home alone.

He just wished for someone to talk to and often found that at Carter's. Carter's mother, Becky, once told him to give his parents a break. "You're blessed to have parents that work so hard to give you a lifestyle they'd always dreamed of. Your life may not be perfect. Hell, one can always see the cracks in the concrete if they're looking down. Force yourself to look up and you'll see everything you want waiting for you. Look forward to a future that has the perfect life and relationship. Then stop whining about what isn't right and go get what is—what can be. Your parents can't control who you are and the sooner you realize that, the quicker you'll find your own place."

Becky Coben was right.

Jackson went to college and found the self-satisfaction he'd never attained at home. Without his parents' legacy, he'd managed to make his own way. He'd studied hard and while his father had wanted him to choose a path in business, law school hadn't been a disappointment. It was the contrary. More than his parents expected of him. In truth, if he thought hard about his life, he'd always exceeded their expectations and it was never enough.

Snap. Snap. His mother's finger clicks jolted him back to the present. "Earth to Jackson. What in the world are you daydreaming about? Are you hung over?"

"I haven't had a hangover in years, Mom, but thanks for the confidence."

"I didn't mean it in a bad way. I was…trying to lighten things up."

Dad chose that moment to turn his head and focus—on Jackson. "Mmmm."

Jackson leaned forward. "What, Dad? Do you want something? Some water?"

"Mmmm." A mist covered Dad's eyes. Hell. It had to be frustrating to lose so much.

The door whooshed open and the attending physician joined them. "His speech will take a while to come back but it will. Slowly. The rehab will help get him on his feet and moving. We'll transfer him to our residential physical therapy program on Monday. Your insurance covers it for two weeks, then he'll need to continue the exercises at home."

"How long will that take?" Jackson wasn't all that keen on filling his father's shoes at work.

The doctor shrugged. Without looking up from his notes, he spoke. "I can't really say. Everyone's different. As long as there aren't any further episodes, a couple of weeks will make a huge difference."

"Will he be able to return to work?"

"Sure, but he may not be the same."

The same? What did that mean?

"Not the same would be fine with me." Okay, maybe it wasn't nice to be critical at the moment.

The doctor's eyes snapped up from his pad. "What's important is getting him on his feet and talking. He needs to relearn a lot of things, simple things like how to use his hands and legs. I can guarantee you he won't be same for a while, maybe never."

Damn.

Chapter Ten

It wasn't until Jackson was in his SUV that he wished it had occurred to him to question his mother about Amanda's revelation. *It was you…you wanted me out.* She'd left the company because of him? The likelihood his mother had any knowledge of the circumstances was slim. At one point, Lynn Holstenar had been entrenched in the day-to-day business strategies and decisions. Not now.

David had knocked heads with her early on which resulted in Lynn stepping back and allowing him room to work. At first, Jackson had been certain David would be fired. No one challenged his parents in business matters.

But David not only survived, he thrived. Jackson was confused at the time but soon came to terms with the man's surly ways, though he often wondered if there was an undercurrent he needed to better understand.

Leaving the hospital felt like shedding a heavy winter parka. The weight of emotion sloughed off temporarily. He rolled the window down and opened the sunroof to breathe in something other than the smell of antiseptic.

He was moving upstairs beginning Monday. He'd fought it for years only to be in the exact spot his parents had wanted him ages ago. The calmness that soaked into his chest wasn't what he'd expected to feel.

As he coasted down the street to turn onto the freeway and head home, music blared from a nearby bar and a thought surged into his mind. Was Amanda with Carter now? Had the date gone well? Had his advice made a difference? Should he stop by and check on them?

He shook his head. Hell, it wasn't like he was her parent. In fact, as much as he'd coached Amanda, the only thought that kept running through his peanut-sized brain was the elevator incident, which conflicted with her interest in his friend.

He flipped a left at the stoplight and headed toward midtown. Carter would want to know about Dad, right?

Twenty minutes later, he walked into the club and searched the room for familiar faces, expecting to see Carter and Amanda on the dance floor. He got it half-right. She was there—her hands in the air, eyes closed, bopping up and down in a group full of people. None of them was Carter. It was a major battle to tear his eyes away.

"She's something else, isn't she? Here." A beer was thrust in Jackson's hand as Carter pounded his back.

"Yeah, not sure exactly what—but something. Having fun?" Should a friend silently wish for a solid 'no' answer? Why was there a tinge of satisfaction at seeing her dancing out there in the crowd alone? He cast it off with a shrug. Hell, the way she flung her arms around, it would have been impossible for anyone to try to dance *with* her. She'd beat them to death.

"This place is awesome. I'm sweating my ass off. Amanda loves to dance, hasn't stopped since we got here. Not sure I keep up but it's a hoot trying. Who said attorneys were boring? I had to take a short break to hydrate a little." Carter tipped a beer toward Amanda. She smiled a huge smile and waved both hands at them.

Yeah, they were having fun—dammit. "I just stopped by to tell you…Dad's in the hospital."

Carter shifted his eyes from the dance floor to Jackson, his voice dropped to a monotone. "Seriously? What happened?"

"He had a stroke."

"Oh shit. I'm sorry. Is he going to be okay?" Carter's concern was genuine and Jackson measured the guilt in his stomach, knowing that he'd intentionally wanted to dampen the spirit of the moment. He'd injected a cloud over their date and it wasn't comforting to know he'd done so intentionally.

"Which hospital?"

Jackson relayed the information and spoke for a few minutes about Dad's state of health. Carter focused intently on Jackson's words. Jackson, however, never let his eyes waver—from Amanda. She was a terrible dancer, yet for some strange reason, it was mesmerizing. Sort of like watching a train wreck. You knew it was going to hurt but you couldn't stop.

When she finally worked her way through the crowd to join them, her hair was dripping and curled up in tiny ringlets around her forehead. It was nothing like the severe and professional look she'd sported in the elevator weeks ago. Nor was it the fresh-but-sloppy/sleepy look of the weekend. It was the look of much-needed escapism. Rapture. He had no idea she loved music and dancing so much.

Carter rushed to get her water and libations from the bar before she melted into the dance floor.

Amanda swept her hair above her head with both hands and held it with one. Was she waiting for her skin to stop perspiring or hoping a breeze would develop inside the building? "Jackson, what are you doing here?"

He wasn't sure. At first he thought he'd be a good wingman— did they call it that for a woman? That was a laugh.

Amanda needed help from no one, especially not him. Carter approached and passed her a drink. She downed it in two gulps; it was incredibly sexy to watch the water pour down her throat and disappear into the crevice of her shirt. "His dad just had a stroke."

The euphoric abandon splayed across her face earlier disappeared. Amanda dropped her hair and clutched into Jackson's arm. "Oh, my God. I'm sooo sorry."

Carter didn't seem to notice the familiarity of the gesture though it made Jackson uncomfortable. Sure, it was just a friendly gesture of sympathy but to Jax, it felt—personal. Carter must have thought otherwise. "I need to go by the hospital, Amanda."

"Now?" Amanda seemed disappointed. Was she upset that her good time had been interrupted?

"He's like a father. Jax and I grew up together. When my dad died, he was—around."

Jackson wasn't going to be responsible for crashing their date, no matter how much his gut told him it felt good to put a little distance between his friend and the girl who tied his brain in knots. Or maybe it wasn't his brain that was the problem. "It's too late. Visiting hours are over anyway. You can stop in tomorrow. I'm sure he'll appreciate the support."

Jackson fought a squirm as Carter focused on him. It was what a friend would do under the circumstances. Carter just didn't understand the full extent of the circumstances. Jackson wasn't just worried about his father but also about the fact that while he pretended to support Carter's interest in Amanda, he secretly wanted it to fail. Carter's shirt sleeves were rolled up to expose forearms a man worked hard to get. He wrapped one of them around Jackson's neck and pulled him into a man-hug. "What about you, man? How are you doing?"

Jackson shrugged. "Just waiting to see how this is going to work out—they're already pressuring me to move upstairs. As if I didn't get enough of that already."

"Then do it. It's not like you can't handle it."

"That's just it—they don't think I can. They're all expecting me to fail." Jackson had felt the loathing in David's words more than once, not to mention the way some of the others avoided him. The conversations sometimes implied he wasn't good enough simply because there was an entitlement to his role. He'd gone overboard to earn his stripes and prove his worth. Yet it wasn't enough.

"You don't know that. You're being paranoid." Carter, of all people, said that? The man who trusted no one and had a phobia about honesty?

"No, just stating the truth. I have a reputation for being the playboy son. No brains and no common sense, just a legacy."

Amanda dropped an elbow on Carter's shoulder in a gesture of closeness. Jackson stared at the sheen of perspiration covering her arms, her neck, her face. She strung a couple of fingers through the sweat-covered tendrils of hair. "Then prove them wrong."

"Exactly how am I supposed to do that? They've already made up their minds."

She sent her eyes skyward. "God, Jackson. Do you really let everyone else make your choices for you? You and I both know you're smarter than most of the people there and know the inner workings of your dad's business better than almost everyone... except maybe your mom. Stop sitting back and pretending to be an idiot simply because that's what they expect and you're trying to fit in."

"I want them to like me, not resent me."

She stuck a finger in his face and Jackson stepped back. "No. You want them to respect you. That's what's important at the moment. It's one thing to be the fun guy who everyone wants to go out for a beer with. It's a totally different story to be the man they decide to rest the weight of their future on. Stop trying to fit in and be liked. You had that covered years ago and I don't understand why it mattered anyway."

She obviously didn't get it, which was a surprise coming from her. She had agonized over and over again that she was the token female and always on the outside when things got dicey. "You can't be respected if you're not liked. They go hand in hand."

"Bingo." She cocked a finger and made a gun-shooting gesture. "*You* just need to start playing it in reverse and concentrate on the respect part. They're looking for a reason to dislike you and can't find one so they label you a party guy, a womanizer, which, by the way, you are...but we'll pretend differently for now. When people envy someone, they look for flaws. We all have them but for some reason, we want someone else to have more. Show them what you're really made of."

He looked at the drink she'd set down. "How many of those have you had tonight?"

Carter had stood silently as she gave the speech. His glance shifted between his two closest friends. For Christ's sake, could he see how much Jackson wanted to rip her clothes off at the moment? She was frickin' gorgeous…and out of his realm. Carter patted Jackson on the back. "See, she gives you a pep talk and the first thing you do is discount it by saying she's drunk. Go be the boss, Jax. You know you can handle it. We all know. The company needs you now more than ever."

Jackson squinted at the haze over the stage as the band regrouped for their next song. "So does Dad."

Chapter Eleven

Was it crazy to be thankful for a quiet hospital room's sanctuary? Being with Carter when his dad died had been brutal and the memories stayed with Jackson. The stench of antiseptic, Clorox, and some sort of cleaner they used to hide the other smells was obnoxious to a young teenager's heightened senses. Add to that the high-emotion factor and Jackson had considered himself a trooper to spend as much time there with Carter as possible.

He had hated it but understood, thanks to his parents' insistence, that presence was key to getting his friend back on track. On what track was a bigger question. After Carter's sister drowned, the boy had never been the same. Anger. Sadness. Withdrawal. All things that made Jackson want to deck his friend but he didn't. Instead he started daring him. First it was to beat him at hangman in the hospital room while his father slept between treatments. Unfortunately, Carter soon tired of it since words were Jackson's forte and not Carter's.

So Jackson switched to math, then after the funeral it was baseball when the summer heat set in. Carter's mother had encouraged them to be outside as much as possible, which was easy since it forced them all to forget. His father had encouraged Jackson to stop pestering Carter all the time and let him "work through his pain." But Jackson understood like no other. He had lost a pseudo-sibling in Carter's sister, Carley, then a father figure that was a better role model than his own dad when Mr. Coben finally succumbed to his illness. There was no way in hell he'd let his friend take the easy way out.

So, when Carter started glancing at Kylee Williams during gym class, Jackson chose a new competition—girls. It worked. They were drawn to Carter's looks and his mysterious moodiness but Jackson would make his best effort to draw them away with jokes and goofiness. Between the two, they were the perfect team and soon Carter returned in mind and spirit.

"Mmmm." Robert was watching Jackson stare out the window.

"What, Dad?" Jackson searched the face that had always scared him. His father had been a demanding man with high expectations. It was ironic, considering he'd been a womanizing, walking ego. "What do you want? A drink?" Jackson reached for the plastic pitcher at the bedside.

Robert moved his head slightly to the right. That was a no, apparently.

"Are you cold? Do you want a blanket?"

Another movement, a little stronger. "Mmmm." His father's finger lifted off the sheet and pointed...at the television. "Mooobie."

Jackson glanced at the screen. "Oh, a movie. You want to watch a movie? I'll change the channel."

Another movement. No. Okay, what the hell did he want? There was already a movie on. It was *Lord of the Rings.* "Mmmmember. Moobie."

Ooooh, of course. "You remember, Dad? We saw this when we went to Cozumel the summer of my sophomore year in college. Is that what you mean?"

"Sssss." Judging by the change in head movement, that was a *yes. Yes.* He remembered. *Yes.* He was talking. The man raised his finger again toward Jackson. "Sssssick."

Oh, not a yes. "Okay, we don't need to remember *that,* do we? Yes, I was sick. I ate enough Milk Duds to fill a dump truck and puked them all over the bathroom. Geez, couldn't you pick something else to remember?"

"Sss...ssss...sss." The man was—laughing? Yep, he was.

His father never laughed. In fact, that summer was probably the last time Jackson had seen mirth cross his father's features, and of course it was all at Jackson's expense. His father returned his gaze to the television, a weird half-smile crossing his lips.

Jackson swallowed back the lump of cotton that threatened to choke him. His dad had shown the first signs of recovery. Well, of mental recovery. Physically, his rehab had gone mediocre. He was able to step off the bed and walk a few short feet, completely unaware or unconcerned that his ass hung out of the hospital gown.

It was crazy. His dad, the man who never wore anything that wasn't perfectly pressed, whose hair was cut every three weeks regardless of its length, and whose car had never seen a crumb from McDonald's or a toy under the seat, didn't seem to mind his bare butt staring them down as they followed to ensure he wouldn't tire and fall.

Should he get him talking more? Try to weasel a few more words out? Why not?

"How far'd you walk today, Dad?"

No answer. It was worth a try.

The clip-clop of heels echoed in the hallway, growing stronger with each tap before Jackson's mother entered the room.

"He talked, Mom."

The clipping stopped abruptly. "What?"

"He talked."

"What'd he say? Please tell me he didn't mumble Ritz or something like that. I'll deck him." Was that a joke? She'd made humor of Robert's infidelity? Oh, God.

"Ssss …. Ssss…ssss." And Dad laughed.

Lynn's mouth dropped. "Are you laughing, Robert?"

The man's chest rose and dropped and the hissing continued until a tear trickled down his cheek. "L…L…L …"

She finished for him. "Yes, Lynn. That's me, honey. Good job."

Jackson's father twitched his head to the side in the gesture that Jackson now understood as a no. "That's not what he was going to say, Mom."

Her shoulders sagged and Jackson wished he hadn't been so abrupt. "How do you know?"

"That little shake there, that's his no."

The doctor joined them and started talking with Robert, explaining how well he'd done at rehab today, and advising that he had about another week before he could go home.

"L…l…liquor." Dad pointed at Jackson. Huh? "Find L…l …"

The doctor laughed. "No, no liquor for a while, though it might keep the blood thin which isn't entirely all bad. Still, it would be a disaster if you tried your rehab while plastered. Better stay off the sauce for now."

Robert grunted and laid back.

Seriously? His father wanted a drink? Great. Some things hadn't changed. Jackson couldn't remember when his father had started the habit of stopping off for a drink on the way home. He only knew it had been a steady routine since he was a senior in high school. One that often appeared associated with his other routine of collecting outside female companionship.

Was it expecting too much to hope his Dad would forget all that crap?

Jackson excused himself and headed toward the office. He'd postponed the inevitable as long as it was possible, now he had to force himself to follow through on his promise to his mother. There was an impromptu board meeting in an hour that he was to attend, at which point he would advise everyone of his father's change in health and begin educating himself on the business's current state of affairs.

"You need to do this solo," his mother had encouraged when he asked her to join him. Jackson thought it would be good to make it appear a team effort. "If you want them to take you seriously and understand your leadership capabilities, you have to go in there alone and take the bull by the horns. David will be there, too."

As if *that* was comforting. David was the last person Jackson could lean on in this situation.

Jackson's phone rang as he strode from the parking garage to the building. He opened it without looking. "How's he doing?"

Amanda. Warmth settled in his shoulders. "He talked today."

"That's gotta be good, right?"

"I thought so. Especially because he remembered something from a trip we took when I was in high school. It wasn't just a hello or something like that. It was a memory."

He could almost feel her smile. "Oh, that's awesome! Does it mean he'll be back to normal soon?"

"I wish it were that simple but no, he has a lot of physical therapy to finish, and a few words isn't much. His vocal skills need some development."

"Still, it could be a lot worse—thank your stars it isn't."

Thank his stars. *There's a good phrase if you believe the stars portend your future.* He didn't. Neither did he think legacy mattered in business. The most important difference in work was results and if he couldn't get the desired results, it mattered little that his father was the founder and CEO. Results were the only thing that mattered in Dad's recovery also. Would he be able to speak again? Would he be able to walk, drive, and make decisions?

Yes, making decisions was a biggie. Jackson had already received numerous phone calls with what seemed rudimentary questions that the caller could make without input. Had Dad always dealt with trivial matters such as the lunch menu for board meetings or the flight arrangement for sales staff? What a waste of time—not to mention lack of confidence in his staff. They were adults and could make those decisions themselves.

"Amanda, I need to ask you something." His mind was preoccupied with the papers on his desk and he didn't think to lead into his question with any background information.

"Yes, I'm busy this weekend but thanks for wanting to take me on that cruise… I've always wanted to do one." What? Obviously, she was teasing and he felt his shoulders relax. He needed a little lighthearted humor at the moment. The mirth in her voice made him smile. "I thought maybe we could do lunch instead."

He let a chuckle go. "I'm crushed. These tickets were expensive. I guess lunch will work, but won't Carter mind?"

"Why should he care? It's just lunch and not like he and I are serious. Besides I thought you'd want to know how things went the other night."

She was right. He did, sort of, but that wasn't the reason for the call. "Sure, and you can tell me why you said it's my fault you left the job too."

Crickets. Not a word came through the phone. Had she hung up? "Amanda?"

"Um…we should probably not talk about that right now. Please tell me that wasn't what you wanted to ask because I might lose it and well, my temper isn't exactly the sweet, feminine kind. I *really* lose it."

He doubted that. She was as cool as an ice cube on the North Pole in his eyes. "My question was business related and we can talk on the phone now if you'd rather, but you're the one who suggested lunch and I'm okay with a little food and business. You dropped a bomb on me the other day and didn't explain yourself and now you want me to ignore that anything was said. It wasn't the reason for my call but I'd still like to know what made you leave."

"I have my reasons."

"Maybe you could explain them because apparently the reason has something to do with me."

Chapter Twelve

Amanda wasn't prepared for vulnerability. Seeing Jackson's face in the business section of *The Chronicle* was disturbing. He looked sad and angry at the same time but the clincher look was—vulnerable. She'd never seen that emotion in him and hadn't expected to care if she did. It would be easy to distance herself from him again, except for Carter. Jackson and Carter were friends, and if she kept seeing Carter, Jackson was likely going to be a regular distraction.

Amanda told herself it didn't matter. Jackson wasn't a problem anymore. Still, there he was in the paper wearing the striped shirt she remembered. She loved that shirt on him. He rolled the sleeves and sometimes untucked the shirttail at work which made him look comfortable and incredibly earth-sexy.

The deli they'd chosen for lunch was a short drive and she made it with time to spare. She waited outside, scanning the article and trying to understand the emotions it invoked. Jackson was touted as the playboy heir to his father's business. It was odd that the article made the papers since their company was small compared to so many others in the city. The description of Jackson was accurate only in that he was a playboy and enjoyed life—but they made him out as stupid and incapable.

Did they not know the man like she did? In college, he had patiently worked through their law class study sessions with the entire group, often explaining what many hadn't understood. At work, they'd collaborated many times on key points related to contracts or issues. Given a chance, he would contribute as much or more than most and do so in an unassuming and non-intrusive manner.

Jackson was neither stupid nor incapable. He was misunderstood more than anything. Was that intentional?

"There she is." Jackson's voice carried on the breeze outside the restaurant. Amanda turned to greet him and stilled. She hadn't expected him to have additional company and certainly wasn't prepared to see someone she'd thought she was rid of forever. A man who'd made her career take an unexpected turn—her old boss. "I told David I was meeting you and he asked if he could join us. That's okay, right?"

Uh, *nooo*. "Sure, fine. Good to see you, David," she lied. The last time she'd seen David, he had informed her the Holsterar family no longer needed her services. Why? Because she was getting too involved with Jackson and not following through on projects she was assigned. Total crap in her opinion because she was never *involved* with Jackson and her projects were not only on schedule but most were ahead of the planned time frame. When she'd asked if her departure had been discussed with Jackson, David had told her it was Jackson's idea.

The words still burned—not that the family didn't want her, nor that David felt her easily dispensable, but Jackson had wanted her gone and didn't have the stomach to tell her himself.

Amanda pasted on a smile and led them in for a meal that suddenly wasn't at all appealing. Once seated, a waiter thrust menus in their faces.

Jackson's phone rang and he glanced at the screen. "Uh oh, I need to take this. Give me just a second." The chair legs screeched against the floor as he stood and stepped toward the door. Perfect. He'd left her alone with David.

Awkward. Amanda pretended to be immersed in the menu for several minutes. When she could bear the silence no longer, she snapped the plastic shut and dropped it on the tablecloth.

"Soooo, how's life treating you? Ran anyone else off lately? Or do you save that special thing for people who work harder than you?"

David frowned. "Look, you know I did the right thing. You're making twice as much money where you're at and there's no one to pick and choose your projects. Besides, this wasn't about you. It was about family. Family is all that counts."

What the hell was he talking about? He wasn't part of their family.

"Sorry about that." Jackson dropped into his chair. "Has the waiter taken drinks yet?"

Dumfounded, Amanda shook her head.

"Well, I need one." He turned his head and signaled for help.

They avoided everything to do with work and when Jackson started to discuss old projects they had in common, David squelched his words.

If David had lived in the sixties, he would have dressed like one of the Mormon boys that came to her parents' door and sold pencils while trying to give a sermon. His hair was always cut a bit short and plastered neatly with a lot of gel. He would have worn a white starched shirt with a pencil thin dark tie and dark pants. The new version was less obvious and didn't stand out. David wore khaki pants and a long-sleeved polo with a white collar. The style of dress wasn't unusual in itself. In truth, Amanda had been fine with his dress code.

Just not with David. He tried too hard. Something about the fact that he was in a constant state of intent-to-impress was— creepy, forced. Disingenuous. David was disingenuous.

Jackson, however, moved with ease and seemed unconcerned with the effect he had on the people around him, though Amanda knew he cared. A lot, in fact, which made his statements and actions more believable. It was ironic that in order to be believed and trusted, one should not care about being either.

The only good thing about lunch with the two men was she didn't have to discuss the anger and hurt she'd felt at knowing Jackson had wanted her dismissed. She wasn't ready to do so and certainly not in front of David. She wouldn't give him the satisfaction. Nope, he'd never know how crushed she'd been. When the two men walked away together after lunch, she was relieved and perplexed.

Why had David wanted to join Jackson? He'd made it clear she wasn't needed any longer. He'd also made Jackson's intentions pretty transparent in the process. Was there more?

A truck horn blared at the same time her cell phone kicked into action and Amanda changed her focus to the phone call. Her mother.

"We need you to come home, sweetie." Mom's endearment was sweet even if she did use the words on all her children. It was her mother's way of putting affection into a conversation regardless of the subject. The Southern way, she always said.

"What's wrong? Is Dad sick? I don't know that I can book a flight that quickly."

"Nothing like that. I meant next month. We're planning to do a little remodeling and need some help, plus your brothers will be here and it just wouldn't be the same without you."

Her mother had a habit of leaving out small, yet crucial points in a conversation, like dates, times, and the importance of events. She'd say something that put one in a panic only to fully explain afterward. It drove Amanda bat-crazy.

After speaking for a few more minutes, Amanda was committed to a family weekend in three weeks. The thought of seeing her brothers and mother together for the first time since the holidays was both foreboding and pleasant.

• • •

Jackson regretted allowing David to horn in on his lunch plans the minute he'd agreed. He'd hoped for some alone time with Amanda—not the personal kind but more the professional and confidential type where he could discuss some of her prior projects without any other ears or eyes involved. He didn't trust David enough to involve him in those conversations yet he felt he owed it to the man based on his role in the company.

Those choices were easier a week ago. Now, after taking on tasks that his father had always handled, the possibility of choosing badly had grown significantly. The company financials sprawled on the corner of Dad's desk were a stark reminder. Dad had made several notes and positioned the list of notes under the document as if to hide them. The notes were cryptic but the triple line under one name seemed critical. He'd found the list last night when it slipped to the floor as he scooped the financial document to shove it in his satchel for night reading. He had retrieved the list and scanned it, then decided to leave all as it was and research further.

When Jackson rounded the massive mahogany desk and settled into the uncomfortable chair, the papers seemed to wave a flag. David had followed Jackson into the office and focused immediately on the documents. Jackson was tired. Tired of David's questions and constant blabber of advice, another situation that Jackson wanted to escape. He tried limiting his responses in the hope that David would get the message and leave.

David pointed a toothpick that he'd been chewing at the papers. "You need to approve those today. They're due to the board next week and the admin staff will need to make copies of the signed documents and bind them in packets for the board meetings."

"I know. I'll get to it this afternoon. I have a couple of calls to follow up on first."

David tossed the toothpick in the ornate copper trash can by Robert's desk. "If you want to sign them now, I'll take them down and save you a little time."

It seemed innocent enough and Jackson should take him up on the offer. But his father's note, well hidden, tapped him on the shoulder as if to say "why the rush?"

David lowered a hand to the financials and pushed them toward Jackson. Thankfully the note underneath stayed. *Is he forcing me to sign?* Jackson's shoulders bunched and the hair at the nape of his neck rose. *No one forces me to do anything.* He had yelled it to a teacher in grade school right before pouncing on another ten-year-old who'd threatened to beat him up if he didn't supply answers to a homework assignment. He'd landed in detention then because the teacher hadn't known what the true issue involved and he saw no need to divulge. He wasn't a rat but he wasn't a wimp either. There had been many incidents over the years where his will was tested. He'd never been good at acquiescing.

Jackson leveled his gaze on David, reached out to the papers, and planted his fist to anchor them in place. He lowered his voice in a manner that he'd learned from Dad, who believed very strongly in Teddy Roosevelt's motto, "Speak softly and carry a big stick."

"I said I'll do it this afternoon. I have some calls to make now, David. Thanks for joining me for lunch. I will see you later." Jackson picked up his phone and punched in a number. It wasn't really business, just Carter, but the point was made. As soon as Carter answered, he dove into conversation and ignored David. Would he get the message or was this destined to go an extra round?

David hesitated, then removed his hand from the stack and strode out of the office. As soon as the door closed, Jackson whispered. "Carter, would you mind terribly if I sought a little legal advice from Amanda? There's something weird going on here and I can't discuss it internally. I want a second opinion."

Carter hesitated. "Why Amanda?"

"Because she worked here and she knows one of the contracts I'm concerned about. Before Dad had his stroke, we were about to close on a pretty large contract with a construction outfit in Philly. The client was overseas and this project had been on and off at least three times. Amanda worked on the first revisions before she left."

"That was nearly two years ago, Jax. I doubt she remembers."

He was wrong about that. Amanda had the mind of a vacuum cleaner. Once she'd sucked it in, it stayed forever. He pitied the man who ever sought a relationship with her. He'd get away with nothing. "Maybe but I'd just like to discuss it with someone outside the company. I need a little advice and don't want to seem inept here." It wasn't exactly the full story but good enough. Carter would understand his desire to prove himself in the new role and hopefully be a bit sympathetic to the cause.

Carter agreed, though he seemed reluctant. Jackson wasn't sure why he had a tinge of guilt for asking. It was just a business discussion, right? Besides, she'd already expressed an interest in his friend and Carter seemed to finally be enjoying himself with a woman. Jackson should be happy for his friend. At least one of them was happy with a woman worth being around. Carter deserved it and Jackson should support that and revel in his luck. All Jackson needed from Amanda was professional advice—he was confident she'd be the best source.

So, why did he feel a storm coming?

Chapter Thirteen

Stop living in the past. It couldn't be changed so why waste the time? She wasn't sure what she'd change if she could anyway—her current job was far above the role she'd played at the Holstenar Advisory Group. Maybe her love life? The only candidate there was Carter. And Jackson? Well, he was entertaining but not a bit serious when it came to relationships, which was in total opposition to her respect for commitment. No, she'd wasted too much time in their weird friendship already. It was time to move on.

Her cell phone summoned and she glanced at the display and sighed. It was confirming her thought apparently; the number was Carter's.

"Jackson called about you."

Her desk chair screeched as she jolted upright. "He did? Why?"

"He wanted to get a legal opinion about something you worked on a couple of years ago. Some contract. I told him you probably had forgotten much of it but I wanted to let you know in case he called."

Forgotten a legal matter? Not likely. "Okay, well, thanks for letting me know."

"Wait. Don't go yet. Look, I had a great time last weekend. You want to come over tonight? I'll cook dinner."

Awww, he wanted to cook for her? "Sure, why not?"

"And we can watch the Astros game." Carter loved the Astros. Amanda had to admit she enjoyed the games too, though it was primarily a people-watching exercise for her.

They talked a little longer and she agreed to show up around eight. It gave her time to finish work, then go to the gym. The gym was a must since most guys knew how to cook only a short repertoire, all of which were extremely calorie-rich. She'd forgotten to ask the menu, but it didn't matter. Her mother's etiquette about invitations had stuck. *When someone invites you to dinner, you go. It's rude to ask about the menu as if you'll only show if the food's right. Invitations are about the visit, not the food. A chance to build something more permanent.*

More permanent with Carter? Did she want that?

Amanda focused on a mass of white puffy clouds in the sky outside her office window. She shrugged. She wasn't sure. He was nice, attentive, and expected little to nothing. That was a great thing since it meant she couldn't possibly fall short of expectations like she'd done much of her life. He was as driven as she was about his career—a great match. God knows she wanted to have a relationship that respected and supported her career. It had been hard enough to make it past the bar exam, then snag her current job. The last thing she wanted was stress in the form of man-trouble.

So why did it all feel so—boringly by the book?

She managed to leave early enough to get a good workout before going home to shower. She wasn't sure if the excitement that bubbled in her chest was due to her exercise or the fact the night promised a little more than dinner alone and watching late night shows on TV. Regardless, she flipped her iPod speakers on high and danced to the alternative rock tunes that bellowed. With mascara in hand, a baggy T-shirt over her shorts, and a headband holding her hair, she applied makeup sparingly. She wanted to look nice but not *intentionally* nice.

Bang bang bang.

What was that? She tapped the volume button a couple of times to lower the blaring to a reasonable roar. Four more thunderous bangs—on her front door.

She pattered barefoot to the door and peeked through the window—*oh my God.* What was *he* doing here? She rolled to the side of the door and smoothed her shirt—a dumb move since T-shirts never looked neat anyway. She yanked the band from her hair and shook it out before opening the door.

"Jackson. What are you doing here…and how'd you find me?"

"Carter gave me your address and number. He didn't tell you I was going to call?"

"Call, yes. Drop in on me without warning? No."

"So you know why I'm here, then?"

"You wanted to ask about a case I worked on. I suppose that's code for wanting answers to the other items, too? Right?"

"Which items?"

Jackson glanced up and down her frame as she kept a firm hand on the door. Amanda was keenly aware that her T-shirt hung down so far that the shorts underneath were invisible.

"My eyes are up here, Jax." She stuck a finger under his chin, closed his mouth, and pulled his face upward until his eyes locked with hers.

"It's not my fault you answer the door dressed in nothing but a T-shirt."

Amanda flashed her eyes skyward. "I have shorts on, and I wasn't expecting to need to answer the door."

He darted a devilish grin her way. "Don't tell me you were singing to that crap on the radio? Or were you dancing?"

She felt the warmth in her cheeks. "As a matter of fact I *was* dancing…while I put makeup on for a date."

The grin on his face disappeared. "Dressed like that? I hope it's a sleepover date. Can I come in? It won't take long."

"No."

He ignored her. As he strode past, his hand brushed her thigh. Yikes. Amanda turned to stop him and ran smack into his chest. Oomph. You would have thought a guy would back up and give a girl some room, but noooo. She put a hand out and shoved. He stepped one step backward.

"Amanda, I need your help, so I thought we could make a deal. I'll help you with Carter and you can help me with work."

Technically, she doubted she'd need help with Carter considering her plans for the evening. "What makes you think I still need your help? He invited me for dinner tonight."

"That's the date you're getting all made up for?"

She lifted her chin. "Yep. And about that sleepover thing—"

Jackson held up both hands. "Don't tell me. He's making lasagna. Wine and lasagna. Carter thinks his lasagna is the bomb and it's his version of an aphrodisiac...or at least, he thinks it is."

"Really? Well, that's interesting. So, his recommendation to watch the Astros game after dinner was a ruse to what? Get me drinking so much I wouldn't want to leave?"

"I wasn't saying that...I don't know what he's planned. We haven't talked about you. Look, I need your help. Give it or not. That's up to you. But don't play around with my friend if you're not interested. He has enough to deal with already."

It was odd that her living room shrunk the minute Jackson stepped inside. It had felt so roomy when she chose to add the space rug and put an antique steamer in the middle as a table. Now, she needed space and there wasn't any to find. She shoved him again. "Would you mind sitting down? I'm getting a crick in my neck trying to look up."

Jackson flopped backward into a chair and stretched his legs over the trunk. He glanced around her home. "You have a lot of stuff."

"Most of this 'stuff' is considered antique, things I've collected from family members or that I've purchased at auction."

"Seriously? You paid for someone's old junk?"

"Not junk. Antiques. They have value."

He shrugged and Amanda registered the disbelief in his expression. "If you say so. Looks like junk to me."

Amanda crossed her arms, ready for battle. "What do you want from me, Jackson? Let's get this over with so I can finish getting ready for my dinner date."

"With Carter."

"Yes, with Carter. Now, spill."

"Look, I don't want to interfere, so we can continue talking while you"—he swirled a hand toward her bathroom—"do whatever you need to do. I can talk while you primp."

She hesitated. Her place was small enough she could hear him from the bathroom but did she trust him alone? She threw her hands up in exasperation. "Okay, fine. I'll listen and you talk." She went back to the bathroom, finished applying her mascara, and drew on some lip gloss. Tossing her makeup case into a drawer, she leaned over and pulled her curling iron from below.

"You really do have shorts under there." Jackson's voice held surprise.

Amanda jolted up and met his gaze in the mirror as it slowly rose from looking at her backside. "What are you doing?"

"I'm talking."

"I get that but I meant in there. Talk in there." She pointed down the hall. "You can hear me from the other room and I can hear you."

He leaned a shoulder against the door jam and stuck his hand in his pocket. "But I can't see you if you're in here and I need to know what you're thinking."

As if he could tell that just by watching. Hell, she couldn't read him at all so what made him think he could do so with her? "Jackson, this is my *bathroom*. Guys don't have conversations about business with a woman in her bathroom. That's off limits."

"Why?"

"It's…it's…private. Personal."

Amanda wrapped her hair in the heating curling-iron and narrowed her eyes at him in admonishment. Surely he'd get the message and tread back down the hall to the safety of the living room. She released the hair and let it fall in a soft ringlet, then wrapped another strand.

Jackson didn't seem disturbed by the comment. He simply sat down—on the toilet. Next to the open cabinet, under the sink, which boldly displayed things even more personal. He glanced at the pink tampon package, the plastic container that held her birth control pills, and the stash of nail polish. Awkward.

Amanda stuck her bare foot against the door and slammed it shut. "See? Personal."

He leaned his elbows on his knees and stared at the floor. "Your bathroom smells like you."

She wasn't sure if that was good or bad. "So what's this contract you're all worked up about?" Thankfully, he didn't glance down too far below his feet, where she'd discarded the bra and panties she'd had on before her shower. How could she retrieve them without notice?

"Right before you left, you were reviewing a contract for a bid proposal on work for a company called BookMyss. Do you remember that?"

"Of course. Their attorney was pretty difficult to work with and refused to allow us any changes. He'd sent over a first draft on the contract and I took that to mean it was negotiable but he wouldn't budge on some of the key items."

He grinned. "I knew you'd remember. Carter said he doubted you would but he doesn't really know you like I do, does he?"

With her hair wrapped around the hot wand, she stared at his lopsided grin. "*You* don't really know me like you think you do either, Jax. We haven't seen each other more than a few hours in two years."

"Yes, but I know your mind is like a steel trap. Once something goes in there," he tapped her head above the curling iron, "it stays."

Amanda let the curl fall and started on another. "So I remember things. Most good attorneys do. That's how we make a living—ensuring our facts are straight and provable."

"Provable. Now there's the word I was looking for. Something about that contract just doesn't seem provable…Do you do that to your hair every day?"

She turned, a big mistake, because he lifted his head and his eyes were level with her chest. He didn't flinch but he didn't look away either. Instead, he grinned again.

"On work days I usually put my hair up. It saves time and keeps it neat all day. I don't like it falling in my face and looking mussy."

"I would."

"Would what?"

"Like it falling in my face and looking mussy."

"Seriously, Jackson? You're sitting on a toilet trying to make a move on me while I get ready to go on a date with your best friend? Are you kidding me?"

He shrugged. "I can't help myself."

She held the end of the curling iron toward him and swirled it like a sword. "You do realize these things are hot, don't you? It would make a nasty scar."

He slid up to full height. "I was only kidding."

She finished her hair and set the curling iron down, then walked toward her bedroom. He followed. She whirled at the door and pushed his chest with both hands. "Oh, no you don't. Go back in the other room."

"But we're talking."

"We can talk in there, *after* I get dressed." Gripping his biceps, which sent a little tingle through her stomach, she turned him around and pushed.

"Talk about a buzz kill."

"Yeah, well, there wasn't really a buzz going yet, Romeo."

Jackson turned back around to face her. He slowly ran his fingers through one of the curls she'd pressed into her hair and let it drop. "No?"

Amanda sighed. "Sorry if hanging out and talking shop in the bathroom doesn't turn me on, Jax, but maybe that works with someone else. Oh, snap. I forgot." She clicked her fingers.

"Forgot what?"

"My friend that I introduced you to a while back wanted to know if you'd like to double."

"Double?" He let that stupid grin curl back up. "As in both of you and…me?"

Amanda rolled her eyes. "No, as in you, her, me, and Carter."

His faced went serious. "Oh, uh, I'll have to think about that and get back to you. When did you say your date was tonight?"

"I didn't say but I'm going over to his place at eight. Now," she waved a hand in a go-away gesture, "wait for me in the living room. I'll be out in a few minutes."

She half expected him to refuse and tromp into her bedroom just as he'd done her home earlier. He didn't. Jackson turned and followed her direction.

Amanda joined him after slipping on a T-shirt, a blue skirt, and open-toed sandals. She had her purse over her shoulder and he frowned when she walked in. She put a hand to her stomach and pressed the shirt down. "What's wrong?"

He shook his head. "Nothing. Nothing. You look great."

"Thanks." She smiled. Why did she care about his approval? She had no need to impress him. "So, what do you want to know about BookMyss?"

"I was hoping you had the old contract lying around somewhere. Or at least committed to memory. I have the current one here." He held up a handful of papers that she hadn't noticed until now. He'd drawn them from a pocket. "I did a little research on the BookMyss Company and if the Internet is accurate…which we know isn't always the case…the company has no possible reason for a project of this type."

She pulled the papers from his hand and flipped through the pages, pausing periodically to review verbiage. The document was forty pages long and she hadn't the time to give it more than a brief glance. "You're right, it doesn't. That's not the contract I was working on. I've never seen it before."

"None of it?"

She handed the document back to Jackson. "I can't say without reading it more carefully but at first glance, no…not a word. If you leave it with me for a couple of days, I can take some time and review it in full. I could let you know by, say, Friday?"

"I'm not sure I can stall that long. This contract goes in front of the board on Thursday for a vote. I also have to approve the financials and there's a couple of transactions that confused me. This contract requires up-front payments to a couple of vendors in order to get started. It points to order placement guarantees required to meet the production timelines."

"So? People do that all the time. It helps to protect the vendor in case you default on the project."

"I know that. Oddly, in this case, we've already paid a significant amount to this vendor."

"Maybe you're using them for another project?"

Jackson shook his head and Amanda squelched an urge to move his bangs away from his eyes so she could see him better. "The contract specifically states the reason for pre-payment is due to no prior established relationship or credit lines. That would imply we haven't worked with them at all."

"Oh, let me see again." She held out a hand.

Jackson flipped to the second to last page of the stack and pointed to a section. "Right there."

She read the section slowly. He was right. How strange. "But there's obviously a relationship if you're already paying them as a vendor."

Jackson tapped her head in a gesture that was starting to both piss her off and make her want to yank him into a kiss again— for punishment, of course. "Ding ding ding, jackpot. The only question now is…why? Any thoughts on that, counselor?"

Amanda concentrated for a second. "No idea, unless someone in your office has a connection. I need to get going so this will need to wait. If you want me to look it over, leave it here."

"I could just wait here and you know, tidy up the bathroom."

No way in hell was he staying in her house. "Why on earth would you want to do that?"

"Because I like the décor in there but you seemed to have left a few things lying around. I could clean the bedroom too if you're planning on using it tonight."

She raised a brow. "Very funny. Wouldn't that be a little difficult if you're already in it?"

Jackson plucked one of her curls. "Depends on who you want to use it with."

"Oh brother. There you go again. Look, I told you I'd review your contract. Now get your smooth-talking ass out of here. You're wasting your breath on me, kiddo. Remember, I've seen you in action and I'm not stupid."

Maybe a little weak-kneed at the moment, but definitely not stupid. Jackson stood and worked his way toward her door. The entire room and entry seemed to shrink with him inside. His height swamped the door which almost appeared as if it were undersized. "Hey, what's your cell number in case I need to reach you?"

She handed him a business card. "The one at the bottom but don't wear it out."

Jackson stepped outside and turned to look her up and down. "If Carter baked brownies too, he's probably hoping to get laid. One of his high school girlfriends loved chocolate and that worked for her. Needless to say, he got pretty good at making brownies, not that adding water and an egg to a mix is all that tough."

Amanda gripped the handle and leaned against the door. Her T-shirt slipped to bare the skin on her shoulder and it pleased her that Jackson soaked in the view. "Well, I always have liked a good—brownie."

His mouth opened as if to say more but she slammed the door before any words came. Let him chew on that for a while. She grabbed her keys and headed to the garage.

Thirty minutes later, she knocked on Carter's door.

Chapter Fourteen

Carter kissed Amanda at the door. It was nothing new since they'd kissed more than a few times since they started dating. She liked the kisses too. Why did it disappoint her that she didn't feel more? What was her issue?

She didn't *crave* them. That was the problem.

"It's almost ready. Want a glass of wine?" Amanda followed Carter into his apartment dining room where he'd set a beautiful table. Or at least as beautiful as a guy can set. There wasn't a tablecloth or fancy dishes but everything matched. A couple of candles flickered in the middle of the table while tendrils of smoke rose from their soft light. He'd muted the lighting a little too. Nice and very romantic.

Amanda suddenly felt a huge lump forming in her throat. She looked around in confusion. "I'm sorry…what did you say?"

Carter smiled. "You must have had a rough day. I asked if you wanted a glass of wine."

She followed him to the kitchen counter where he held up a bottle of chardonnay. "Oh, sure. That sounds nice."

While he worked the corkscrew, she inhaled the warm buttery chocolate scent of—brownies. *Gulp.* The lump in her throat plummeted to her stomach. Was she ready for this? Did she even want it?

She wasn't sure.

Carter's cell broke the awkwardness and he set the bottle and cork down to answer. There were a lot of monotone yeses and noes, then he made an excuse and hung up. "Sorry about that. Jackson wanted to check up on me."

Yeah, right. "How's his dad?" She had completely forgotten to ask when she saw him earlier which made it easy to show concern.

"Struggling but better than the alternative." Carter's voice was distant and Amanda felt a crushing guilt for asking since the alternative was to be in Carter's shoes—without a father.

"Oh, I guess that's good."

"He can't speak very well but the doctor thinks it will come back in time…at least enough to understand him. He has the use of one hand and leg but the other is useless. They're forcing him through a lot of rehab exercises which, despite not talking, he's able to protest in a way that only he could manage. Jackson goes in for dinner every other night and helps him eat. His mother alternates."

Amanda tried to picture Jackson spooning soup into his Dad's mouth. The thought was too strange to conjure up and she questioned whether he really helped or just sat while the nurse did the work. "How sad." She sighed.

Carter poured two glasses of wine and handed one to Amanda. "So, you want to start with dessert?" He motioned to a stack of brownies. *Hmmm. Clever.* "The lasagna has about ten more minutes."

She turned and carried her glass to the living area and stood to stare out the window at the traffic below. Carter's apartment, while very modern, was definitely a man-cave. Stark, mismatched furniture with very little adornment on the walls. No plants, no knickknacks, a few piles of sports paraphernalia placed with little thought. She found that oddly comforting.

"I like your place. It's nice."

"It's dull. I don't spend much time here. My job requires a lot of travel and I keep thinking I will get a few pictures to put on the walls or something but I never have time."

She smiled and sipped the wine. It warmed on the way down. "I can relate to that. I still have unpacked boxes lining the wall of my spare bedroom. They've been there for two years. It's funny, because I'm anal about the details of my work but when I get home, all bets are off."

"I take it you're not a neat freak."

She shook her head and sipped again. "I'm clean but not OCD. You?" Amanda glanced around, noticing the neatness of his kitchen. She already knew the answer.

"I'm probably a little OCD but it comes in waves."

In waves, yes, that would be an appropriate description for her level of effort as well. They were more alike than she thought—and she'd thought them very similar to start. "So tell me about your travel."

Amanda moved to the couch, slipped off her sandals, and settled into the cushions. She sipped and listened until a ding on the oven signaled lasagna time. Carter refilled her wine glass and they met at the table. The more she drank, the more comfortable she was with him. He was a genuinely nice guy.

Then he started talking about Jackson. She wasn't sure how the conversation veered that way but wished it hadn't. "Jackson and I grew up together mostly. His parents moved to our neighborhood when we were both ten. We were friends by default and I can't tell you how glad I was to have a guy move into our world. As the little brother, I'd played enough girly-shit to last a lifetime. He saved me in a lot of ways."

How could she change the subject? The last thing she wanted was to hear martyr-making crap about the guy she wanted to detest. "No kidding."

"The guy has a non-confrontational way of getting people to make changes without being pushy. When my sister died, he was always around. I hated it at first and we competed in *everything* but it probably kept me from dwelling on the negative. We both changed after that. We became meaner. More competitive."

"Well, he's probably got that pegged."

Carter was relaxed. He lifted his wine glass and stared at the remaining claret-colored liquid. "Why do you say that?"

"Nothing. I don't know…wine talking, I guess." Amanda's plate was empty. So was Carter's.

"Time for my famous brownies."

She giggled. Yep, the wine was definitely sinking in. "What are those brownies famous for, Carter?"

He wiggled his brows. "I'll never tell."

Double-gulp. No need, she already knew and she wasn't ready for what it all suggested. Not with Carter. Still, it would be rude to skip something he'd taken the time to cook. For her.

The warmth of wine and fatigue was comforting. Talking with Carter was like visiting with her brother. Or a long-lost friend. Like Jackson.

Amanda watched him return and clarity sank into her stomach, making the lump more solid. No, it wasn't like talking with Jackson. Not even close.

And *that* was the problem.

"Carter, I'll need to leave after the brownies. I have a case I need to review tonight for a client who's waiting on a response. I promised him something tomorrow." Should she mention it was for Jackson? Probably not.

• • •

Amanda pulled into her drive two hours later, thankful she'd remembered to switch on the light over the door. It wasn't until she trudged up to the step that she noticed a silhouette leaning against the wall.

She stifled a scream when the lump moved.

"Hi. I thought I'd wait up."

Jackson was sleeping on her doorstep?

"Wait up or *check* up? Has your curiosity got the best of you, Jax?"

"Curiosity about what?"

Amanda reached down and slipped her sandals off, then strung them between her fingers and tried to push her key into the locked door. She missed. Despite the light above, the wine fog made it a little more difficult. She tried again, unsuccessfully trying to think up an appropriate answer.

"You wanted to see if Carter's brownies were successful, I guess? I don't know. You tell me. You're the one lurking around on my porch."

Jackson lifted his arms above his head and stretched. "I wasn't lurking. I just hoped you'd be back and we could talk about my contract thing more."

With her back turned, she growled as the key once again missed the target.

Jackson yanked the key from her fingers and opened the door, then shoved it to allow entry. Amanda stared at her darkened and quiet home. She couldn't bring herself to step inside.

Instead she whirled around and clunked her forehead hard against his chin. The crunch of bone on bone sent them both backward. Jackson recovered first and wrapped his big hands around her arms to steady her. "You okay?" he asked.

Was she? She shook her head; the acrid sting of water puddling in her eyes made it impossible to focus. Especially with him front and center equally blurring her vision. She sighed and let her head drop. "What's wrong with me, Jax?"

"Wrong with you? What makes you think anything's wrong? What'd he do? Did Carter make an ass out of himself? He didn't …"

Amanda shook her head slowly. "No, it's not him. He was great, better than great. He was—amazing."

Jackson's eyes softened, though there was a stiffness to his frame that seemed restrained. "Amazing. Should I ask 'how amazing' or am I destined to regret the words?"

She lifted her eyes and let the liquid spill. Too much wine had made it impossible to hide her emotions and at the moment, she didn't care. She'd regret it tomorrow but now was all that mattered. "Really, really amazing. That's the problem."

"Normally that isn't a problem. It's an asset." Jackson sucked in a breath and stepped backward two steps.

Amanda almost lost her balance as he removed his hands from her arms. She caught herself and hiccuped. "He's just not *you.*"

Oh shit. Why'd she do that? It was stupid. Too much wine, all that good food, and those damn brownies. Carter's magic brownies definitely worked with the women—unfortunately the target wasn't him. She was an idiot.

Amanda looked up, expecting to see anger. Or maybe even laughter. Instead she saw a depth of smokiness in Jackson's eyes. Something that had never been there before. It appeared like *longing.* "Hell, Mandy, he's *better than me.* Way better."

Amanda blinked. Did he seriously believe that? Anger grew within her chest. Not because of the realization that the man she actually *wanted* was standing in front of her, though that was a definite frustration. The heat bubbled up her spine and she adjusted her shoulders despite the wine-soaked softness of her prior emotions. "Who the hell made you think that?"

Chapter Fifteen

After all these years apart, Jackson could look at the situation with an open mind. So he thought. He wasn't a young college kid seeking to get laid. He was a man who had been around the block enough to know there was a helluva lot to Amanda Gillespie beyond her fancy clothes and sharp mind. Her immaculate dress was all a front to hide what was underneath. In the depth of her heart, Amanda was a person very few knew. She was soft, kind, and right now, with tears in her eyes—so fricking vulnerable that he couldn't breathe.

Here she was at—he checked his watch—two in the morning and she was telling *him* how he measured. Against his best friend. She was trying to pump up his self-perception. God knows why.

"Does it really matter?"

Amanda shrugged. "Not really, I guess. It's just that…as your friend…it really pisses me off when you measure yourself so poorly against the rest of the world. What makes you think Carter's a better man? Sure, he's nice, but so what? So are you."

As his friend. Yes, they'd been that for years. It was time for a change. "About that friend thing, Amanda—we really can't be friends. I don't believe men and women can *ever* be friends."

Her mouth dropped open and her eyes glistened wet again. "No? I thought that's what you wanted when you—"

He shook his head and moved into her, half expecting she'd back away. She didn't. She dropped her head to his chest in a weary, tired-of-the-world way, which made the warmth in his chest surge to the surface of his skin. He palmed her cheeks and lifted her face until her eyes met his. "I don't want to be friends with you, Amanda, because if I'm honest with myself … I never did. I always wanted more, I was just too stupid to recognize the fact. It crushed me when you ran out on me two years ago."

"I didn't run—" Amanda stopped when Jackson put a finger over her lips.

"It's okay. We can't go back, and I don't think either of us wants to. I realize I'm just a lazy, rich boy in the public eye but I have a chance to change all that now. With Dad sick, there's no way I'm going to let things go down the toilet in his absence. I'm not asking you to be my friend again—I'm asking for your *help*. There's nothing wrong with us helping each other even if we can't be friends." Because he wanted so much more.

Her eyes clouded and a single tear streaked down her cheek. Why was she crying? "Why me, Jax? There are a hundred other attorneys out there who understand the law well enough to work with you. Why me?"

"Why *not* you? We get along, we think the same way, you've already seen this contract, and know better than me what the goal was originally. You're the best person among us to do this work. Surely you know that as well as I do? I promise I'll behave and keep all the personal stuff out of things."

"See, that's the problem, Jax." Amanda hiccupped and another water droplet rolled down her cheek. It settled in the corner of her mouth and damned if he didn't want to lick it away, to taste the saltiness. "You like me for my mind, and, ironically, I like that part of you too—I just happen to like everything else equally. In fact, as much as I wish all that was over, it isn't. Not for me, and if you ask me to do this work for you, it means I have to keep hanging around you and pretending that I don't feel anything. I have to pretend that it didn't completely ruin me when you made David fire me. I can't—"

A cold wave of fear washed down his spine. "Made David fire you? What are you talking about? I didn't make David fire you. He said you quit and that you didn't want to work with me because I was causing you issues."

Her eyes returned to his, widening in surprise. "He told *me* you suggested I leave because I was distracting you from work. That it was awkward and you didn't know how to handle the situation. He suggested I save you the trouble by exiting gracefully since you could never leave."

Jackson shivered. The cold flooded him from head to foot. He let it soak in, let it overtake him completely before rage rushed in behind.

"That fucking bastard."

Jackson wanted to deck the asshole. Just not now. Right now, all he wanted was to—he dropped his mouth to Amanda's. In fact, he came in so fast he probably crushed her lips or perhaps slightly bruised them. He didn't care. Amanda Gillespie was no distraction. Not in a bad way, at least. How dare David give her that impression? Why would he do it? What possible motive could he have to run off one of their best employees?

Jackson gave in to the earlier desire to lick the tear from her mouth and enjoyed the saltiness of Amanda's skin. She mumbled something against his mouth, then opened so he could delve into a deep-throated kiss full of the fire he knew was there.

In the back of his head, the words Carter had said on the phone just before she showed up flickered as if thumping him to remember. *I really like her, Jax. I think I want to take it to the next level and make a commitment.*

Jackson stilled. Yeah, he should back off—but Amanda strung her left hand into his hair and continued to kiss him as if he were ice cream. She thrust the fingers of her right hand between the buttons of his shirt and trailed circles against his collarbone. *Sorry, Carter.* Jackson trailed kisses down Amanda's neck and ran his fingers along the smoothness of her skin until he felt the tip of her nipple straining against the cloth in invitation. *I really like her too. In fact, I think—whoa. No.*

"Stop." He pulled Amanda's hand from his neck and stared into the hazy lust that egged him to keep going. Somehow they'd made their way into her house and down the hall during the kissing. A dark doorway loomed ahead and he knew where it led. Knew it was only a few feet away from a decision that would change his friendship with both Carter and Amanda. And probably detour his life.

"You're telling me to stop? Jackson, you're the one who started this. You kissed me. Take a look at where your hands are at the moment and tell me what you're thinking."

He glanced down at his traitorous body. One hand on her right breast, the other clenched into the soft fabric covering her ass. What was he thinking? How completely awesome it would be to strip every inch of fabric off her and throw her on the bed that had to be in that dark room. That was what he was thinking. "I'm thinking the only thing wrong with you is this: you have way too much clothes on and the last thing I give a shit about is your mind." Oops, he should clarify. "Not that I don't love your mind but right now, I'd rather worship this part of you."

He cupped her breast and lifted to his mouth so that he could bite through the fabric of her shirt. She let out a squeak of pleasure, then ran her tongue over lips that were already swollen from his kisses. There was a small amount of satisfaction at the way they plumped. "So, I take it we're not talking shop, then? Wasn't that why you came here?"

Jackson shot his eyes at the ceiling and ran his hands around her waist. "Okay, here's the truth, Amanda. I didn't come here to talk shop or to go over that contract. I didn't come here to be friends either. The only reason I was sleeping on your doorstep at one a.m. was pure green-as-hell jealousy. I couldn't stand the thought of you sleeping with Carter and I was just praying you'd come home and he wouldn't have convinced you to—you know—eat those damn brownies."

Amanda's eyes glistened in the darkness. "Oh, but I *did* eat the brownies. They were good too."

Uh oh. "Does that mean what I think it does?"

Amanda tugged at the top button on his shirt until it came open. She moved to the next one and it cooperated quickly by opening at first try. "It means I ate the brownies, thought about what you said they represented to him, and realized I couldn't go through with it. As much as I like Carter…I meant what I said earlier. He's not you."

The sweet warmth of relief trickled through his veins. Her words were all Jackson needed. He scooped her up and walked her backward through the darkened door.

Chapter Sixteen

The following morning Jackson opened his eyes and evaluated his situation while watching her sleep. Amanda was a restless sleeper. For someone who always seemed calm under pressure, she was anything but in her sleep. She rolled and kicked—and mumbled. He tried desperately to decipher the words but couldn't. At one point during the night, he woke to find her head lying on his stomach and a hand played across his chest. It was oddly comforting. She must have liked it as well because she stayed like that the remainder of the night.

He didn't mind her hair tickling across his waist, tempting him to move it back so he could see her face. When his watch signaled time to move, he slipped from underneath and searched out his clothes. She propped her chin on elbows and tossed her head to get the hair from her eyes.

"Hey."

"Hey, yourself." He smiled. "Are you okay this morning?" He didn't mean it in a trivial, hey-how-are-you way and she knew as much.

She shrugged and the hair threatened to fall back over her eyes. "Yeah, fine. Guess I'd better hit the shower. There's probably something in the kitchen if you're hungry." She walked to the bathroom and it took every ounce of willpower for Jackson to watch and not follow. Amanda's skin was perfection.

"Nah, I need to get to the hospital. It's my day to help dad with his therapy. See you?" He wasn't sure whether to ask when or not. It was awkward, sleeping with someone you cared about enough to want to stay.

He heard a squeak of metal, then the swish of water spray as she started the shower. Her voice rose above the sound. "Sure, I'll look over that contract and get back to you by end of day. Don't make any rash decisions until you hear from me, okay?"

That was it. Professional. Cool. And—finished. It was neat and tidy. Jackson hated neat and tidy.

"Okay." His keys rustled in the pocket of his pants as he slipped a foot into the leg. He wasn't ready to go. His stomach knotted. Jackson looked at the hallway, knowing Dad was awake and waiting, then back to the bathroom with an open door and steam wafting his way. "Fuck it." He dropped the pants and strode to step into the shower. The sting of warm water rushed over his shoulders as he slipped between the spray and Amanda. Her eyes popped open and he smiled. "Mind if I look over this particular contract a bit more? The you-and-me contract? We wouldn't want to make any rash decisions, would we?"

A lazy, satisfied grin crossed her lips and he realized she had wanted him to follow. What would have happened if he hadn't? Would she have written him off forever? Ticked him off the list? It had been a rash decision to join her—thank God for rash decisions.

"Of course not. Level-headed people like ourselves never make a decision without evaluating all the facts."

He ran his lips across the slickness of her wet shoulder. "That's right."

Jackson began evaluating every nook and cranny of those facts, spot by spot, until Amanda let out a soft sexy squeal. She then turned to him and layered kisses down his chest and other regions until he lost control himself. He left over an hour later, knowing that the facts were about as clear as he'd ever seen.

He was in love with Amanda Gillespie.

• • •

When Jackson entered the hospital room, his father's bed was empty. He headed to the nurse's station where the attendant was actively listening to a phone receiver perched on her shoulder. With a single head motion, she directed Jackson toward the physical therapy room.

The one good thing about his Dad's stroke—Jackson could talk without any pending argument since the man couldn't respond. His words were beginning to come but so stilted that Robert used them sparingly. Sweat spackled his forehead. Therapy was grueling but he seemed to improve daily.

"Dad, I need to tell you something and please don't repeat it to Mom, okay? It's a secret."

"Sss, sss, sss." His father chuckled. The chances of repeating anything at the moment were pretty unlikely and thankfully he appreciated the humor.

"I met someone and I'm pretty sure she's going to stick."

"Sssssick?"

Jackson wasn't surprised to hear the word. Robert was piecing together more and more words as the days passed. He seemed to have trouble with R's and T's, hence "sick" instead of "stick."

"Yes, that's right. There's a couple of problems, though. One of them is pretty major and I'm not sure what to do."

His father grunted as Jackson moved his leg, bending into a tight curl. "Dooo I."

"What?"

"Dooo I." Was that I or eye? What was Dad trying to say?

Jackson puzzled for a moment. *Oh.* "Yes, I'll try to do right." Just like a parent to burst your bubble. "Now, let's stop talking and work your legs and arms. Concentrate on that and don't talk, okay?"

More conversation would just make Jackson reveal how wrong his relationship with Amanda might be and he wasn't ready to divulge further.

Jackson rolled his father to his side with the help of his therapist and began working the leg from hip to knee in a circular motion.

His cell chirped in his pocket and he debated answering. What if it was Amanda?

"Excuse me a minute, Dad." With one hand holding his father, he used the other to retrieve the device and glance at the display. Not Amanda. He answered anyway. "Hey Carter, what's up?"

Carter's voice was chipper. "A lot, actually. Remember my neighbor, Maddie? She broke her leg again and now I'm babysitting her dog."

Jackson feigned interest. "The big beast that sounded like a freight train bouncing around her place?"

"Yep, that's the one. He's actually pretty good on a leash."

"You're keeping him for her? At your place? How are you managing that with all the travel?" Jackson was glad to discuss anything but Amanda. Avoid that subject, please.

"No, I just walk him at night for her. Which is great because it gives me a chance to scout the park for that runner we scoped out a while back. Remember her?"

Yeah, he remembered. Black hair, fit as an athletic trainer or yoga instructor, but with a serious focus on her steps as if she were counting each one. "What about Amanda?"

Crap, there he went—avoiding the subject like an idiot. "Hey, just because you're on a diet doesn't mean you can't look at the menu. Isn't that what your dad always said?"

Jackson watched as foamy spit bubbled from the corner of his dad's mouth. His dad said that, all right, but he wasn't exactly a model to follow. He'd definitely done more than just look at the menu on multiple occasions. Ironic that he was now totally dependent on the very woman whom he'd betrayed. "I guess. Look, I'm with Dad right now."

"Oh, how's he doing with his therapy?"

Robert grunted an "ow" and Jackson glanced his way. Oops. Somewhere in the conversation, Jackson had lifted his Dad's leg to a point that had him somewhat dangling mid-air.

"Uh, sorry Dad."

"What's wrong?" Carter's voice came through the phone.

"Nothing. I just kind of overextended the therapy a little." The bubbles on the corner of Robert's mouth spewed as his father huffed a strong breath.

The old man lifted an arm and grasped Jackson. "Ssssay hhhhhi."

Carter nodded and lowered his father's leg. It would probably be better to just do a few ankle rotations while talking. "Dad says hi. So, why'd you call?"

"Hi back. Nothing much. I just wanted a little advice. It can wait."

Jackson stuck the phone between his ear and shoulder and grasped his dad with both hands. He held the instep and with the other hand worked the foot in a circular rotation. He noticed a bit of tension releasing in his back muscles. Obviously, Carter wasn't aware of Jackson's night yet. He should say something. "Go ahead. Shoot. I'm here."

"Amanda was here last night for dinner. It was great."

Wait, he thought it was a work-related advice thing. "Great, as in you made your famous brownies?"

Jackson heard a snicker. "Yeah, I made them all right. It was great. Listen, I think I could actually do this. You know."

"Do what?"

Two seconds ticked off in silence. "Commit."

Jackson felt his heart screech to a stop. Shit.

"Sssssssop."

Jackson dropped his eyes. "Oh, sorry, Dad." Jackson halted his efforts since he'd twisted his father's foot in circles like a helicopter blade. Was the therapist watching? He looked over his shoulder and measured the deep frown. His dad's therapist was a big burly guy with ripped muscles that belonged in a gym. You had to admire the guy for choosing to be a physical therapist for stroke victims instead of spending his days teaching fitness to a bunch of middle-aged housewives. Right now, the guy looked like he was one step away from casting Jackson out of the room. Jackson shrugged sheepishly and dropped his father's foot.

He patted his dad's arm. "Give me just a minute, okay? Carter wants some advice."

"Fffffom y-y-you?"

Jackson shot an eyebrow up. "What are you trying to say? I'm not capable of giving advice? Come on, Dad, have a little faith."

Jackson focused on the phone call. "So, you're trying to tell me that after all these years of distrusting the world, you decided out of the blue that now you'll put all that in the past? All because of Amanda?"

Carter coughed, and the sound smacked Jackson's ear as if he'd been slapped. He pulled the phone from his ear for a second, then returned. "I'm saying I want to take it to the next level."

Jackson didn't buy it. Not because it was Amanda and whether Carter liked it or not, she was *his*. Nope, his friend had enough baggage to fill a freighter. "Exactly what level would that be? What the hell does that mean, anyway? Take it to the next level? Is that an 'I want to move in with her' statement? Or maybe a 'let's get married' thing? Surely you haven't fallen that far out of the stupid tree, Carter? Slow down there, Romeo—when I said you need to take a chance on a woman now and try trusting a little, I didn't mean buy the whole ranch house. I just meant spend more time together and see if it fits."

His head was spinning. Carter was talking about *Amanda. His Amanda.* Whatever level he planned to take, there was no way in hell Jackson could just stand by and—

Carter sighed. "I'm not talking about any of that. Hell, we've only been dating for three months and I've been gone half the time. I just wanted to do something nice. Something that shows I like her and want to be with her. Something that shows I want to share more time together."

Oh, okay. Well, what should he say? What's a good response? *Hey, don't bother because I just spent the entire night with her and you can't have her?* Or perhaps, *sure, just make it something we can all three do together because you'll have to share with me?* Uh, nope. *That* wasn't going to happen. As much as he liked Carter, there wouldn't be any sharing. Maybe he should just admit he'd had crazy aerobic-style sex with Amanda, and Carter needed to move on.

And lose his best friend for eternity.

"Okay, I have an idea or two, then."

He spouted off a few ideas and hung up the phone. Would Amanda fall for that? Would she still see Carter after all they'd been through—or done, rather? A lead stone sunk into his gut and he knew it wasn't going to dislodge any time soon. Not until Amanda made a choice.

Jackson returned to his dad and met his father's eyes with a pasted-on smile. "Okay, let's get back to work."

Robert waved a hand in disgust. "Ickesss are supid."

"What?"

"Ickesss are supid." More spit flew from his dad's mouth and Jackson found it rather humorous. Trying to understand Robert was not just a lesson in deciphering his improvised language, it also required a certain amount of duck and dodge tactics in order to stay dry. What the heck was he saying? Jackson sounded it out in his head.

Oh. "No, they're not stupid. Amanda loves the Astros. Season tickets are a great idea."

His dad rolled his eyes—or at least made the attempt. His right side was slow to cooperate. "For you. Bbbbad idee for Carrrer."

Still Jackson smiled innocently. No, season tickets to the Astros were a perfect idea. Carter could give them to Amanda and they could go to the games. It was something to do but it wasn't too *personal*. It was the kind of thing you'd do with a friend. He should feel guilty for recommending something so unromantic. He wasn't.

The only thing he felt at the moment was—satisfaction. He picked his father's arm up and started to work.

Chapter Seventeen

Amanda replayed the first voicemail from Jackson again before moving on to the second and third. Had she stopped at the first, her temper would have hit an all-time ceiling.

First message: Had she found anything in the contract of concern? She frowned as his voice sounded light and soft. Was the contract all that mattered? His precious contract, his precious company? After the second listen, she started to hit delete on all three, then decided to continue. After all, his voice was rather like a nice cool glass of tea on a hot day. It soothed even while dropping a bomb. What a talent.

Second message: Would she have time for him to stop by and pick up the document? Hmm, that depended on whether the entire conversation would revolve around the contract and not touch on what had just happened. Touch, bad choice of words—a brief vision of his hands flitting across her stomach in the shower made her temperature boil. If business was his only focus, he could take his *business* elsewhere. She growled. Maybe his voice wasn't so soothing after all, more like fingernails on slate.

Third message: *Oh, I'm sorry—I should have started out with this…last night was fantastic and I can't stop thinking about you. Can I stop by on my way home? I am craving to see you again. We can talk about the contract if you want—or not talk at all. Your choice.*

Okay, that was more like it. Tiny violets and rosebuds blossomed in her chest, wrapping their little green leaves around her heart in a tight squeeze.

She picked up the phone and dialed Jackson's number. She glanced at her watch and started to hang up. It was noon. He might be at lunch. When Jackson's voice echoed through the receiver, she smiled. "How can we have a one-night stand if you keep calling?"

She heard a sigh on the other end and could feel him smile. "Mandy, that wasn't a one-night stand, it was a one-night start."

"So, I take it you like my little shower? I almost didn't buy the place because you can barely turn around in it. The entire bathroom is dinky."

He groaned. "You had to go there, didn't you? I was doing great, concentrating on work like a good boy, and you went straight to putting that vision in my head. Yes, I love your tiny little shower…barely enough room to do anything clean at all. Thank God we didn't."

She giggled as heat rose to her cheeks. A quick glance around ensured none of her coworkers was approaching. She covered the mouthpiece and whispered, "You're trouble, Jax."

Did he laugh? His voice lowered to a sexy rumble. "You have no idea. So, can I stop by?"

• • •

A couple of seconds ticked away as Jackson waited for Amanda to agree. He'd buy flowers at the little shop by the parking garage opposite the police station. It was on his way. Roses? No, didn't she once mention her favorite color was purple? Maybe something in deep and passionate—

"No, um, I'm sorry. You can't."

Wait. No? Jackson blinked and pulled the phone from his ear to stare at the receiver as if it would change the answer. Reeling it back in along with his bruised ego, he spoke. "Oh, uh, okay. Well, maybe another time then. Tomorrow?"

There was a tapping noise coming through the receiver as if she was clicking a pen or tapping her foot. "Jackson, you can't stop by because I won't be there. I'm meeting Carter this afternoon for coffee. He wanted to tell me something…or give me something…I couldn't really understand him. I'll be home later tonight, though. You can come by then if you'd like."

After her conversation with Carter? That would likely be the conversation where he gave her the Astros tickets. Would she take them? Wait, did he buy something else more personal? The thought of her attending games on a regular basis with Carter didn't sit well. The thought of her doing *anything* with Carter made his head hurt. Okay, maybe not his head. "Ummmm, no. You guys have fun." *Click.* He couldn't get off the phone fast enough.

He hit speed dial for Carter. The phone rang for approximately an hour—or perhaps just a minute or two. Voicemail. He didn't leave a message, which was probably good because his mouth would have overloaded his brain enough to make a complete ass of himself.

Badeep deep.

A text message came through. He stared at the screen.

Carter: *Sorry, can't talk. Took ur advice—meeting Amanda later for coffee and dinner.*

Jackson frowned. Dinner? She had told him she'd be home later. Nothing was said about dinner. And which advice was he taking? The one about trusting more and choosing to get serious rather than waiting for the world to come to him? Or the one about buying Amanda something to show he cared?

Jackson thumbed in a response and waited. The screen took forever to buzz a response but when it did, Jackson felt sweat bead up on the back of his neck.

Carter: *Yes…I bought her something. Hope she likes it.*

Crap. What should he say? How do you wish your best friend failure for the first time ever? He couldn't, but he wouldn't wish him luck either.

He typed: *Let me know how it goes.*

The next few hours would suck if he didn't find something to concentrate on. He pulled out the copy of the contract he'd given to Amanda and tried to focus on the words.

Within minutes Jackson had highlighted certain portions of text that were questionable. The contract stipulated an advance that seemed exorbitant with terms that were easily avoided and non-binding. In addition, the delivery terms and payment schedules didn't follow normal patterns or have dependencies that protected the company. It put them at significant risk. Why had Dad agreed to this? It didn't make sense. He glanced at the bottom of the document and deciphered the typist's initials. DR/saw. David Radigan, the head council, drafted the document and one of the pool administratives typed it for him. Normally a legal team would be assigned to a contract of this monetary value.

Jackson wasn't on the team. He had no idea if any of the other two legal staff members were involved. Duties had been shifted around quite a bit when Amanda left in order to balance the load until they decided how to handle her departure, according to David.

No decision had been forthcoming and they still juggled her workload between three staff members, himself included. Until recent events.

There were several parcels of land involved in this particular contract, not uncommon. That was what real-estate developers did—develop property to meet the needs of their client. He waded through land surveys, environmental surveys, documentation on mineral rights assessments, and oddly one archeological survey. Interesting. Flipping through the pages, he grimaced at the complexity of the deal.

Ten parcels of land, all different sizes in acreage. All but three were individually owned. The three others were owned by a trust, probably a family trust. He opened the folder for the three and scanned it, seeking information on the trust. The contract mentioned nothing about a trust fund.

Jackson needed Amanda's input *badly*, but he wouldn't call. Not while she was with Carter. Of course, he wasn't sure she actually was with Carter at the moment. He picked up his cell and typed in a text to Carter.

Did you give her the tickets?

A response came immediately.

Carter: *Waiting for her to show.*

A few seconds passed, then another message showed: *Hope ur right about the tickets.*

Jackson ignored the guilt that stabbed at his conscience and responded: *If she not like, you can take me.*

No answer came. Maybe she'd showed up? Were they having that coffee? Or talking about last night? His stomach turned.

Jackson sighed. He should have told Carter everything. Of course, if he had, it would have just accentuated the man's trust issues. Nope. It would be better to wait and see what happened. If he never talked with her again, was it worth the trouble?

Jackson reviewed five more pages of the contract, then looked at his watch. He typed another message: *She seen them yet? What she say?*

Crickets. Nothing. No answer. He waited an hour before trying to call Carter. The call went straight to voicemail. He sent another text. Silence.

Had she told him? Hell, she could have at least allowed him the courtesy of being there, or let him break the news instead. After all, Jackson had known Carter much longer. Like all his life. He tried again to call and text without success.

Jackson finished his notes on the contract, tossed the document in his satchel, and headed for the door. No way in hell could he concentrate another minute. He needed to find her—or them. But where?

Wait. No, what he really needed to do was relax. Leave it alone. Anything else would just make it worse. On his way home, he decided to detour by Baker Street Pub for a beer and sandwich. He wasn't up for being home alone with his paranoid thoughts of two lost friendships. By nine thirty that night, he'd given up on a call. From Amanda or Carter. Why did he feel even worse than if he'd confessed?

He sat in his lounger in front of the TV, switching between ESPN and The Weather Channel. Back and forth. Rockets up by ten over Seattle. High of eighty-two degrees tomorrow with 30 percent chance of rain. Seattle scored a three-pointer. Chance of rain over the weekend went down to 20 percent. The northeast was getting pummeled with unexpected showers and flooding.

Jackson turned the television off and stared at the dark screen.

Amanda was with Carter.

Or was she? She hadn't called, but had he asked her to? No. What he had done was tell her he'd stop by that night. Or maybe she'd asked Jackson to stop by? He couldn't remember and it didn't matter. That happened before she agreed to see Carter.

Regardless, it was too late. He'd figure it out in the morning. By then he'd hear from one of them, right? He'd be a basket-case if not. He dropped the remote and went to bed. An early workout tomorrow would clear his head. That would get his mind on business and back on track.

Bam. Bam. Bam. Bam. Bam.

Jackson opened his eyes and stared at the dark ceiling. What the hell was that? The pounding started again. He bolted out of bed in his briefs and grabbed the bat from his closet. More pounding.

Someone was at the door? He glanced at the clock in the hall as he tiptoed toward the noise. Two forty-three in the morning. Nothing good could possibly be waiting on the other side of that door. He peeked through the window.

"Open the door, Jax. I saw you." Yeah, he saw her too. Okay, maybe he was wrong about good things behind doors in the middle of the night.

After placing the bat by the hinges, he twisted the lock and pulled the door. "Hi."

Amanda's eyes were wet, mascara streaking down her cheeks. "He bought me tickets, Jax. Season tickets. What the hell was that about? Did you know he was going to do that?"

Jackson rubbed his left eye, then strung his fingers over his hair, trying to imagine an appropriate answer. She was already pissed so would it worsen things to tell the truth? He wasn't sure. "What happened?"

She shoved past him and threw herself on his couch, crushing the pile of newspapers he'd read yesterday morning. "Carter wanted to meet me to give me a gift. Please tell me you didn't know."

There wasn't any point to lying and he wasn't a dishonest guy, so he pushed the door shut. A cool breeze wafted over his back as it clunked closed. "He mentioned it."

"Did he tell you *why* he wanted to buy a gift?" Amanda asked the question but didn't wait for the answer. "It was a celebration gift. Our *three-month anniversary*, apparently. I didn't even know. Or care, to be honest. Isn't that *terrible*? And he's doing something so incredibly thoughtful and sweet that I—"

Jackson stepped closer and lowered to sit beside her on the couch, half afraid to touch her. "You what?"

Amanda's hair clung to her wet cheek as she rattled her head back and forth. "It doesn't matter. It wasn't right anyway. I messed up. You. Me. All of it. I shouldn't have ..."

Somewhere along the line, he'd missed something because she was making no sense at all. What didn't matter? She was regretting last night? She thought it was a mistake? He grasped her arms and tried to be calm, not an easy task when his stomach was so close to hurling he couldn't breathe. "What happened tonight, Amanda?"

Tears were streaming from her eyes and the black streaks of mascara on her face trailed deeper down her neck. She hiccupped. If she kept this up, she'd have black mascara running down the pink T-shirt she was wearing. Her shoulders rose and fell as she pulled in a deep breath in an effort to calm down. "I'm sorry. I shouldn't have come here. I—"

"It's okay. I'm glad you did but I can't help if you don't at least give me a hint what's wrong." Jackson focused on her face, a hard task because he was pretty sure there wasn't anything under that T-shirt and the pajama pants were untied and so low, he could see bare skin between the two. *Focus, asshole.* "Talk to me."

"I broke up with him. Technically we didn't break up because we were never officially together. But he was talking about anniversaries and season tickets and fancy dinners together. It was all so, so relationshippy. I couldn't do it. Not after last night."

The quiet sound of a car passing on the street emphasized the calmness that began to dislodge the sick feeling in his stomach. "Mandy, it's going to be fine. Everything will work out…fine. You want some tea? Or maybe a shot of bourbon?"

Though her eyes still rained, the torrential downpour slowed enough for her lips to curl slightly. "Tea might be good. Bourbon would be better, but probably not a safe idea."

Safe? Who needs safe? Jackson disagreed but thought it best not to say anything. He walked to his kitchen, made a glass of tea, and returned. The time elapsed was enough for her to collect herself. When he set the glass down on the table, she was hunched over and reading the notes he'd made on the contract.

"So David is working this contract now? Last I heard, it had been assigned to Gabe Dennis, the new guy." Her voice was stronger now.

"Dennis left a few months after you. David took over about half of your old contracts and I took the rest. This one changed hands twice, which might explain why it's such a mess."

Amanda nodded without looking up. "You're right about that. This is going to the board this week?"

"In two days but I'm debating whether to take it off the agenda. There's too many questions." Jackson was glad for the change of subject. He had no idea how to handle tears. Without any sisters, his only experience dealing with emotional women included his mother and Carter's sister, before she died. That had been years ago. His mother wasn't exactly a normal woman with normal emotions so she was a bad example.

"Your note here says 'why?'" Amanda pointed at his chicken-scratch on the page. He hadn't really planned for anyone to read his remarks and hoped she hadn't seen the pages toward the back where he'd used a few choice words.

"I didn't understand the archeologist. I mean, how many people just decide to start digging for artifacts out of the blue? What prompted that in the beginning and why had it been relevant enough to require review by an expert?"

Amanda nodded, her eyes glued to the pages. "There wasn't an archeologist review in the first contract."

"No?" That made it even more puzzling.

She shook her head and took another sip of tea. "Have you talked to them?"

"The archeologist?"

A wisp of hair fell into her mouth when she shook her head once more. "No, the contractors, or the property owners, or the attorney that drew up that document."

"I haven't talked to anyone except you. To be honest, I'd never seen this at all until a week ago. I probably wouldn't have if Dad hadn't been incapacitated to do so himself. I just didn't want to go to the board meeting without looking over each of the agenda items and knowing what was encompassed in the document."

Her eyes rose to his and the scrutiny of Amanda's tear-stained expression held a depth of curiosity. He shrugged. "I know—don't say it—why do I care, right? I'm just the spoiled rich son. Why should I get involved?"

Her eyes stayed steady for a couple of seconds. "Actually, I wondered if your father would even look at this under normal circumstances. Perhaps he's lucky you *are*. Tell me something. Do you think things like this happen for a reason? I don't wish your father in the hospital but this contract is huge for the company and maybe, just maybe, it needed more eyes on it. Have you asked him about it?"

His dad? How was he supposed to ask him anything in his current state? "No, but I don't want to worry him. He needs to concentrate on his health. The business can manage for a while."

"You're a good son. I hope your parents know that."

Oddly, it occurred to him he'd never heard those words from them. Other important words—love, pride, appreciation—sure. A *good son*—those words were never spoken. He wasn't even sure he'd thought of it until that moment.

Jackson didn't respond. He wasn't sure what to say.

Instead he picked up the remote and turned on music to break the silence that filled the gaps in their talk. It was too early in the morning for anything too loud or busy so he set the station to soft music that would have fit nicely in a dentist's lobby or an office reception area.

Amanda wiped her face and stood to leave. "You should take it off the agenda."

She was right, and he'd thought of doing so. "David said my dad wanted it moved so that we could get this project going. Apparently, it's been on the back burner for a while. He said Dad was insistent. There was a narrow window with one of the vendors to get started."

She raised a brow. "Maybe it's not your dad who's in a rush. Besides, if it's waited this long, one more month won't matter. Tell them, you need it to wait until he's better. They'll understand. At least go ask your mom what the urgency is. David's not exactly a nice guy. Maybe he has a hidden agenda. Tomorrow, I'll get in touch with the archeology survey company and see what I can dig up—no pun intended. I'll contact the property owners also."

"You have time for that?"

She straightened her hair and ran a hand over her shirt as if smoothing the wrinkles. T-shirts always had wrinkles so it seemed a little humorous. "Billable time, sure. You'll pay me for the work, right? Or were you expecting this to be pro bono? I'm not a public defender so I don't normally do that type of thing."

"We'll pay you…but can we save the bill until the work is finished? I don't want to raise any red flags at the moment." Not to mention, he had no idea how to get outside legal counsel approved without going through *inside* legal counsel. Especially since they'd wonder why he felt it necessary considering his legal background.

Amanda held out a hand to seal the agreement. How professional. Her hand shook a little as she waited for him to grasp it in an equally professional and firm grip. He didn't. Instead he put one hand under her graceful fingers and traced each individual digit of her hand with his free one. Very slowly, he ran his index finger along the quivering lines of her soft skin. Amanda had long slender fingers void of jewelry. She'd obviously spent a little time at a nail salon recently as the nails were perfectly manicured.

She attempted to pull back. He squeezed the hand, keeping it tightly in his own. "Who would have thought such a tiny little hand could wrap around a man's heart and deal a death blow?" he whispered.

Amanda blinked eyes that no longer had a stitch of makeup. Her mouth dropped. "I wasn't intending to hurt him."

She yanked her hand from his grasp and was out the door. Jackson couldn't move fast enough to stop her.

"I wasn't talking about Carter."

She was gone before the words were said.

Chapter Eighteen

As Amanda drove away she recognized the fact that truth was a personal thing. What one person considered honest disclosure might be evasive to another. People never really told the whole story anyway. They chose to leave out minor details or skew the facts for various reasons. Perhaps telling all the details was cumbersome, a waste of time, or simply certain details were forgotten. Some people believed themselves noble for not telling the full truth because it might hurt someone.

Amanda wasn't even sure what the full truth entailed nor if she knew and understood enough of it to disclose anything. Jackson's contract was so incredibly different from the one she'd seen and worked on while at their company. The archeological review hadn't been part of the original contract because the artifact discovery occurred while the contract was under edits. One of the property owners died and everything was put on hold.

None of that mattered under the present terms because the new contract had different people involved and stipulations that covered the new find. She doubted she'd be able to add anything relevant above and beyond Jackson's current concerns. Still, she should have mentioned it, right?

She hadn't given him the full story about Carter either. Jackson had texted Carter while she was with him, asking about the tickets. He *knew* Carter bought them and from what it seemed, it was *his* idea. Why would he suggest something that meant a long-term attendance at public events together? Did he want her to be with Carter? Had she completely imagined the connection with Jackson? Was he trying to push her into a relationship with his friend in order to gain distance?

Amanda wasn't naïve enough to believe that one night with someone meant a relationship. Nor was she planning to rush over and confess her feelings—first she'd have to understand them. Yet she'd done exactly that—she'd rushed over and cried all over Jackson about the breakup.

Earlier Carter had followed her into the street, astonished that she had broken his phone and dumped him in public. The phone thing was simply a frustration with his texto-manic personality. Then she'd dropped an even bigger bomb: she told him she was involved with someone else.

She'd lied.

It was only a partial lie but still dishonest. She wasn't in a relationship with anyone else. To be in a relationship, a person had to know how the other one thought and felt. She didn't. It wasn't like the night with Jackson was earth-shattering or life-changing either. Did that really happen? Nope, this was more real than that, not something in a storybook. It was simply so warm and nice, she could imagine staying there for days. Touching each other in so many ways until she knew every inch of him. Amanda sighed and checked herself in the rearview mirror. Lovely. She wiped the smudges below her eyes.

Traffic was sparse on the roads at three in the morning and her car sat at the red street light, the only vehicle awaiting a change of color in order to continue home. Her story to Carter was similar to the light. The traffic signal had turned yellow as she approached, the warning to prepare to stop.

The light was like Jackson's eagerness to switch to discussions of his contract—a warning to tread carefully. In all honesty, she'd swayed toward the contract because she was so wound up about the breakup, she had needed some breathing room to think. Then he launched into work discussion and moved to put distance between them.

During the breakup she had told Carter, *I'm involved with someone else.* But she had no idea if her words were true or if she even wanted them to be. Should she have told him the "someone else" was his friend? No, that was cruel. Wasn't it?

It would destroy their friendship.

Amanda pounded her head against the steering wheel a couple of times before hitting the gas when the light turned. *Hell, Jackson, I thought I'd gotten away from you.*

At home, she dropped her clothes on the floor and crawled into bed in her bra and panties. Her head throbbed from her emotional outburst—or maybe it was dehydration from all the tears. Her bones ached and every movement made her body feel as it weighed a ton. Perhaps it was the guilt. She knew she'd face it eventually. At the moment, she craved rest and a thorough analysis of the inside of her eyelids. Thank God for the weekend and the pleasure of sleeping late.

Thud. Something had fallen.

Amanda opened one eye and peered at the nightstand where the sound had come from. The clock blared eleven a.m. She felt like she'd had less than an hour of sleep. Nothing else was there. She lifted her head and peeked over the bed. Her cell phone danced on the floor beside a puddle of water. Had it rang so much it knocked over her nearly empty water glass?

She snagged the phone as it veered toward the puddle and answered.

"Open your door."

"Wow, nice way to greet someone, Jax. Gets me off to a real good start after a long night. Why not try 'good morning' or 'hello' or—"

"Good morning, sleepy head. I'm outside your door and I have someone with me. Do you have time to talk?"

"Oh. Okay." She dropped the phone and searched the room for her clothes. Um, no, it would be gross to put them back on.

She rushed to the closet and pulled out a sundress and threw it over her head. The zipper caught in her hair. She tugged. "Ow!" The zipper gave but took a couple of strands of hair with it.

Amanda ran to the bathroom, grabbed her toothbrush, and quickly scrubbed a couple of times. She grimaced at her reflection in the mirror. *Oh my God, I look like death warmed over.* She ran water, scrubbed her face, then brushed her hair. Not great but better. She stuck out her tongue at the woman staring back.

She rationalized he had to look as bad as she did; he'd been up most of the night too. Her footsteps fell like logs on the carpet as she rushed to the door and pulled it open. Damn Jackson. Why couldn't he look as worn out as she felt? Nope, not him. He was his cool, collected, normal, and annoyingly attractive self in a T-shirt and shorts. He even smelled like soap as he stepped past her into the living room followed by a random—girl?

Without turning, Jackson waved a hand at his guest. "Amanda, this is Celia Hovart. She's going to help us."

Celia Hovart was the size of a string, tall and lanky with barely enough meat on her bones to make a steak. Amanda nodded as she took in the hiking shorts and sports bra tank that served to accentuate her litheness. She wore dusty boots with socks rolled down over the laces. She wasn't the norm for a legal eagle.

Amanda gave her best professional smile. "You're an attorney?"

Celia shook her short-cropped brown hair. "Nope. I'm a geologist but that's not why I'm here. Jackson asked me to help you guys with the climb."

Amanda raised a brow toward Jackson. "Climb?"

He had the audacity to return her look with a sheepish grin. "Uh, yeah. When's the last time you climbed a rock?"

"The last time…well, that would be the first time…which isn't going to be today, Jax. You want to tell me how this relates to your contract and why I need to be involved?"

"Sure, but you'll need to change clothes first. We're going out to look at the property on the deal and it's a little dirty. Mostly rocks, trees, and a lot of dust. That dress would be ruined. Put on some shorts or maybe jeans."

"You're assuming I didn't have something else planned, aren't you?"

His eyes widened. "Do you? If so, we can come back this evening or maybe tomorrow. Celia's gone after that. She's just here for the weekend visiting."

"How nice of her."

"She's not visiting me. She's visiting her parents who live across the street from mine. I was there this morning and saw her outside. I knew she liked to rock-climb so I asked her to help."

"You keep bringing up climbing. Don't think you're getting me to scale a wall or something this weekend. I don't know anything about that and—"

Jackson held up a hand. "You don't have to. It's just that I called the trust for the family that owns the property. They forwarded me to someone named Big or Biggs and he agreed to meet us at the land site to show me the archeological find that's holding this whole thing up. He said it would make sense once I saw things for myself."

"Did he tell you what it was?" Amanda envisioned a national archive team showing up and a team of scientists with picks and brushes at work.

"Not exactly."

"What does not exactly mean?"

"I don't know. Look, are you going or not? Because if you aren't then we're leaving. I have to get this done and go by the hospital to get Dad."

Amanda felt a tinge of guilt for stalling. "How is your dad, by the way? The rehab efforts are going well?"

"He's being released today. Rehab will be a lengthy process but all in all, he's good. His speech hasn't recovered very well and he's a little gimpy. His memory seems pretty fuzzy still."

Celia stuck a hand in her pocket. "Jackson, I didn't know your father was in the hospital. What happened?"

"Stroke."

"Oh, God, I'm sorry."

"Don't be. He's fine." Jackson moved from foot to foot.

Amanda questioned his analysis but kept her mouth shut. Jackson stepped toward the door he'd just entered and met her eyes. "What's it going to be? Are you coming or not?"

She desperately wanted to say "not" and head back to her rumpled sheets. "Oh, okayyy. Give me a minute." She went back to her room. It actually took ten minutes but when she returned in shorts and tennis shoes, he said nothing. Jackson pushed out the door and the two women followed.

Chapter Nineteen

Mosquito spray would have been a great idea. Amanda swatted the pesky bug from her face after its one-millionth attempt to take a nip of her cheek. She tilted her head back and peered through the trees. The sun beat down upon them with laser focus. At least she'd remembered sunscreen.

She trudged behind Jackson and Celia, her eyes focused on the terrain, regretting the decision to abandon her wonderful mattress and pillows.

They cleared the trees and the road leveled, which allowed her to concentrate on something other than her next step. She lifted her gaze to Jackson's back pockets. Nice.

He chose that moment to turn and catch her staring at his ass. *Crap.* Busted. A slow grin spread across his face while an equally slow burn filled her cheeks. He enjoyed her embarrassment, the jerk. She shook it off and lifted her chin. "So, you and Celia have known each other a long time?"

"Yep." He turned and trudged forward leaving no alternative but to follow, which she did.

Celia's thin athletic figure bounded forward, daring them to keep up. "We've known each other most of our adult lives. He was a bratty pubescent thug when he moved to our neighborhood."

Jackson broke off a twig that threatened to take the cap on his head. "Yeah, and you were a scrawny bean pole."

Celia laughed. "It takes one to know one."

Amanda stopped walking and watched the two. His footsteps followed hers effortlessly as if he'd done it for years. Followed her wherever she went. Had they? She couldn't bring herself to ask.

As if he sensed her question, Jackson held back and waited for Amanda to reach him, then leaned down and whispered in her ear. "Just so you don't embarrass yourself—Celia has a live-in girlfriend. They've been together for eight years."

Oh. "She's—?"

He nodded.

"So the two of you never …?" Amanda hesitated.

His eyes widened at the thought, then a look of disgust crossed his face and he shuddered. "Ugh, no. No way. She's like a sister."

Ahead of them, Celia bounded over a dead tree that had fallen across their path. Jackson followed. His long legs cleared the debris with little effort. Amanda tried to clear the mess with equal athletic prowess but caught a toe on a wayward limb. She pitched forward and landed face-first in the dust. Jackson's fingers clutched around her arm and pinched as he pulled her to her feet.

Amanda dusted off her shirt and shook back the hair that threatened to fall into her eyes. "Don't you mean like a brother?" Celia was well out of earshot and out of view too. The path ahead was quiet.

He shrugged. "I guess that's why we get along so well. Watch yourself. There's a lot of snakes in this area and they like to hang out under rocks and stumps."

Amanda cringed and searched below the wood debris she'd just been splayed across. Nothing moved. Whew. She squinted up at his sinewy frame shadowed by the sun behind. The twitch at the side of his mouth was barely a tick. If it hadn't been kind of cute, she would have punched him. "You *had* to say that, didn't you?"

Jackson had one dimple and it only showed when he did something devilish, like try to put the fear of snakes in a woman. She'd noticed it in college and ignored it, unlike many of the other coeds that had trailed his way. Time had lowered her reserves, though, and ignoring it now wasn't as easy. The tiny indention only served to make her insides warm and tighten. He was oblivious to her discomfort as he gave her a faked innocent grin. "What? You don't like snakes?"

"Are you kidding me? Does anyone?"

"They're harmless for the most part. At least, the no-legged kind are. You might want to watch out for the two-legged kind, though."

Hmmm. Fair warning. "Would that two-legged problem be you? Or someone else?"

Jackson stopped walking and let her catch him. She chose to keep moving and the narrowness of the path made it impossible to pass without brushing his chest. How can a guy smell so good while sweating in the morning heat? He put a hand to her arm and held her against him for a brief second. "Men are never harmless, Amanda. Every last one of us wants to get in your pants if given a shot."

She met his gaze and instantly regretted raising her eyes. "Then that would make you the safest of all, since you've already been there."

His hand rambled up her arm and clutched into her hair, pulling her head back to hover his lips closer. It was impossible not to focus on that mouth and the warmth of it that she'd felt only hours ago. The nervousness in her stomach spread to her chest and she gulped as he leaned closer, hovering. "I'm the least harmless of all."

That was meant to put the fear of God in her but she wouldn't cave. "You don't scare me, Jax."

He put his lips right against hers for a second, then spoke softly. "I should because you scare the hell out of me."

"Where are you guys?" Celia's voice echoed from the distance, breaking their trance. Amanda felt relief flush through her veins. She stepped past Jackson and kept moving. "Coming."

Did he mutter *not yet* or was that her imagination?

• • •

The musky smell of the Texas hill country filled Jackson's nose as he entered a clearing to find Celia standing with her hands on hips and Amanda tiptoeing up a rocky path to meet her. Two ropes hung from the rock face near them and jostled in the wind.

Wait. The wind had died; there wasn't even a stir. He squinted upward to see dangling legs and the harness of gear strapped around the small ass of his newly found friend, Bigby. The man had a shaved head that glistened with sweat and his sinewy muscles bulged as he reached for a rock, then pulled his weight to an apparent twenty feet above them. He slipped a rope into a tie-anchor, looped it, and grasped with one hand. He tested the hold before stopping to look down. The man lifted two fingers to his forehead and soared a quick salute. "Hello there! Glad you finally made it…I was climbing up to see where you were. Just get your gear on and come up when you're ready. I'll meet you on the ledge."

"This is my attorney friend, Amanda. The one I mentioned," Jackson shouted, though it wasn't necessary. They were the only ones within miles and the stillness made their voices echo.

The man kept climbing but nodded. "Bigby Hernandez, ma'am. I'm the caretaker for the estate's property."

Jackson's adrenaline started to hit warp speed. It had been a couple of years since he'd tried climbing but there'd been a time when he was pretty decent. He joined a local climbing group for a while, then work became too much and he slowly extricated himself from the planned outings. It was a shame because he loved the challenge. That was part of the reason he'd decided to join the adventure club where he'd found Amanda.

"Ahem, Jackson?" Amanda's face held a universe of skepticism. How would he talk her into the climb?

By the time Jackson reached the two women, Celia had dropped her pack along with all the gear and was sorting and organizing. "What's up?"

Amanda bugged her eyes, an expression that was both cute and irritating. She pointed toward Bigby. "I'm not doing that.

Whatever is up there, it's ancient and dirty. Take pictures and text them to me. I don't need to kill myself for this consulting gig."

He watched her blow hair from her face in a huff. She tried so hard to be prissy but he knew under that cool façade, an athletic competitiveness simmered. He'd seen it many times over their school years and the short time they'd worked together. "What's the matter? You scared?"

Her gaze shot up, then back to him. "Me? You're kidding, right? I just don't want to get filthy dirty…and besides, look at these clouds up there. They're probably going to burst open within the hour and we'll get stranded and wet."

She had a point; the clouds had moved in quickly and the stillness in the air was foreboding. In fact the change was a little too quick for his comfort. When did that happen? Probably about the time he'd been focusing on little else but the scent of her skin and the pockets of her shorts. "I checked the weather on the way to your place. There was only a twenty percent chance of showers, which means the likelihood is slim. Besides, I've never seen you back down from a challenge before."

Celia stepped toward her and nudged her arm with a sling of sorts. "Here," she said. "This is your harness. Wear this and you'll have nothing to worry about. You step into it like…a diaper." Jackson appreciated that Celia assumed Amanda would comply and gave her no option. She simply held the contraption open and waited for Amanda to lift a foot. After a moment's hesitation, she did.

"I am so charging you double-time for this."

He shrugged. "I don't have a problem with that. As long as we can double on a few other things too." *In particular, the shower thing.* He decided not to wait for her to grumble further and retract her decision to climb. Maybe if he'd already gone part of the way she'd have less concern. He strapped into his climbing gear and started scaling the wall. Celia stayed below, giving Amanda some brief instruction before urging her to follow.

When he glanced over his shoulder, she was ten feet behind and seemed fine. He couldn't see her face but he expected there was the same measure of intensity he remembered from when she was elbows-deep in a study session or legal matter. Amanda had the fierce concentration of a starved dog focused on a bone. When she wanted something, the fool who stood in her way had better expect to be pulverized.

He loved that about her. It was infectious. Jackson pushed up and grabbed the ledge. Bigby wrapped two gloved hands around his wrist and pulled him the last few feet. Once securely on solid ground, Jackson rolled to his stomach and peered toward Amanda. Specks of gravel and dust rattled down the rock wall and pelted her shoulders. She had only a few feet left.

Amanda ducked and stuck her tongue out to spit the dirt away. "Hey! Do you mind not spraying me with rocks here? It's hard enough to hold on without dirt in my eyes."

Kaboom.

The ground shook from the sound of the thunderbolt. Jackson jolted, Amanda screamed, and before he could grasp the hand that was extended she fell backward. With his rope still secured, he shoved over the edge. The rope whirred as he sailed to her side. Two big leaps and he was there beside Amanda as she hung from the rope, dangling like a needle on a thread.

Jackson pulled her tight, his chest thumping at Mach-One speed. *Holy shit, that was close.* The thought of her falling to serious injury made him sick. Her fingers dug deeply into his flesh but he didn't care. *Get a grip, dumb ass. She was never in real danger. The rope made sure of that.* He peered down at Celia latched on with all her strength. The rope plus Celia's deceptive strength kept the danger at bay.

"Jackson, don't let go. Please." Amanda's voice was muffled by his throat as he held her tight and pulled them to a rock outcropping just below the ledge.

"Never." He hooked a leg over the outcropping and readjusted their weight. "We'll go the rest of the way together."

"You mean down, right?"

He shook his head. "Up is closer."

"But you heard the thunder—we'll get soaked."

"Better on the ledge under the rock overhang than down there with all those trees jutting above us like lightning rods. I don't know about you but I'm not in the mood for a little electrocution today."

She darted a glance from the ledge to him and back. He knew she was considering her options. He wanted her with him—where he could make sure she was safe. He hooked his rope to the loop on her harness. "We're going up. Together. Just follow my lead. We'll be there in a couple of minutes."

Jackson reached for a rock and waited for her to do the same. When she did, he lifted a foot and found a hold for his shoe. She followed the action and ten minutes later, they reached the ledge where Bigby pulled Amanda into safety.

Seconds later the rain began.

Bigby motioned for them to move against the inner wall and use the sanctity of the stone overhang to shield them from the pounding drops. The scraping of their shoes as they crawled into the miniature cave was drowned out by the rainfall.

Would Celia wait for them? Of course not. He wouldn't. Why should she? She'd get drenched. Jackson pulled the ropes in and rolled them neatly into a pile and tied them together. He kept one rope anchored to Amanda's belt and latched to one of the anchors on his own belt. Call it overprotective, but he'd nearly lost ten years off his life earlier.

Jackson stared at the blur of rain as it splashed into their cubbyhole. "We should do this another time."

Bigby seemed excited about the turn of the weather. Or maybe it was more relaxed than excited. Undisturbed. "Too late for that now. We're here and there's no sense in trying to climb down in these conditions."

The guy seemed to enjoy their discomfort almost as much as he enjoyed the anticipation of whatever he planned to show them. It had been impossible to pry any information from him on the phone. Jackson didn't give him the satisfaction of asking as soon as they arrived. He expected it would be met with some sort of avoidance tactic. All the man had said was he was going for a nice climb on the property and would like them to join him so that he could show them the importance of the land. Would Bigby be so happy with the situation if Jackson chose to call the entire excursion off and take Amanda home?

Doubtful.

"Bigby, the rain could cause a problem for whatever relics you wanted us to see."

The man knew he held them hostage. Or at least the rain had, which was probably better anyway. If they left at the moment, the least they'd get was drenched to the bone and risking pneumonia. Not that they were completely dry anyway. The rain hit the stone ledge and sprayed them with mist almost as much as it delved to the ground below. Amanda's blond ponytail was dark, and limply curled around itself toward her neck. Lucky hair.

The worst that could happen? Struck by one of those massive lightning bolts that made the ground shudder.

Bigby lifted a hand toward the inner wall of their respite, drips of water running down his wrist and dripping to his lap. He ran the fingers across the wall above him. "Check this out. Ever seen anything like this?"

Until that moment Jackson hadn't spent more than a second or two evaluating the space they were in. As if a light bulb—or lightning bolt—struck her, Amanda gasped. "Oh my God, it's some sort of Indian hieroglyphics, isn't it? Wow! That's amazing."

Bigby laughed. "I wish. No, it's nothing that old or precious, but it is a great message. Especially if you combine it with what's in the box I found up there." He pointed to a small hole that appeared to be freshly dug into the stone, except for the pile of bird shit streaming down the rocks and the knot of sticks and leaves that signified a bird had taken up residence.

Jackson lifted a brow. "Behind the bird nest?"

"Yep. The bird's been gone for a while but it served as a good way to cover up what's there."

Amanda crawled closer and peered behind the nest. "You're sure it's gone? I'd hate to mess with Mother Nature. Or have a big angry bird attack us for desecrating her home."

Bigby reached a hand up and yanked the nest from the hole, then tossed it to the ledge. "I'm sure."

While Amanda searched the small hole, afraid to remove its contents, Jackson started to review the chicken scratches carved into the wall. No Indian had made those marks. Judging by the clothing of the stick figures, he guessed it was much more recent. Still, the first portion of the drawing was worn away by wind and time so it hadn't been made recently. There was no mistaking the final message, though. There was a man with a bandage on his head—or at least that's what he thought it to be—then a tree, a woman, and a child, plus the message *Find me* scrawled below. Jackson wasn't impressed with the person's artistic ability. "Is this our big archeological find? A bunch of chicken scratches on a wall?"

Amanda frowned. "It's a love story. Look. Start at the beginning." She pointed toward the opposite end. "Two kids playing. Two kids holding hands. Two lovers kissing. Then one waving—not sure about that. Maybe he was leaving? Or she was? Then the last picture. Maybe they got married?"

Jackson didn't exactly see the romance in it. "Or pregnant."

He looked down when she shot him a reprimanding glare. He shrugged and attempted an innocent tone. "Hey, depending on how long this has been here, it could be. Or maybe it's just a couple of kids playing around by drawing pictures in the stone to kill time after climbing all the way up here."

Bigby nodded. "That's what I thought at first. Then I found the box there. Go ahead, get it out and take a look."

Amanda shook her head. "You do it. There might be snakes in there."

Jackson snickered. "She's a little paranoid about things that slither."

Bigby smiled. "So am I. That's why I have this stick." He pulled a twig from his pack and poked it into the dark crevice. *Thunk.* It hit something hollow. He wiggled the twig for seconds as if to flush out any current residents.

Jackson had never achieved a normal amount of fear in his lifetime. It was probably a weakness but he'd never considered it such. Instead he fancied himself blessed with a larger sum of common sense than others which kept him calm under pressure and focused in situations of duress. Like he had been when Carter's sister died.

He sighed. "Here, I'll get the damn thing." He shoved his arm into the crevice and felt around in the dampness. His fingers enveloped something square and sandy. A box.

Amanda's voice whispered at his shoulder, "What is it? Is it moving?"

God help him, but Jackson couldn't resist what came next. "Holy shit!" He jolted and pretended that his arm was pulled into the crevice. He yelled.

Amanda shrieked. "Oh my God! Get him out. Pull it out. Kill it! Kill it!" Her eyes were the size of half-dollars.

Jackson stopped, no longer able to contain his mirth. The laugh rolled up inside and eventually bubbled out. Slipping his fingers around the box, he pulled it from the opening and laid it at her side. "There you go. One…dead box."

Her face shriveled up tight and her cheeks flushed crimson. She thrust a finger into his face and Jackson lunged backward. She opened her mouth to speak but said nothing. He watched her move like a guppy in a fishbowl. "You! You! Dumb ass."

"I was just playing around, Mandy. Lighten up."

She huffed but opened the lid to the box. "Well, it's a good thing it wasn't alive because there's no chance I'd try to save you or help you. Now, what do we have in here?"

Bigby didn't budge and Jackson had to assume that he'd already done a fair inventory of the contents of the box. *I wonder if he took anything?*

Amanda lifted out some plastic bags and turned them over in her hands. "Letters. It's a bunch of letters."

Bigby interrupted, no longer able to hold his excitement. "Yes, and some pictures. Look at them." He took one bag from her fingers and tapped the address. "These are from her to him. The others are from him to her. The ones from him were opened. The others weren't. See?"

Jackson noted the pink index finger label stamped with the words, "Return to Sender." He darted a glance over both packages and did a quick count. Ten letters from her to him. Six from him to her, all appeared unopened. "Did you read any of them, Bigby?"

"A few."

"So what's in them? And why do we care?"

The rainfall continued to spray their backs but Jackson had situated his frame to shield the box and its contents. The thunderous downfall had weakened to a steady shower and the wind had come and gone as quickly as the saturation.

Bigby squinted at the sky. "That's the coolest part of this. I can't tell you—you need to read them. Just know that it has everything to do with this land and why one of the owners will be a problem for you. Unless, of course, you find what can't be found."

Jackson hated evasiveness and Bigby was oozing it simply because it added to the drama. "Don't you mean who? Unless we find the person *who* can't be found?"

Bigby snapped his rope back into his harness and shrugged. "Whatever. Look, the rain's stopped and I have to be at work at two so you're on your own now. If you take anything with you, be sure to bring it back. I've inventoried everything and it has been claimed as part of the property."

Amanda grimaced. "You claimed a bunch of old letters and a cigar box? Are they lined with gold or something?"

"Ha, not exactly but close."

Bigby's rope whirred as he descended the rock face in several short lunges. Jackson searched the ground and a few minutes later saw Bigby striding into the trees.

"Wow, that was helpful." Amanda's sarcasm wasn't a surprise. "We're stuck up here. Celia left when the rain started."

"Amanda, I've climbed a lot and can handle this. Don't worry, I'll get you down." He held his tongue before his thoughts spewed the words *unless you take another dive like earlier.* No need to frighten her.

The rain stopped. The sun peered between the trees and lit the water droplets on the ledge like crystal in a chandelier. It was an opportunity that Bigby was smart enough to use and they should do the same. As if reading his thoughts, Amanda grabbed a rope and clipped it to her harness beside his clip. "We should go, too, before it rains again or the sun fades."

She had a point. "You don't have to tell me twice. Should we take the cigar box?" Jackson shoved the plastic bags of letters into the box and dropped the lid into place.

"Yeah, but first let me take some pictures." Amanda dug into the pocket of her backpack and retrieved her phone. Leaning to the side but staying clear of the ledge, she snapped shots of the carved artwork that adorned the wall of their shelter. Once satisfied, she dropped it back into her pack, added the cigar box, and zipped the bag closed. She slung it over her left shoulder and slipped the right shoulder through the strap. "Ready?"

He had already attached his ropes and slung their safety ties over the edge. He'd made sure her rope was secure before testing his own. "Let me go first. When I get to the first clip, you start down. Watch my footings and try to follow. I'll clip to your rope too just in case something happens. That will let my weight counter yours."

Amanda didn't argue. "Wow, you really do know what you're doing."

"Of course. Why would I lie?"

"I wasn't saying you did. It's just…this isn't something I thought you would be interested in. I guess I had you pegged more as the pretty-boy party type."

Jackson lowered himself over the ledge and with one hand on the rope and the other working his lead, he dropped to the first tie-off. "Don't tell anyone, okay? We wouldn't want to ruin my rep."

"Pretty boys can be outdoorsy too—it's not a crime."

Ten minutes later they had worked down to the midway point. Within thirty minutes, they were packed up and hiking to the car where Celia was huddled in the back seat—sleeping. She bolted upright when Jackson opened the door and tossed the ropes on the floor. "A lot of help you were," he said.

Celia yawned and stretched. "Sorry. I wasn't too thrilled about a potential lightning strike so I figured I'd hang out here until it let up. I guess I dozed off a bit."

Jackson stepped out of his sling and added it to the ropes. "I guess you did." He tossed Amanda's equipment and backpack on the seat.

Amanda didn't complain when he dropped Celia in her drive, then drove to his place and pulled into his garage. As if to explain why he hadn't taken her home yet, he motioned to her bag. "Let's take a look at those before I run you home, okay?"

She nodded. Amanda's face was pale and though the sun had returned and warmed the air, her clothes stuck to her like a second skin. It had taken every ounce of control to keep his eyes on her face and not focus on the way her nipples strained through the fabric or the goosebumps that speckled her arms and legs. She was damp and cold. He wished he'd thought to tell her to bring a change of clothes but how was he to know they'd get stuck in a rainstorm?

Inside, she placed the cigar box on his table and headed toward the back. "Have to make a pit-stop. Be there in a sec."

He followed, taking in every line of her soaking wet five feet, eleven inches. He'd already investigated them up close but seeing the way the cloth slinked and clung against those curves was— disturbing. "Amanda, if you're not opposed to wearing an old T-shirt and sweatpants, I'll give you some dry clothes. They won't fit but at least they'll be warmer than what you're wearing."

She shivered and while she said nothing, he knew she'd wear a tent if it meant it was dry and warm. "Th-th-thanks."

He searched through his closet until he found something that might work and hung it over the bathroom door. "It's outside the door when you're ready. I'm going to make us something to eat."

Jackson wasn't a great cook. His parents had a knack for entertaining, but not him. He scanned the fridge for anything edible, settled on some hamburger and cheese, then got to work.

When Amanda walked into his kitchen in his T-shirt and sweatpants, his breath caught. Not because she looked amazing in his clothes, although she did. No, he stopped breathing for a second because it was so—damned—intimate. That should have bothered him because as much as all his friends thought him a man-whore, the truth was he normally didn't like having a woman underfoot. Until that very moment, he would have panicked to see a female wearing his clothes and making herself comfortable in his kitchen or home.

This was Amanda, though, and he'd known her for years. They were like best friends. Like him and Carter. He looked at the way his T-shirt hung over her breasts. It draped dangerously over her shoulder as if one move would make it fall to reveal the creamy skin hidden below. The softness of her collarbone was exposed above the cotton.

No, *definitely not like him and Carter.*

"What?" She met his gaze with glassy blue eyes full of concern. Should he confess his thoughts?

He buried his head into the fridge and pulled out a couple of beers. Opening one, he handed it to her, then opened the other for himself. "Nothing. I just—nothing."

He took a long draw on his beer, searching for something that wouldn't make him feel a complete idiot before lowering the bottle. "Amanda, don't take this the wrong way, but I like you in my clothes."

She twisted her fingers through her hair and cinched up the waist of the pants with her free hand. "Thanks. They're a little big but comfortable. I hope they don't fall off."

He took another drink. He should probably stay silent but—

"I hope they do."

Chapter Twenty

She could have gone the rest of the day without him making a comment that turned her insides to Jell-O. Was that necessary? He didn't need to pour on the schmooze to get her involved in helping with the legal work. She was getting paid and she loved her job. That was enough.

Jackson, on the other hand—well, she wasn't sure how she felt about him. The only truthful part had been what she told Carter. She was seeing someone else—or was she?

Not by most standards. They had spent one night together and barely spoken since. In fact, they both seemed to avoid the topic. Regardless, it made sense to blame their "encounter" on her emotional state at the time and try to counteract his charismatic charm with—staunch professionalism. She cleared her throat and moved to sit at his kitchen counter. A pile of bills graced one side and the newly found box of letters filled the other.

"Okaaay, so let's do this." She flipped the cigar box lid open, took out one of the bags, and laid out the contents in a line.

"You want to start with the unopened ones?"

"Sure." It was comforting to know that he was just as concerned about prying into unopened messages as she. She chose an envelope, and opened it.

Jackson followed her lead and retrieved another envelope. "We should put them in date order and make sure we have everything in perspective. This one looks like the first. December 14, 1950. Knowing which letter came first might help to understand the chain of events. Is it just me or does this feel like spying?"

Amanda looked at the first line, *Dearest M.* He had a point. "He just used an initial—how cryptic is that? Yes, I suppose it feels a little like digging in someone's panty drawer but apparently we're supposed to read these so we understand your legal dilemma."

Jackson slipped his opened. "Mine says *Dearest Marion.* So, not too cryptic, though digging in each other's panty drawer sounds a lot more interesting than reading a bunch of crusty old love letters."

"You don't know they're love letters. Marion could be his sister or his mom."

Jackson turned to her and raised a brow. "You seriously think he called his mom by her first name? I'd get backslapped if I did that with either of my parents."

Good point. "Your parents are really that picky about manners? I wouldn't have guessed."

He didn't miss her sarcasm; his voice had a soft tone as he laughed. "Manners? Nope. One of my dad's favorite phrases was, 'Only one person in the world can call me Dad, so use it.'"

Amanda warmed a little toward his old father. "He had a point. So, want me to read this out loud or just pass them to you?"

A bell dinged. Jackson dropped his letter and strode to the kitchen. "First, we eat. Then we read."

Amanda breathed deeply as he shoved his hands into some oven gloves and pulled something steamy from the oven. Jackson knew how to cook? What a surprise. He placed a casserole on the cooktop and lifted the foil. Steam gushed into a small cloud. Another wave of garlic and oregano filled the room. It smelled fabulous, and suddenly Amanda was ravenous. She tiptoed into the kitchen and stood at his side to see the masterpiece. "I didn't know you cooked."

He laughed. "I can make three things really well. My famous chili cheeseburgers on the grill, a rib-eye that can rival Ruth Chris's, and my mom's famous meatloaf. I wanted to make the burgers but didn't have any buns so you get the meatloaf."

"It smells fantastic. You use cheese in yours?"

He nodded. "This is my mother's recipe and yes, there's cheese. Always. My mother's philosophy on cooking is easy—everything tastes better with cheese or butter. The meatloaf has a layer of cheese in the middle that melts and flavors as it cooks. It's pretty good. There's French fries too." He pulled the oven open with a creak and retrieved a sheet full of crinkle fries.

Amanda was in heaven. "I'm starved. Point me in the direction of plates."

Jackson reached above her head and grabbed a couple of plates, then pulled utensils from a drawer. With both hands gripping plates of heaven, he nodded toward the table. "Would you mind clearing us a spot?"

Amanda did so, and they enjoyed the meal while laughing about her first attempt at rock-climbing. She shrugged. "Hey, I can't be perfect at everything." Not that she was.

Jackson leaned toward her, fork in hand, and dropped a kiss on her nose. "So true. But we should go back and try again when there's no rain in the forecast."

The meatloaf was magnificent; his mother had a hit there. Amanda gobbled it up, then chased it with half a dozen fries. They washed the food down with two more beers and all Amanda wanted afterward was—a nap. She'd eaten too much.

The letters sat on the counter, taunting them to read. She carried the empty plates to his sink, scrubbed them, and placed them in the washer.

"Are we ready to start reading?"

Jackson pulled himself to a stand. Lifting his arms above his head, he stretched. "I am if you are."

They sat and read Marion's letters, one by one. While it felt like intruding in someone's privacy, the letters were well written and sentimental but not over the top. The kind of letters one would imagine a soldier writing to his love before heading into the trenches of war.

Which was exactly what the letters were. The man writing them—his name was Jacob—served in Korea during the Korean War. According to the letters, he was nineteen when he walked into battle for the first time. The letters were a lot of mush with small amounts of details about the people around him. Never about the war.

Amanda sighed. "It was a different time then, wasn't it? He could say the sweetest things but never tell anything about the horrific violence he witnessed."

Jackson stared at the letter she'd finished. "That hasn't changed. It's a matter of national security. They're not allowed to divulge anything about the war or their location."

"I know, I know. I meant that all these men went over there and were exposed to all sorts of things they'd probably never dealt with before. They came back home and just walked right into their old lives as if it never happened. There wasn't any PTSD diagnosis or counseling. They just—went on. Things are so different now. Now, soldiers are encouraged to explore their combat experiences and feelings with professionals and are given all sorts of opportunities when they return. It was harder then."

"Harder? I suppose. Listen to this." Jackson lifted a handwritten note and started reading.

"*Today, we scaled the side of a hill and dug foxholes so we could prepare for the advance. I can't tell you where I am but know that it's not a good place and this is a tough war. On my first day, I was assigned to a weapon that would have surely gotten me killed. Then the commander's driver took some shrapnel and just like that, my job here changed and I became a driver to the head guy.*

When we scaled the hill, I thought of us and our little piece of heaven in the rocks. I wondered how many people before us had reached that ledge and looked out over the Texas hill country. No matter where I go or what shape I'm in when I come back, know that

I love you and that little spot is the only place in my heart that means home to me. I dream of walking through the trees to find you there."

Amanda's eyes misted and she watched as he folded the pages and slid them back into their envelope.

"You're a softie, Amanda Gillespie." Jackson's words were teasing but his voice was kind. Yeah, she was exactly that. As a teen, she'd hated the way she cried at sad movies, weddings, funerals, and even graduations. It was embarrassing, and several of her friends hadn't skipped the opportunity to tease her for the weakness. As a result, she was sensitive about being sensitive.

"Shut up."

He cupped her cheek and pulled her face toward him. "No, I think it's adorable. Come here." He eased her closer and dropped his mouth to hers, a feather-light dotting of kisses that trailed along her mouth and cheek. It was sweet.

"We should get back to the letters. I think we should make some notes." She couldn't concentrate because Jackson had slid his hand across her shoulder and eased his oversized T-shirt down. He followed the movement by trailing kisses along the top of her shoulder and down.

He whispered against her skin. "The letters have been there for fifty years. They're not going anywhere. Besides I think we should make notes too—right here. Note to self, Amanda has a tiny mole at the very spot that her collar bone meets her heart." He kissed the spot.

"I have a lot of moles."

"Note two, there's another one on the outside of her ear. A tiny speck that looks almost like it was drawn there for decoration. I think I need to get a pad and do a massive inspection. Maybe I should catalogue them so you know where they all are." Jackson nibbled her earlobe and Amanda squelched the urge to squeal with delight. How would she not know her own body?

He ran a finger up her back and dipped into his massive sweats that were threatening to fall from her waist. Circling a finger at the lowest part of her spine, he snickered. "You probably haven't seen this one."

"I have a mole *there*? Seriously?"

His gaze held hers, his eyes smoky and dark while he nodded. Hmmm, okay, so she didn't know every nook and cranny of her own body. She did know what it felt like and at the moment his hands were making ripples of heat that she expected would turn to fire as soon as he decided to change things up.

She curled her bare toes together and kept still. "While we're taking notes, did you know there's a little scar right here?" She trailed a finger along his chest, inside the collar of his shirt.

"Little League. I played outfield and went after a fly ball. The fence and I had a little argument over who could have the ball."

"I'm guessing you lost?" She quirked a brow.

Jackson laughed, a soft low rolling grumble that made her stomach flip. "Nope. You should have seen the fence. Even then I was a big, lanky guy. I tore it to shreds."

She smiled at the thought of a gangly pre-teen wrestling free from chain-link. Before she said the next words that came to mind, Jackson blotted her vision by dropping his mouth solidly to hers. She let him intensify the kiss for a few moments, then reared back.

Digging her fingers inside his pants behind the back pocket, she clutched his right glute. "I think I should take a few notes myself. For instance, there's a little bump right here …"

"Little?" He gave her a wicked smile with a half-raised eyebrow.

She clutched the spot harder and he jerked. "Yes, tiny…but I couldn't really see it the other night so I'd better check it out and make sure there's nothing—life-threatening going on with your backside."

Jackson sucked in air and kissed her hard. "I'm pretty sure the only thing life-threatening at the moment is not happening on my backside, babe. I know that for certain. But if you bring those claws of yours around to the front…there's definitely something there that needs serious attention."

Amanda stuck her tongue to the side of her mouth and tried to give the most provocative look she knew. "Serious?"

Jackson nodded. She liked the sound of that. He tossed his head at the table. "Grab the pad, counselor, we have some work to do."

Awesome.

Chapter Twenty-One

So many people thought authors are wordsmiths. But the best author in the world had nothing on a fine-tuned, well-experienced legal mind with gorgeous blond hair. Jackson knew that firsthand. He glanced down at his palm splayed across Amanda's back. Secondhand too.

The woman was vocal about things that surprised him at the strangest moment—almost randomly. Jackson realized if you let her finish the thought, it was always a profound insight she'd come upon and needed to share. Unfortunately her timing sucked. For instance, she waited until he was in a passion-filled hold on her hips and an intense lip-lock to say, "Do you think Marion and her solider had sex on that ledge?"

He groaned. "Amanda, at this very moment I can honestly say I don't give a shit but I sure hope so."

She blinked and widened her eyes, a move that always made his breath catch. "Why do you hope so?" With minx-like intention, she gyrated her hips a little and heat flooded his veins.

Amanda Gillespie knew exactly what she was doing and she enjoyed his agony while waiting for an answer. He, however, wanted things to move a little faster. He frowned. "Because it's a hellaciously romantic spot and someone needs to christen it if it hasn't happened already."

"You think so? Really? Because that's exactly what I thought. I mean, you could be all alone and private but still see for miles. It's like being on the inside of one of those privacy windows and looking out over a nature trail or something. The only thing that struck me when we were up there was how in the hell had they found it in the first place? It's not visible from the ground or at least not completely. It just looked like a shadow. So, how did someone wander into such a remote spot surrounded by trees and just happen to find a ledge that's thirty plus feet above them? None of the trees even reach that high."

Jackson laughed. "Yeah, and I'd be happy to take you back with a blanket…just not right now."

She blinked again and he soaked in her wide-eyed stare. He could drown in those eyes. "Do I have to climb up?"

God, she was stalling. His body wasn't tough enough for this kind of game. "Either you climb or I carry you over my shoulder like a sack of potatoes. You can choose. Now…Mandy…I love where your thoughts are, but can we please…stop…talking?"

But just like that she'd killed the mood—and raised his curiosity. How had she come to such an important observation about the ledge? And why mention it now rather than earlier while they were there and could search further for clues? Jackson squeezed his brows over his eyes with a thumb and forefinger. "Hell, Amanda, does your brain ever stop going full throttle?"

She batted her eyes again and he wanted to deck her—or kiss her, he wasn't sure. "What?" She gave him the doe-eyed innocent look that he was beginning to think she practiced in front of a mirror. "Is something wrong?"

He ran a hand over her thigh and grabbed her wrist, then wrapped his fingers around the other wrist and drew them both around his neck. "Before we go any further, I need you to promise me something."

"I don't make promises I can't keep so be careful what you ask for and know that I have a right to say no."

Jackson dropped his forehead to hers and sighed. "You have a right to say whatever the hell you choose, but do you really need to do it when I'm trying to feel you up? I know we're working on a project here but just for a second, babe, put your lawyer hat in the drawer. Be here, okay? With me?"

At least Amanda had the decency to look ashamed. She chewed on her lip for a second and he half expected her to keep talking about the letters and the ledge. She didn't.

Amanda shoved him onto the couch and crawled on top of him one leg at a time. The effort had dislodged the string on the sweatpants he'd loaned her. They lowered dangerously around her waist. She grinned, then straddled his chest and leaned down to put her chin on one hand while the elbow jabbed him in the sternum. "Wellll, you *did* say you wanted to take notes."

"About each other, not a couple that is either as old as my grandfather or dead."

"Okay, Mr. One-Track Mind, I solemnly swear not to discuss any legal matters with you while we're horizontal or naked." He seriously doubted she was a Boy Scout so the fingers she held up were a ruse.

"We're horizontal now."

She grinned and patted his cheek. "You're brilliant, counselor."

He quirked a brow at her insolent tone. "But we're not naked."

An evil glint in her eyes made him wonder what was going on in that brain he'd just asked her to turn off.

"I suggest we come to an agreement then, and fast."

"Seriously?"

"Uh huh. I'll take all your clothes off, then we can stop talking about the contract."

"What about yours?"

She giggled. He liked the sound of her voice, teasing and tempting, as she grabbed a chunk of the sweats from her hip. She pulled the fabric generously to allow a view of the skin below. "Oh, these? Well, isn't that something—these are yours too."

Ohhh. He really *was* brilliant.

• • •

By seven that night, Jackson's stomach was growling—again. Mom's meatloaf recipe had been a huge hit. Unfortunately, it had worn off due to a very robust workout with Amanda. He had no regrets.

She was a tiny bump in his blankets, covered from head to foot in his comforter. He reached out and pulled her close, spooning against the long legs that always made any skirt look like designer-wear.

His cell phone jolted both of them to a sitting position. She dropped back with a bounce. Wait, his was on the table in the kitchen. *We both have the same ring tone? How kismet is that?* Jackson scruffed a hand over his hair, knowing it had to be rooster-tailed in back. It always did that after lying around. He smiled.

For all Amanda's graceful ways, she slept like a guy. At the present moment she was flat on her back with legs all over. At least they were all over *him*, which was where he intended them to stay. She rolled onto her stomach and reached into the pile of clothes to find the phone.

"Ugh. My brother." She tapped a button and the ring stopped.

Jackson's stomach clenched. "You have a brother?"

She sighed and glanced over her shoulder his way. "Two. Both are older than I am. Is that a problem?"

He shook his head. "Of course not. I just can't believe I didn't already know. Tell me about them."

Her phone jolted back into action, then a voicemail message beeped almost consecutive to the ring. She growled. "They're a couple of busy-bodies, to be honest. If I did half the things they'd done as kids, Dad would have tanned my hide. For some reason I can't get away with anything."

She read her screen, then slapped a hand to the tousled hair falling over her eyes. "Oh, crap. I forgot."

"Forgot what?"

"They're coming over in an hour to help me paint my kitchen."

Jackson couldn't remember the last time he'd picked up a paintbrush. "You like to paint?"

She gave him the *you're crazy* look. "If I liked to paint, they wouldn't be headed to my house at this very moment. I promised beer and pizza in return for a new paint job."

Jackson grinned. "Sounds like they ended up with the short end of that straw." He slapped her hip. "Get up. Let's move it. We'll have to hurry if you want to beat them to your place."

He didn't really have to mention it; she was already stepping into the clothes he'd brought from the dryer earlier. She balanced like a stork over the leg of her shorts and shot him a glare. "Oh, no you don't. You're staying here."

Yeah, that would have been a good idea except for one thing. "I drove, remember? You don't have a car. How are you getting home in a hurry without my help?"

"I'll call a cab."

"And wait thirty minutes for them to show? Probably not a good plan. Why don't you just call and cancel?"

She struggled her leg into the shorts and cinched the waist. "Are you kidding? I've wanted to do this for months. If I don't take their help now after shaming them into it for weeks, it'll be a year before I get another chance."

Jackson thought for a second. As much as he wasn't really keen on the idea and needed to get back to their research, he knew it would wait. "Then I guess I'll be on the dumb end of a paintbrush for a few hours. Let's go."

He second-guessed the decision as soon as they arrived at her house and two burly men with shocking blond hair lifted off her porch and stared him down. *Oh, this is going to be fun.*

He had barely stepped out of the driver's door when he was toe to toe with one of the men. Jackson had at least two inches of height advantage but they were very likely equal in weight. The man squinted and spat. "Who the hell are you?"

Amanda stepped between them and groaned. "Oh, my God, stop it. Jackson, this is my older brother, Rory. He loves to intimidate but don't worry—he's about as tough as toilet paper. The ugly one on the step is Danny but I call him Dan-Dan."

Jackson smirked. "As in Dan-Dan Noodle bowl from the Chinese restaurant?"

Dan-Dan stood and Jackson sucked in his breath. The height advantage was lopsided with Danny—along with the weight. There was no way in hell Jackson would be a match for the younger Gillespie. Dan-Dan strode forward and Jackson was certain he would *not* use Amanda's pet name for the boulder-sized brother— or any other smart-ass nickname. In fact, the safest bet would be to call him straight-up Daniel. Or perhaps Sir.

The younger but bigger brother reached for Jackson with one hand. Jackson reared back, ready to duck. Daniel chuckled. "Ease up, buddy, we don't bite. At least, not until we know you better."

Jackson let out his breath slowly. "I was kidding about the noodle bowl thing."

"Yeah, I figured as much. So, back to Rory's question—who are you?"

Amanda growled and grabbed Jackson by the arm. Her nails dug into his bicep as she drug him toward her front door, bypassing the two brothers. "Guys, Jackson is a colleague, an attorney friend. We used to work together and now I'm doing a little contract work for his company."

Jackson wasn't so sure he liked the label she'd applied but it wasn't worth arguing over. A colleague? Hmmm.

Rory attempted to stare him down again but Amanda wasn't having it. She unlocked her door and shoved through, pulling Jackson along. Both brothers sauntered behind. Amanda jerked her head toward the kitchen. "Paints in there. Brushes and rollers in the garage."

Daniel came up behind and thumped a fist on her table. "Oh, man. I thought you said you were ready for us. You haven't even packed or taped. I've got a date tonight and I wasn't planning on staying here more than a couple of hours. Mandy, I am *not* packing up your crap *and* painting."

Jackson wanted to laugh. For all the man's size, his sister ruled his world without even trying. She batted her big eyes and gave the fakest sheepish grin he'd seen. "Sorry, brother. I've been swamped and haven't had a chance. I'll do it now, and don't worry…you'll make your date. Who are you going out with?"

Big Dan, as Jackson wanted to christen him, darted a daring look at his little sister. "You really think I'm going to tell you? I'm no idiot." He pulled a box from a closet and with one arm, swept everything from her counter into the cardboard.

Amanda's relationship with her brothers reminded him of Carter. He hadn't spoken to his friend since Amanda ditched him, and he missed their talks. He watched her tease with her brothers about dates, paint, and all sorts of stupid topics and it hurt to realize that the only brother he'd ever had was likely never going to forgive him for what he'd done. *Don't be stupid, Jax, she didn't break up with him because of you. You didn't ask anything of her. You simply—cared.*

"Amanda, have you talked to Carter since you kicked him to the curb?"

Screech. All three of them stopped grab-assing AKA childish wrestling and opened their mouths. Amanda squinted. "I didn't kick him to the curb. I just told him I was involved with someone else."

Rory picked up on one word and only one. "Are you telling me you're involved with this string bean? Please tell me no."

Jackson felt the skin on the back of his neck rise. "You have a problem with me?"

Rory held up both hands. His left palm had a stripe of blue paint and Jackson wanted to laugh but knew the timing wouldn't work. "I'm not saying that but if my sister's going to be *seeing* someone, I think maybe our family ought to know the person before she starts telling the world."

Apparently Amanda had a problem with big brother's overprotectiveness because her face went from pink to crimson in two seconds. She shoved a finger in Rory's face, then switched to Daniel and back. "You and you don't have any say in who I do or don't date. You never have and you sure as hell never will. The minute I ask your permission to *see* anyone would be the minute I need to be committed to a psych ward somewhere. Need I remind you of the time Daniel tried to set me up on a blind date with his buddy at work?"

Daniel immediately turned his attention to spreading cloths and placing paint cans. His mumbled response wasn't missed. "Hey, I thought he was a nice guy."

Amanda lurched her hands skyward, then dropped them with a loud slap. "That's just it—a nice guy to a *guy* is not always a date-able one. All you see is how much beer he drinks or if he can compete at golf or softball. You have no clue whether he's an octopus on steroids or takes baths once a month. Besides, I'm an adult whether you like it or not."

Daniel didn't turn around. "I think we'd probably notice the bath thing." Jackson snickered. Amanda's younger brother was a mumbler but he liked the dry wit.

Rory darted a glance from Jackson to his sister. His voice was flat as he reached for a paintbrush. "So you are involved with Tall, Dark, and Dumb ass, then."

Her face went crimson again. Jackson wanted to intervene but damned if it wasn't funny watching her mouth pop like a guppy.

Besides, even though the nickname made Jackson want to go a couple of rounds with Rory, he wanted to know the answer too. Were they involved or was he just a sex buddy? He wasn't sure. Nor was he certain which he wanted.

Amanda stomped a foot. "*No.* I'm not involved with anyone. I just said that because he, as in Carter, wanted to make a commitment and I…it doesn't matter, it didn't work out."

Daniel whirled around, brush in hand and drips of paint splattered his jeans. "Commitment! Jesus, Amanda, don't you think you should slow down a little? Mom and Dad would go through the roof if they heard you."

She shot her eyes at the ceiling. "He wanted to give me season tickets to the Astros. Actually it was just one ticket. He intended to keep the other one. Still, that would have meant we'd go to all the games together and that kind of means something, doesn't it?"

Daniel and Rory exchanged glances and shrugged. Daniel turned back to the wall and started slathering paint. Jackson had a sneaking suspicion she wasn't going to like the end result of the paint job. Daniel snarked again, "So, Jackson, since you're not all that important now, do you think you could pick up a paintbrush and help get this done so I can get the hell out of here?"

"Hmmm. Thanks man." Jackson dug through Amanda's supplies and found a paint roller. "Think I'll use this instead since I don't want to be here all day and like you said, I'm not hanging around."

Rory coughed, a noise that sounded distinctly like *dumb ass.*

Jackson grinned. "Look, Rory, the only dumb asses in this room are the ones who planned to paint the whole space with those baby-ass brushes. You'd be here for a week at that rate. Call me what you want but stupid sure doesn't fit."

Three hours later Jackson was cleaning rollers and brushes in Amanda's backyard. The brothers left and she went inside to pick up trash and pull tape. They'd spent the entire time razzing each other about one thing or another. It felt—natural. Invigorating.

"Jackson, your cell phone's ringing on the counter." Amanda stood in the doorway with arms crossed over her waist.

"I'll get it as soon as I'm done."

"This is the third time. Someone really wants to find you."

He twisted the spigot until the water slowed to a drip, then met her gaze. "Then answer it, beautiful."

Shoving her hands into the pockets of her shorts, she looked away. "I can't do that. Someone might think—"

"That you answered my phone because I wasn't able to? I don't care."

His phone jolted into action and she rolled her wrist to show the phone. She held it out without looking at the screen and he realized she was afraid to look. She didn't want to know who was searching him out. "Answer it, Mandy."

Amanda sighed and punched a finger to the phone. "Jackson's phone." Amanda's eyes bugged and she reared back and frowned at the screen.

The expression was a little scary. "Who is it? A telemarketer?"

Her hair flipped in her face as she shook from side to side. "From your display he's known as Roger Dodger. I'd probably give him a better descriptor, though. Maybe something like Creeper-In-Training or Telephone-Asswipe." She shoved the phone his way.

Uh oh. "What did he say?"

"Apparently he had bet Carter you'd have a blond stacked chick answering his phone within a week of taking over the reins while your dad was sick. He seemed to think that would be me."

"You're kidding." He knew his voice insincere since Roger was a caustic failure when it came to diplomacy or phone etiquette. Hell, any kind of etiquette was a loss on the man. Jackson grabbed the phone.

"Nice guy." Amanda crossed her arms.

Jackson stared at the screen, wondering what more was said. "Rog, what's up?"

He heard a familiar laugh. "Guess I won twenty bucks off of Carter. Tell me, is she has hot as her voice?"

Jackson met Amanda's eyes and she quirked a perfectly arched brow. Had she heard the comment? "Better."

A groan from Roger was followed by a crashing sound. Had he fallen? "I *knew* it. You didn't waste any time. What's her name?"

"Amanda."

"Wait. Not *the* Amanda. You didn't. Oh my God, I thought I was a slime-bag. You're seeing Carter's girl?"

She's mine and she was right about you. You're an asswipe. "No. Hey, have you talked to Carter lately? I've texted and called. He hasn't answered."

"He won't. He blocked you."

Jackson's chest lurched. "He blocked my calls? Is he really that mad? This wasn't about me, you know. She—"

"Technically *I* blocked you. The first time you called, we were in a meeting and he was in front of the group. He asked who it was. I saw the number and lied—told him it was a telemarketer and I blocked the number. Remember the girl from the park? The runner?"

"Yeah, what about her?"

"He met her the day Amanda bolted. I had already tracked down her number so I just typed in her number on his phone with your name. He always texts you instead of calling so I thought it might be fun to see what happens and get them talking more."

Jackson shook his head in disbelief. Only an idiot would think that could lead to anything but hang-ups. "You're a moron, Rog."

"Yeah, and you're boinking Carter's girlfriend. Which is worse?"

Jackson hit the end button. Before Roger made things into a disaster, he'd have to stop by and see Carter. He needed his friend—his brother.

Amanda had gone back to admiring their handiwork. He admired her backside as she stood facing the wall with one hand on her hip. She flipped a light on. "I suppose that was a friend of yours and Carter's?"

"You're not going to believe what a mess he's made of things for Carter. I have to talk to him."

She turned and swayed from side to side. "I never meant for things to get awkward for you two."

He shrugged. "He'll get over it. Eventually."

Jackson's phone burst into action again and he started to let it ring. A quick glance at the screen and he chose otherwise. "Hey, Mom."

"Your dad's home, no thanks to you."

"I know. Sorry. I tried to call earlier. We were stuck in rain over on the property I told you guys about."

"How'd it go?" Her voice was all business but Jackson knew that was her coping mechanism. His mom wasn't overtly emotional but she had a sensitive side. She just kept it contained pretty well.

"You're not going to believe what we found. I'll show it to you later. How's Dad?"

"Sleeping. He had a rough day in P.T. and he was sore. You need to come by, though. Want to eat dinner with us?"

"Tonight?"

"Sure."

Amanda left the room for a few minutes. Jackson guessed it was time to make his departure anyway. "Um, okay. I guess."

Jackson said goodbye to Amanda, scheduled a time to get back together to finish their review of the letters, and took off.

· · ·

Technically the color on her walls was "Perry Winked At Me," a catchy and cute descriptor for periwinkle blue. The transformation was amazing. She wanted to hug Jackson for helping without complaint. Surely he had more important things to do. Amanda turned and noticed the stack of letters he'd forgotten. Like research for his board meeting.

She'd been an incredible distraction. *Don't be ridiculous. If he'd wanted to leave, he would have.* Actually he just did.

It was unnerving the way he settled into the vocal effusions her brothers adored. She wasn't sure whether she should be concerned or glad. Jackson wasn't a good risk for long-term commitment, or long-term anything. Having him get too comfortable with her family would be risky.

She grabbed the box her brother had dumped her belongings into and placed things back on the counters and table. There. She stepped back. Perfect.

The letters seemed to wave for her to move them too. Or read. Should she continue the work without Jax? It took all of two seconds to make a decision. *He's paying you to dig into the deal. This is part of the deal.*

It felt suspiciously like spying.

The following morning, Amanda dressed for work in a rush. How long had it been since she'd slept so well? In the car, she flipped the mirror down on her visor. She looked rested. Would they notice?

Of course not. Her first two hours of work were spent catching up on email and reviewing a legal brief for an afternoon meeting. She turned her music on softly and tapped a foot as she read. Concentration was tough.

Bzzzz. Her phone jolted her from the page.

"You have a delivery at the front desk, Ms. Gillespie." Sara, the receptionist, had a pleasant voice. Perfect for phones—or radio and television.

"Me? What is it? Can you just hold it for a few minutes?" She wanted to finish the next four pages. The phone went silent for two seconds.

"Um, no, you should probably come down here."

Amanda sighed and rustled the pages together neatly on her desk. "I'll be there in a minute."

Her office was hidden two corridors from the entry to their office. The tuft, tuft of her shoes on the carpet was the only noise as she worked her way through the hallways.

Sara smiled brightly and nodded toward a woman in the lobby. Or at least she thought there was a woman behind the massive mountain of flowers. A voice called from the depths of roses and lilies, "Amanda Gillespie? We have a delivery for you."

Flowers? He sent me flowers? "They're huge. Where are you?" She put a hand into the fence of flora and tried to peer through to the deliverer. The person shifted them sideways. Wham. Amanda took a lily to her left eye and winced. With one eye closed, she laughed. "You just belted me. Those things are dangerous."

From the depths of the artwork, a voice spoke. "There's a card." She shifted the bundle to display the paper.

Amanda breathed deeply, inhaling the scent of roses. Heavenly. She slid her arms around the crystal vase and took them. Setting the arrangement on the reception counter, she pulled the red envelope from the depth of leaves.

She smiled at the flower girl—a tall, dark-haired woman with her hair pulled back in a braid—as she slipped the note from the envelope and read. The woman averted her gaze to the framed artwork above the desk. Amanda read the note and a heavy weight sunk into her heart.

Dear Amanda,
Thanks for letting me off the hook before the hook sunk in further. The good news? I have a new smartphone! Even better news? I won't waste another minute of its service talking to you AND I have season baseball tickets to share with someone who actually DOES want to go. Have a good life.

She stared at the paper. Why had she assumed they were from Jackson? Oh, God. Nope, they were from *his best friend.* What had she done?

"What's wrong? You don't like them?" The girl's voice was way too chipper. Of course she didn't like them. They were *hate flowers.*

Amanda's gut tied up in knots. She was *not* going to tear up. *No.* She was going to laugh it off. Only she couldn't, because she'd treated Carter terribly at a time when he'd needed something more, something better.

"No, it's not that. It's just—he's really a nice guy. I shouldn't have gotten involved." Snot started popping from her nose and oozing down her lip. Crap. She knew she was babbling. "He's been through so much. He didn't deserve…Oh, shit." Her words were salted heavily with tears and hiccups.

The flower girl leaned over the counter and grabbed a tissue box. She yanked four out and pushed them in Amanda's face. "Hey, it can't be that bad. Someone sent you flowers. That's a good thing."

Amanda looked at her through a fog of tears. She blinked. The tears continued. "I mean, how was I supposed to know that would happen? They were both soooo…nice. I never thought. I couldn't help it."

"You couldn't help what?" The flower girl patted her back in a get-me-away-from-crazy-girl look. She obviously had no idea where this was going. Amanda pushed the note at her chest and waited as the woman glanced over the note. She coughed.

Amanda sucked in a stilted breath. Could she be honest? Why not? She hardly knew the chick anyway. She wasn't even sure it was true.

"Falling in love with his best friend."

• • •

The following Wednesday, Jackson stood in yet another elevator listening to Barry Manilow. He hated Barry, thanks to a high school English teacher who would make the class memorize the words to every song. She had a thing for Manilow and thought life's problems could be solved by knowing and adhering to some of his songs. Jackson couldn't get past his oversized nose.

He wanted to settle things with his best friend. It was a long shot, but after hearing Amanda's outburst and Roger's story, he had to see Carter. Had to find out if they were done permanently. He needed someone to talk with and get advice. His dad was off limits for two reasons. One, he was incapacitated. Two, he wasn't exactly a shining example of relationship material, even with all his wits.

The elevator to Carter's floor took half a century to ding the right floor and slide open. The carpet absorbed his footsteps as he strode past the empty reception desk to see Carter sitting with his head buried in a computer. A woman in a green top and black pants watered the greenery in the corner of his office. Since when did Carter have plants?

Jackson rapped on the door, then entered. "Hey."

"Oh! Jackson. What are you doing here?"

Had the woman with the huge watering can gasped? Jackson shot a glance at her black hair but she didn't turn.

How should he approach the subject? What was the best way to keep their friendship and let him know that Amanda had been his all along? Sure, they'd competed over women in the past but this was different.

"I thought we should talk." Jackson stood at the door unsure what to do. Sit down? "It wasn't like I meant it to happen."

Carter glanced from Jackson's face to the black-haired woman's back. She was a post. He held up a hand in protest. "Let's not talk about it, okay? I don't want to know."

Jackson swallowed and moved to the chair. He had to try. "I met her a long time ago. Before you did, actually. It was just—random. We were having fun and then somewhere along the way everything changed."

Carter hitched a brow. "Changed?"

Jackson shifted feet and glanced at their audience. Damn, he wished the woman would finish her work and get the hell out. "Yeah. I would have told you but it all moved so fast and all of a sudden you were asking about a—"

A sharp pain ran through his back as the water-woman shoved an elbow in his spine and spilled water—on his pants. Not just a little either—it looked like he'd pissed himself. *Did she really do that? Wow.*

"Oh, uh. Sorry about that, Jackson. You should probably go change or something, right?" The woman stared at the wet spot. What the hell? How'd she know his name? Oh right, Carter had called him by it when he entered. Jackson's mouth opened then shut. He darted back to Carter's face with disbelief.

Jackson felt a hundred-pound weight on his chest. It was worse than expected and Roger was full of shit about the running chick. Carter was furious about Amanda. Even this unknown worker sensed the animosity and came to Carter's aid. Seconds ticked as the two men glared at each other. Acceptance finally kicked in and Jackson shrugged. "Yeah, I guess I should. Later, man." He stood but hesitated. "Where's Roger? I need to kick his ass."

Twenty steps later he stood in front of Roger's desk. "You're an idiot if you think he's over Amanda."

Roger blinked as if he'd been clocked. "What are you talking about?"

"I just talked to him. He's pissed. Big time."

"What did you say?"

"I just told him I met her first. I knew her before."

Roger nodded as if all-knowing and Jackson had the urge to make the earlier blink come back by actually throwing a fist his way. "That's good. That's good. Jealousy—not exactly what I intended but it might work. What else was said?"

Jackson slammed a fist on the desk. "Not a damn thing because the plant girl dumped a can of water in my lap."

Roger took in his dampened crotch and snorted in an attempt to hold back laughter. He failed miserably. His laughter fueled Jackson's rage. "You're crazy if you really think he's into someone else. No one acts like he did if they're over a breakup. Whoever this runner is, I'd bet it's just a revenge game."

Roger sobered. "Nope. Actually, the chick that hosed you— that was her. And here's the funny part: She's also the manager who had him fired."

What the hell? Roger dove into an abbreviated explanation that had Jackson's head spinning. Amanda had trashed Carter's phone when she ditched him; oddly, she'd never mentioned that little fact. With a brand-new phone, Carter asked Roger for Jackson's number and Roger gave him the runner girl's number instead. It was brilliant, since they'd failed miserably in trying to get the two together the first time. The first time they'd tried, it had ended in Carter's unemployment when Roger and Jackson mouthed off inappropriately in the conference call. So Carter was texting *her* and thinking it was Jackson.

It was crazy and stupid. Still, once he caught up, he decided maybe there was a little merit. Not much, but a thread. "You could have at least told me the story earlier so I had a clue."

"Well, if you'd answer the damn phone I would. Seems Carter isn't the only guy with his nose buried in a woman's—"

Jackson held up a finger to silence whatever vulgarity came next. "That was the stupidest idea ever."

Roger stared at the door behind Jackson. "No. Give it a little more time. I think it'll work out. Besides, you could have done a better job with your part, you know. Mouthing off like that wasn't cool."

"Maybe not, but how was I supposed to know she'd do that? You'd better know what you're doing. Personally, I think it'd be better just to lock them both in a room and let 'em duke it out. Or whatever else comes naturally."

Jackson strode out of Carter's building. Which drama should he tackle first? His father's rehabilitation, the contract dilemma with an unknown trust partner that was stalling, Carter's convoluted love problems, or—his own?

He clenched his fists and headed for his own building with the hopes that nothing more earth-shattering would happen.

Chapter Twenty-Two

Amanda stared at the woman in the mirror, certain that she'd be asleep at her desk by nine a.m. She rattled her head side to side and slapped her cheeks hard. "Wake up, sleepy-head. You have a big day ahead. Jax had better appreciate your combat effort."

Once he got past the fact she'd opened all of soldier boy's letters.

She hadn't intended to read every last one but the very first one was such a shocker, she just kept going. After the third letter, she'd emptied the tissue box and had mascara running down her cheeks as she ran to the bathroom for the toilet paper roll. What an amazing story.

It was a story worth pursuing rather than sleeping. She called her office and asked them to reschedule her one appointment for the day. Thankfully her schedule was light, and she needed time to digest what she'd read, plus enlighten Jackson. She dialed his cell.

"You're not going to believe what I found."

Jackson's voice was light, jovial. "Is this a puzzle? Should I ask person, place, or thing?"

She grinned and yawned simultaneously. A funny pop escaped her mouth and she clamped a hand over lips. Oops. "No game but someone could make a movie about this. What's your schedule today? Can I stop by?"

"You're not at the office?"

"Um, nope. I've been up all night and had enough coffee to make a pilot bounce out of the cockpit. I read one of those letters and was so sucked into the story, when I looked up it was six a.m. and the sun was starting to silhouette the skyline."

She heard a masculine cough. "Amanda, you're sleep-deprived drunk?"

She nodded, then realized he probably couldn't hear her brain rattle, though the coffee probably sloshed when she dropped onto the sofa. "I guess you could say that. Can I come by or not?"

After a couple of seconds, he agreed. Geez, why'd she have to convince him? He acted all concerned about her driving half awake. She returned to the bathroom and grimaced. Hell, she looked like she was half dead. "Oh my God." She lifted an arm and smelled her pit, then scrunched her nose. Maybe she wasn't in *that* much of a hurry. The shower knob squeaked as she turned on the hot water. She'd clean up first.

One of the best rules a woman could follow when either exhausted or feeling overwhelmed—dress like you were on top of the world. Power suits weren't named by accident. After she'd dried off, applied makeup, and fixed her hair, Amanda slipped into one of her two best suits. She couldn't get the red out of her eyes but at least the bright blue suit would offset the color. Grabbing her belongings, she strode to the car and sped to his office.

She tapped the controls for her hands-free connection to her phone and selected Darlene's number.

Darlene skipped the greetings. "When are you going to pay me my five hundred bucks?"

Amanda grimaced and slipped through a yellow traffic light. "I don't owe you five hundred bucks."

She heard tsking on the phone. "You welcher. You missed the zip-lining last weekend. That means you lost the bet."

Crap. She'd forgotten. Amanda slammed a hand on the steering wheel and the light turned green. "Pardon me, I was too busy *rock-climbing* a forty-foot cliff to show up for that thing."

Silence. That'd show her.

"Rock climbing. Right. I think you're telling me a windy."

Amanda grappled for a response. "Nope, Jackson and I went out to review this property that his company's looking at and we climbed a cliff. So, technically I haven't lost. You never said I had to do the same adventures you did—you just said I had to pick three. Technically, our bet is still *on*."

Darlene's laugh on the other end didn't sound promising. "You expect me to believe you scaled the side of a cliff? Seriously?"

"Seriously. I'll have Jackson send you a notarized statement if that will be more convincing. Look, I'm not going to be in the office for a while. His company offered me some contract work on the land project and I need to stop by there and discuss the details. Okay?"

A horn blared to her right as a minivan swerved in front of another car. Yikes.

Darlene's voice held skepticism and concern. "You okay there? Hey, contract work is fine as long as it pays. I'll let the boss know… and you can fax that notarized statement over whenever he signs it."

Amanda growled, "I can't believe you're being such a pain."

"I can't believe you want me to believe you went rock climbing. See you later."

Amanda clicked the hands-free and drove to Jackson's office.

• • •

One of the many things Jackson despised at work included the bland colors in his father's office. Though his father had portrayed an austere vibe that reeked of professionalism, his personal life was over-the-top vibrant. Perhaps that had contributed to his stroke.

Jackson had come to terms with their odd family dynamic and chosen to set it aside and help. Just because the man wasn't the most wonderful husband in the world, hadn't meant he wasn't a good father or businessman. In truth, Jackson could only hope to do as well.

Vivid blue shot across the periphery of his vision. He glanced up. Warmth skittered across his shoulders and settled deep in his chest.

God, she was amazing.

She'd been adorable in his oversized clothes with her bony hips protruding over the drawstring waistband. But this suit was one he'd seen numerous times and he knew when she wore it, she meant business. It was her go-to for occasions where she had to impress.

Should he be nervous? Was there a time bomb about to explode? Jackson searched Amanda's face for any sign of conflict. If his perception was correct, the only thing on her face at the moment was *elation*. Or was that affection? Hell, he hoped it was that and a lot more.

"You look like you just won the case of your career…or maybe the lottery." Her arms were heavy with a box. He stood and took it without leaving her eyes.

"I think we did." She shoved her tongue against the inside of her mouth as if to swallow a grin.

Jackson waited. "Okay, spill."

She did exactly as instructed, tipping the box on its side and letting the contents tumble onto the conference table by his desk. Amanda tossed the box on the floor. She beckoned him to join her while sorting and stacking envelopes. "I put them in order by date. There had to be other letters that were opened because some of hers refer to things he'd said. These letters are all marked returned so I'm guessing Marion kept Jacob's unopened ones with hers. It makes sense that they're not opened because why would she open a letter she'd written herself? She already knew what was said."

She was so proud of herself, he couldn't just nod. "Very organized."

"Of course, so…here's where the letters take a turn. This one has a fairly long and sappy apology for her parents' behavior—just a guess but it sounded like Mommy and Daddy didn't approve of

Marion's soldier boy. Sounds like he did something crazy and they forbade her to see him before he shipped off."

Jackson remembered all the times his own parents had tried that tactic. Telling a teenager no was like opening the gate to trouble. "I bet that worked real well."

Amanda giggled. "You know it. This one"—she tapped an envelope with frayed edges—"talks about what a wonderful time she had while he was there and that her friend, Sophie or Sara, can't remember…covered for them without a problem."

Jackson raised a brow. "So we're talking about a little weekend rendezvous? Or shore-leave snuggle?"

Amanda clicked her tongue and pointed an index finger his way. "Bingo. There were three more letters, each of them more intense than the last. You should read them sometime. Pretty sexy stuff for that time, definitely made my face flush. The second to last one is the prize, though. Seems our little shore-leave snuggle was quite productive. Or should I say re-productive."

Whoa, so the weekend snuggle was a lot more than just a campout. Way to go, soldier. Why the hell hadn't he used a condom? Or—wait, it was early 1950s. Good girls didn't *do* those things. "She got pregnant."

Amanda nearly giggled. "Uh huh."

Jackson felt for the woman. "And he never answered her letters after? What an ass. He could have at least sent some money or something."

Amanda frowned. "Is that what you'd have done? Sent her some money to 'take care of it'? I wouldn't have pegged you for that kind of guy."

Jackson growled. "That wasn't what I meant. Come on, the guy's overseas. He can't *be* there but at least he can help financially until he returned."

Amanda's eyes widened. "Oh, yeah. I get it—but I don't think he ever did return. I think something happened. Why else was there a picture of a stick man with a bandage on his head up there on those rocks?"

Good point. "So what's in the last letter?"

"Apparently her parents were torched about the pregnancy and decided to move away, taking her with them. It was a letter to tell him where she was…where *they* were. She had a baby girl. There's a picture."

Jackson lifted the black-and-white image and evaluated the elfin-faced child in a white lace gown. The hair was dark and wafted about the child's face like cotton. The pudgy face looked ruddy, as if the baby had been crying right up until the shutter clicked. "Chubby little kid. I'm confused, though. Why would Bigby think any of this interesting if he hadn't seen it? He'd never read these."

Amanda frowned. What was it about women that they thought all kids were adorable regardless of how round, bald, or red-faced? He was just calling it like he saw it. She tsked. "I don't really know…and all kids are a little pudgy when new…that's why they call it 'baby fat.'"

Jackson shrugged. "Okay. So, they had a kid but he never came back. It's a great story, very romantic and all, but it has nothing to do with my contract."

"Ha!" Amanda punched a finger at him and Jackson crossed his eyes to be sure he wasn't going to lose an eye. "That's where you're wrong. It has everything to do with your contract. The baby is the daughter of Marion and Jacob Rickert. Jacob is the fourth person in the trust. The missing sibling. If he's dead, then Marion and/or the baby are the ones we're looking for to make the deal."

"So, how do you prove she's the daughter? And they weren't married so Marion doesn't count."

Jackson cringed as soon as he'd said the words. Amanda's face turned red and she slammed a fist to her hip. "Doesn't count? Doesn't count! You really didn't say that, did you?"

Holy crap, she had fire in those beautiful eyes. For all her professionalism, Amanda ran the gamut of emotions. Since they'd been together, she'd cried twice and lost her temper more. It was—fun. *Note to self, though: don't make Amanda mad.* She looked like she was about to implode.

"They didn't get married."

"As a matter of fact, they did."

That got his attention. "I thought you said the letters…"

Amanda pulled a paper from the pile she'd dumped. "The letters never mentioned it but it was there. Look, they ran off and got married that weekend. It wasn't just a shore-leave romp in the hay. It was their wedding night. Isn't that awesome? It's so…" She met his eyes and closed her mouth.

Jackson knew what she'd intended to say. Romantic. It was romantic. A typical guy wouldn't notice, which made him atypical. Crap. Look what she'd done—changed his whole perspective. Hell, she probably spent her nights watching chick-flicks and eating chocolate. No way in hell was he stepping that far out of his realm. "Amanda Gillespie, you're a hopeless romantic—a soft-hearted sap."

She lifted her chin. "I am not. Okay, I am, but what do you care? This isn't about romance."

No, it was about closing a deal for Dad's company. Wasn't it?

Jackson was running out of time on the contract. The board had tabled it for a month. He was already deep into that grace period and had to close the deal. His dad's legacy and the company's bottom line required success and by God, he'd make it happen.

If coddling to Amanda's fantasy about love and romance helped make that happen, he wasn't opposed to playing along. As long as she had no expectations that he'd get caught up as much as she was.

Chapter Twenty-Three

Amanda expected a little flack and the normal machismo from him that went along with a story of this magnitude. *Settle down now, girl. It's not a story—it's a contract case.* Or was it a project? She shook her head at his attempt to trivialize her emotion. "You're laughing at me. Stop."

Jackson better wipe that smug grin from his face fast. She clenched her fingers into fists.

He sobered. "Sorry. Okay, so the family tree has an unexpected branch popping out. Where do we find this person?"

Amanda smoothed her skirt. "That's what I spent most of the night working on. It appears that Jacob, our soldier, didn't die."

"That's good."

"He was injured and sent stateside for medical treatment. I think he must have wandered away or something. There was a missing persons report filed about a month after his discharge."

"Was he found?"

"There's no record of it that I can see. No police reports, no further legal documents with his name."

"Do you think he's still alive?"

She shrugged. "Not really sure."

"So another dead end then?"

She tapped the pen in her hand against the table. "Uh-uh. I found the kid."

Jacob's eyes widened. "Marion and Jacob's kid? Really? Where?"

Tap. Tap. Tap. She couldn't stop the nervous energy. "Right here in town. Well, actually it's the daughter's kid. Marion has a granddaughter and she's right here in town."

"This is confusing."

"Well, that's the crazy part of the puzzle. See, Marion remarried after Jacob disappeared—to this news guy. From what I can tell, he was a friend before. There's a news post about the wedding. He adopted the kid, Mary Caroline."

"Good of him."

"Yes, but you're gonna love this…if Jacob isn't dead, then…"

"Our girl Marion is a polygamist? Wow, this one's getting pretty tangled." Jackson reached out and put his massive hand over Amanda's fingers to still the tapping.

"Oh, sorry."

"No worries."

"Very tangled. I was curious though—why wouldn't she file for separation or abandonment? Or maybe just have him decreed dead? If you were going to get remarried, that would be pretty important, right?"

"Unless maybe she knew he wasn't dead or missing."

Amanda held up a forefinger and lifted a thumb like a pistol. "Exactly. It was the only explanation so I started researching. I found a state document from the Texas Mental Hospital in Austin that listed a man whose first name was Jacob. It had his last initial but not name. R."

"How do you know it's our guy?"

"I just have a feeling—I don't know."

"Why don't we just ask Marion?"

Amanda dropped the pen and Jackson strung his fingers into hers. "Well, that's the one thing I *do* know. Marion passed away three years ago and her daughter, Mary Caroline, moved to an unknown location."

"So let's go to the mental hospital."

"It's a four hour drive from here, shouldn't we just call?"

"And take all the fun and anticipation out of a good mystery? No way. Come on, gorgeous, let's go be detectives for a day." Jackson leaned over his desk and punched a button on an antiquated landline. "Rena, I'm going to be out of the office the rest of the day. There's a potential lead in Austin on some things related to that contract I was talking about. We're going to go check it out." Jackson turned to Amanda. "Do you need to check in with your office before we leave?"

She made a few calls. They loaded up the documents she'd dumped on his table and headed for the parking garage. An hour later, they were on the outskirts of the city. Would they find their lost trust fund member? She'd been to the state hospital before and wasn't keen on the place. It was depressing. She couldn't put a finger on the reason but imagined how dismal it would be to have so much going on in your mind that you have to be locked away from society. Was it to protect the individual or the people made uncomfortable by the person?

Chapter Twenty-Four

According to the hospital, Jacob Rickert had left years earlier. No one knew where he went or who he went with. The files pre-dated computer databases and were scanned copies of handwritten paperwork that had been uploaded to their system. He had been visited much of the later years by a young woman named Mary Caroline and was suspected to be the daughter, though she never admitted such relationship. In fact, she'd been listed on the visitor logs simply as a friend.

After a little digging, Amanda was able to find birth records that showed Mary Caroline later married and took the name of Sanders.

Mary Caroline gave her daughter her middle name. Caroline owned a florist's shop. Co-owned, according to the business filing. Amanda wanted to learn more, to meet her, to understand why her mother had visited the mental hospital all this time but never told who she was. Was she embarrassed? Doubtful, her father was a war hero. Nope, the only logical explanation was…she didn't know? If she had no idea he was her father, why would she visit?

Nothing made sense.

"Let's go by her shop and see what's she's like."

Jackson watched the snap of her hips pacing along under the blue skirt. "Amanda, what are you planning?"

"I want to understand why a girl visits a man in a mental institution when she has no reason. Does she know he's her father? If so, why does she purposely hide it from the staff?"

He didn't like the sound of her statement. "So you're going to stalk the poor woman's daughter?"

She whirled around and met his gaze. "No, we can pretend to be there for a reason, maybe ordering flowers or something. I know, we can pretend we're planning a wedding. That way we can ask a lot of personal questions without making her nervous."

•••

Less than a week later, Jackson followed Amanda into a cute little flower shop downtown. It was conveniently located across from the police station and a couple blocks from fire and rescue. How the hell he'd let her talk him into this façade was a mystery. She grabbed his hand as they entered and he remembered their talk that night about his contract. Apparently it was his karma to have been thrown into the mess, and for some divine reason, he was expected to clean it up. Had she really believed all that hype?

He'd wanted to argue at the time but she sat on his lap and her orange-scented body lotion wafted over him. Images of him rubbing the stuff over her legs made him swallow his pride and agree to their pretend engagement. Hell, he would have agreed to just about anything at that moment. She had gorgeous legs. Gorgeous everything.

"Ready, babe?" Amanda moved in and gave him a ridiculous kissy face. Hmmm, was he?

"You bet, *babe*."

He drew the door back and they walked into the store, linked together like two people deeply involved in each other. It should have been uncomfortable but it wasn't.

A girl in crazy colored leggings approached. Her hair was spiked out like a punker and her eyes were lined with black. Bright round earrings dangled from her ears like saucers. She smiled and it transformed her entire look. She was pretty in a wild-eyed in-your-face way. "Hi there! You must be our newlyweds."

Jackson cringed and shot Amanda a look. "Not yet."

Punker girl laughed. "Of course not, sorry. That's why you're here. So, our manager Abby should be out in a second. She ran back to the stock room to get…something." The girl shot a nervous look at the door near the back of the shop. A mirror next to the door was obviously a two-way used for observation.

Jackson wanted to get things moving. "Hi, I'm Jackson and this is Amanda."

Punker girl took the hand he'd offered and gave it a quick shake. "I'm Caroline and…"

Amanda reached in front of Jackson. "Caroline Rickert?"

Caroline's spikes rattled stiffly as she shook her head. "No, Caroline Sanders, and this is our caterer, Samantha. She'll talk to you about anything food related. Did you have anything in particular in mind?"

Amanda sighed, obviously disappointed. "For food or flowers?"

Jackson had to hand it to the girl, she may look punk but she had huge eyes that captivated and a smile that wouldn't stop. He wondered if her face ever tired of the customer service pleasantries. Caroline flipped a book open and turned it over the counter toward them. "Here's a few pictures to look over. If you don't mind, I'll go check on Abby to see what's taking so long."

Caroline's flat shoes were silent on the floor as she trounced to the back room. Her friend Samantha shrugged apologetically. Jackson heard laughter and soft voices. He leaned into Amanda pretending to snuggle her ear and whispered. "I thought you said she worked here."

Amanda returned his pathetic stare. "She does according to the hospital. That has to be her, but…"

"I'm sorry, Abby will be out in just a minute. She's taking care of something. We'll just wait." Caroline's approach startled them. Her face was red and her eyes watering. Either she'd had a good laugh with the unknown manager—or a good cry.

Amanda shrugged. "No worries. I'm curious. Is Caroline a family name? I have an aunt who's named Caroline but we all call her Carley."

"Actually it's my mother's middle name."

Amanda shot Jackson a smug *I told you so* look. "No kidding? What's her first name? Please tell me her dad didn't make her take his name and it's Bobbie or Randy or something."

Caroline laughed. "Nothing that terrible. It's Mary, after *her* mother, Marion."

Amanda's eyes turned to marbles and she nodded. "Ahhhh. Nice." The woman was acting delusional and Jackson had a strong desire to escape.

Except this was the person they wanted to find. Jackson cleared his throat. "Well, it's certainly better than Bobbie or Randy. This shop is new, isn't it? I come this way for work sometimes."

"We've only been open a short while." Caroline jumped right into a lengthy story about her business partner and how they met overseas and traveled together. Then they both decided to take the business-owner plunge together. Hearing her enthusiasm was infectiously inspiring.

Jackson rubbed Amanda's neck as he listened and smiled. Amanda started to pull away but he pinched to hold her in place. She shot him a look.

"Ah, there she is!"

Jackson and Amanda turned and both of their mouths dropped. He didn't even hear the rest of Caroline's words. "You!" He and Amanda both said the word at the same time. Holy shit, it was the chick that had poured water all over him in Jackson's office. But—did Amanda recognize her?

He frowned. "You know her?"

Amanda stepped toward the woman and tossed her hair back. "You're the hate flowers girl."

Jackson popped his eyes. "What?"

"She sent me hate flowers from Carter. I mean *she* didn't send them, he did but…"

Jackson stepped back. "Flowers. You didn't say anything about Carter sending flowers."

Amanda stomped a foot. "Yes. He sent me flowers. Remember when I came over to your place that night and was crying? *She* delivered them that day. Don't tell me—" She dropped a hand to her hip. "You sent Jackson hate flowers too?"

The manager, Abby, rattled her head back and forth as if embarrassed. She pointed to Jackson. "No, he got a bucket of water on his crotch."

Jackson and Amanda both dropped their hands and stood side by side, touching. For all observers, they were definitely a couple completely in sync with each other. "Seriously?" Amanda and Jackson said in unison.

"You two are engaged?" Abby said.

"We're here to discuss a wedding, aren't we?" The two broke their confrontational stance and Jackson shifted to look at the floor. "So, do you make a habit of sending hate flowers to ex-girlfriends, or pouring water on their boyfriends? Or did Carter just sweet talk you into it? Hmmm?"

"Of course not. He didn't talk me into anything. It was my idea. I met him at a restaurant and we had too much to drink, then we started talking about all sorts of things and he told me about you and how you ditched him for another guy then we started—I don't know. It seemed like a good idea at the time. Then I delivered the flowers and you started crying and saying what a great guy he was and you seemed like you *missed him* and I thought, wow, maybe she wants him back or regrets it. I didn't know. So, I didn't tell him what you said because—well—that's *your story* and I don't want anything to do with it. But he keeps texting and Jackson—i.e. me—keeps answering."

Jackson popped his head up. "I'm not answering anything. I haven't heard a word from him since they broke up. I was afraid to talk to him. I went by there and tried, but you doused me."

Caroline and Samantha's jaws dropped. Jackson knew the feeling. Abby kept going. "I had to shut you up. You were telling him about our relationship and I was afraid he'd find out—"

Amanda's face went white and she spun around. Slamming a hand on her hip, she swung her head side to side. "Did she just say *our relationship?* As in you and her?" Her hair swayed as she pointed her perfectly manicured finger between Abby and Jackson.

Jackson raised both hands and stepped back. "I don't know what the hell she's talking about. She's crazy, if you ask me. I'd never seen her before I stopped by Carter's office."

Abby stepped forward and punched a finger at him. "He thinks I'm you, dumbass." She swung to Amanda and moved the finger her way. "He thinks I'm you, too."

Caroline popped up onto the nearby counter and swung her legs as she grinned. "This is getting gooood."

Abby growled. "You're no help. You're the one who started all this lunacy. Why don't *you* tell them?"

Caroline grinned. "Oh, I think you're doing great, partner. You're on a roll. Don't stop now. Just take a breath and keep going. Samantha, what do you think?"

Samantha sidled up to Jackson and hitched a thumb his way. "I'm with him on this. I think she's crazy."

"I'm *not* crazy. Gullible, maybe, but not crazy."

Amanda sighed. "So Carter thinks you're Jackson, or me, or— what was it you said?"

Abby rolled her eyes. "Check. Check. Check. You win the prize. He thought I was Jackson and he kept texting me. Only it wasn't you—" Abby pointed to Jackson and he felt like crawling into a closet or under the flower pots. "It was me. Then Caroline grabbed the phone and answered for me. Thanks for that, by the way. Remind me not to ever call you when I *really* have a problem. Then he thought I was you, Jackson, and kept texting. I answered again because *she* had just dumped him and I felt bad for him." Her accusatory finger moved to Amanda.

Abby stopped for air. "Can you believe that? He sees me running at the park for what, five minutes, and now they all want to talk about the status of my breasts?"

Jackson shot Amanda a crazy-woman-talking glance. She returned an equally astonished expression. They were on the same page, thank God.

Caroline snickered. "Well, they are good ones—as far as breasts go. I mean, from what I can tell and all."

"How juvenile. So, I just texted them back that they weren't fake. Only technically, it wasn't me texting."

Jackson put two fingers in his mouth and whistled twice, then made the time out sign. "Whoa. You mean you're the running chick from the park that he talked about?"

"Oh, great! So, I say fake boobs and running in the park and you automatically know who I am? What the hell else has he said? Yes! I'm running chick. So, I answered his text. Only it wasn't me answering because he thought I was you, and when I told him they weren't fake—well, he put two and two together and figured I'd slept with you."

Amanda's face shriveled up and she squealed. "*You slept with her?*" She threw her purse over her shoulder and marched toward the door.

Two steps away, Jackson grabbed her arm and yanked her back. "Hell, no! I didn't sleep with her. I don't even *know* her."

Abby followed. "He's right. He didn't. Carter just thinks he did because your intended went down to his office and marched in and confessed."

Both of them turned. "Confessed to what?"

"To being with me before Carter was, only—"

Amanda thundered, "*So you were with her?*"

"No!"

Abby continued, "Holy crap, you're dense. Listen up, girl. He confessed—only it wasn't me he was confessing about—it was *you*. Get it? When he said he'd met *her* before Carter, he was talking about you. Carter and I had been sort of seeing each other so Carter thought it was me—because of the texts. He hasn't got a clue it was you, because I never had the heart to tell him. Apparently, neither has lover-boy here. When you cried over the flowers, I just—chickened out."

Jackson cringed. She did *not* just call Amanda dense, did she? He could feel the steam coming off Amanda from two feet away.

The sound of Abby's cell broke the seconds of silence that followed and he took the opportunity to yank Amanda's hand. "Let's get out of here before she does something else crazy like throw a potted plant our way or use those ribbon snips on us. Okay?"

Amanda blinked but let him lead her.

They were almost to the door and safety when Abby pointed at him. "*Stop*." She held up a finger, daring them to step out. What would she do if they tried to go? He swallowed.

"Hi, Carter," she said into the phone. "Hang on a second." Abby clamped a hand over the phone. She glared at Jackson. "You need to tell him. Straighten it out. It's not my place to air your shit."

What the hell is she talking about? Me? Amanda? My shit or—ours?

He heard Carter make a loud noise on the phone.

Abby spoke to the receiver. "Technically, it's not Jackson's."

Abby held the phone Jackson's way and wagged it. When Jackson didn't move she shoved it against his breastplate. *Ow.* She gestured for him to speak. He hesitated, then lifted the phone.

"Hey, Carter. What's up?"

A loud gasp burned Jackson's ear. "You son of a bitch." The phone went dead.

Chapter Twenty-Five

Jackson's stride was fast and long. Amanda clipped quickly in an attempt to keep pace. Her head was reeling. What the hell just happened? He whirled around and the dark cloud over his face was threatening. "If you ever decide to play charades again, don't put me in the middle of it, you hear?"

What? "Me? What in the world are you talking about? I had nothing to do with that crazy woman's ranting. Besides *I'm* not the one who's apparently boinking the dark damsel in dementia."

Jackson rolled his eyes and returned to his race down the sidewalk. If she lost him, she also lost her ride and judging by his mood, he wouldn't wait. Why was this *her* problem?

"Oh, *please*," he said. "Stop acting like some jealous housewife. Your acting job was hysterical—maybe you should have majored in theatre instead of law. You'd have won a Grammy."

"Tony. The Grammy award is for music." Amanda tried to run a couple of steps as the stretch between them increased.

"Whatever. Look, I've wasted an entire day from work hanging out with you researching a girl named Caroline who we spoke to for less than twenty minutes. What we know about her is nothing more than when we walked in there. *But—*" He whirled and poked a finger in her face. "And this is a big but…you gave some random woman the third degree."

"She wasn't random, Jax."

"Ah hah! You admit it, then. Of course she wasn't random. Because she's Carter's girlfriend. The one he's been seeing since *you* kicked him to the curb. What the hell were you trying to achieve by prancing me down there in front of her?"

Amanda stopped running. She stopped walking too because her bottom lip had hit the pavement. What was he talking about? "You think I did that because of Carter?"

"I don't know. I don't care." Jackson kept walking and waved a hand in dismissal.

Amanda ran after Jackson, grabbed his arm, and yanked him to face her. "I do."

"Then tell me what the *hell* all of that was about back there? Because if I hadn't seen it with my own eyes, I'd have thought you were—"

"Jealous. I was jealous."

"That makes zero sense. You dumped him, remember?"

"*No.* Not about Carter, idiot. About you."

Jackson unknitted his eyebrows for the first time since they'd left the shop. "Oh."

"You seriously thought I was pretending?" Amanda had skills but controlling her temper wasn't one of them. Her mother had always warned people growing up, *Amanda has a very long fuse but when she reaches the end of it, you'd better run. Something's gonna blow.*

Jackson shrugged. "I've never seen you act like that. You were— out of control."

Yeah, she was.

She shrugged. *No way am I going to apologize either.* She blinked and focused on his eyes. After a couple of seconds, he cocked his head. Then laughed.

"I like it."

"Really?"

"Yeah, just do me a favor and warn me next time. I had no idea whether that was real or just part of the show for Caroline." He stepped closer to her, clearly not upset anymore. "Listen, I have an idea. The sun will go down in a couple of hours, but want to go on a quick hike out to the property first?"

"What if we get stranded out there after dark? How will we get back?"

Jackson's devilish grin implied he hoped that would happen. He shrugged and laced his fingers through hers. "I don't know, leave some breadcrumbs?"

Amanda rolled her eyes. "Yeah, and draw the raccoons, coyotes, and whatever else is out there straight to us. No thanks."

"Relax, I'll take a lantern and a pellet gun." Jackson pulled on her arms and she thudded against his chest.

Amanda tilted her head back to look into his eyes. He was serious. "You really want to do that?"

"Yeah, I do. Shouldn't we see it from their perspective?"

"Would that happen to be a horizontal and naked one, because I'm warning you…I am soooo not the outdoorsy-in-the-woods type. The thought of limestone and clay dust on my silkies just sounds gross."

Jackson darted a brow up. "Silkies?"

Amanda shoved him back. "Back up, hot stuff. Okay, I'll go, but can we stop and get some bug spray and a blanket at my house?"

He grinned, a look that started to melt Amanda's reserve. "Sure, and you can take off the power suit and stilettos and put on some shorts with hiking boots. In fact, why don't I drop you off to change while I go get the gear?"

"You realize I don't *own* hiking boots, don't you?"

He laughed. "I would have been shocked if you did."

Forty-five minutes later, Amanda peeked out the window at the sound of a car door. She hated that Jackson was punctual. It was one of her strong suits also but this time she needed him to be late. He wasn't. She kicked the slip and heels into the closet, followed by the blue suit. That would have to go to the cleaners but she'd worry about that later. She pulled her hair back and knotted a band around it, then grabbed her sneakers and a beach bag she'd filled with essentials. She was at the door the second he tapped, and followed him to the car barefoot. She'd slip the socks and shoes on as they drove.

The shadows under the trees were long and dark. Amanda peered through as light filtered between the limbs, fighting for its last chance to glisten on the day. Had she really volunteered for this outing? "They don't really have bears in those woods, do they? I heard once that someone saw a huge mountain lion close to here."

Jackson shrugged. "Beats me. I've never seen any. Skunks, raccoons, and bobcats are all—"

"Bobcats? Seriously?"

"They stay far away from humans. They're more afraid of us than we are of them. Raccoons, too."

Amanda darted a glance up and down the road as they pulled over to park. "So that leaves skunks. Woohoo." She lifted her palms above her head to do a raise-the-roof dance.

"I'd be more concerned about ticks myself."

She rolled her eyes. "Thanks. Bloodsucking insects that bury their head in your skin. Even better."

She stepped out of Jackson's Jeep and was blasted with the scent of pine and earth. Okay, *that* part was nice. It was like a step into a candle or potpourri shop.

Jackson watched for a second, then grabbed the gear from his vehicle and tossed ropes and packs over his shoulder. "You'll need to carry this, please."

He held out a cardboard box. Amanda peeked over the edge. "What is it?"

A loaf of bread sat on top of some bags and foil packets. "Breadcrumbs in case we need them. No, just kidding. It's dinner."

Amanda took the box and dug around to see the contents, which were completely wrapped in foil. Bummer. How were they going to get that up the side of a rock wall? Surely he'd thought that through?

Jackson strode off toward the trees, burdened like a pack-horse. Amanda shuffled the box to her hip and followed. Dinner above the trees as the sun went down? It sounded almost—romantic. And scary, if she dwelled on the climb. Three steps into the trees, Jackson veered right.

"This is no time to explore, Jax." Amanda stopped walking.

"I noticed this path from the ledge last time we were here. I think they intersect. This is the shortest of the two."

"Oh, in that case ..." Amanda stepped after him. She was all for the shortest walk. Jackson trudged quickly along and she worked to keep pace.

"Hey, check that out. Someone carved a message into that tree." Amanda pointed to their left.

Jackson followed her finger and stopped moving. "*Find me.* Think it's related to the messages on the rocks?"

Amanda's hands were cramping. She jostled the box to her other hip. "No idea. Usually people carve things like *Joe hearts Sandy*. I would think if you want to be found, you should include a little more info. Something like an arrow pointing in the general direction the person went would be helpful. Of course, I guess if you're carving on a tree, you're not exactly—"

"I think I got the picture. You ready to climb?" Jackson dropped the gear and pointed toward the ledge above.

Uh, not really. "You're sure this is safe without a spotter person?"

Jackson stepped into his harness and handed one to Amanda. "I'm going up first and I'll take care of the ropes. You handled it great before so this should be a piece of cake."

Amanda watched Jackson wrap the box in a blanket he'd extricated from his pack before he started upward with the blanket strapped across his shoulders above the pack. Forty minutes later, she pulled herself over the ledge and grinned from ear to ear.

"I did it." Sweat beaded across her forehead. Hell, it dripped. Everywhere.

He smiled. "You did."

Amanda lay on her back staring at the stone crevices above them that formed a ceiling. She wheezed from exertion but the exhilaration that flowed through her veins was euphoric. If she weren't in such a cramped space, she'd do a happy-dance. She'd hauled herself up the wall with no assistance and not one single tumble. Her chest heaved up and down as she gulped in air while her pulse calmed. "That was awesome!"

The rocks above were gray, brown, and pink—terra cotta was probably the accurate descriptor. They were darkened to black where the edges jutted down. She reached up. "Looks like there have been a lot of people here over the years. Don't rocks change to smoky black over the years from the oils in hands and body touches?"

Jackson was wrestling around beside her and until that moment, she'd not bothered to look his way. A piece of clear glass interrupted her thoughts. "Oh, you brought wine?" She blinked and rolled to a seat before taking the golden liquid.

Jackson nodded. "Yes, and a few other things to celebrate your new success."

"Success?"

He waved over the ledge.

Amanda sipped before glancing at a blanket covered with paper plates, cheese, fruit, and a mysterious Tupperware container. "How could you possibly know I'd climb up here without your help?"

He shrugged. "Okay, it was just dinner. I thought we should come back without the torrential downpour and see what else we can find."

Jackson turned his back to Amanda and filled a couple of plates, then handed one her way. "Fruit, cheese, and some ham. It's all I could throw together on a whim."

"Yum."

They ate and drank the wine in silence. Watching the sun dip further below the tree line was peaceful. The birds swooped over the trees periodically searching for a last-minute workout—or dinner. Their calls carried across the wind, a beautiful backdrop to the view.

Jackson poured more wine into her emptied glass. She peered through the liquid. This must be what rose-colored glasses felt like; looking through the world with a golden pink hue was damned romantic.

After a few minutes of sipping and enjoying the view, she reminded herself why they'd come. "The carvings on the tree have to be connected to this, don't they?" She ran a finger over the stick figures that sported the same phrase.

Jackson didn't shift his gaze from Amanda, which made her want another bird to dart by or a sound to distract him. "That would be my guess. It seems too much of a coincidence to have the exact same phrases in both places. What do you think?"

He was asking her to give a judgment but she hadn't exactly been thinking or acting logically lately. She'd done many stupid things—like staying up all night reading love letters between a soldier and a girl, and showing up at a flower shop to spy on their suspected daughter—or granddaughter?

"Logic tells me not to answer that question."

Jackson lifted an apple slice from one of his plastic containers and dipped it into brown, silky caramel. Amanda knew she was practically drooling as she watched. He lifted it, caught her staring, and changed direction. Jackson slipped the caramel-covered fruit between her lips. She bit down and he smiled as she closed her eyes in pleasure. "Forget logic for a moment and tell me what you really think. Don't talk like a lawyer with a vested interest. Be human."

What was that supposed to mean? "I *am* human."

Jackson leaned forward and dropped a kiss on her mouth "I know. You're a great attorney as well, but right now I'm not asking the attorney, I'm asking the woman. What do you think about all this stuff? Is it important to Dad's contract, or are we just chasing some nice little fairy tale because it sounds cool? The attorney in me wants to say it's all a bunch of crap, but the man wishes—"

"It were more? Me too. I want to think that if we can just find our soldier boy, the contract will all fall in place."

Jackson nodded and fed her another apple. "Or not."

She hated to wish for his company to lose a deal but something about the story made her heart ache for these two lost lovebirds. Had they found each other before she died? Was he still searching? "Maybe they actually *did* find each other and strolled happily around with their matching walkers in a retirement home somewhere."

A screech split the air. Amanda bolted toward the inside wall and stared into the shadows of the trees. Her eyes ping-ponged from left to right, searching for trouble. "What was that?"

Jackson spilled his wine glass as he darted around. "Sounded like a scream."

A booming male voice thundered through the trees and a few birds flitted into the distance above the trees. "Found you!"

Was that laughter? "You did, you did! Silly goose." That voice sounded feminine.

The trees shook in the distance.

"Silly gosling."

More laughter, and two figures burst onto the walking path below. Jackson watched over the edge while Amanda played it safe and stayed against the wall. Would they see the ropes? Would they climb up the wall? Amanda swallowed the massive lump in her throat.

There was no escape.

Amanda found her voice and whispered, "Should we pull the ropes up so they don't find us?"

Jackson kept his vigilance on the figures. "That would call more attention than just leaving them. I think they're gone anyway. They disappeared into the trees. Did you see the girl?"

He leveled his gaze on Amanda and her face turned pink. No, she hadn't seen a thing because she was curled up in a ball against the rocks. Okay, she was a coward. "Hey, that was a blood-curdling scream. They could be dangerous criminals and we're hiding in their turf. They could be armed."

"Well, the guy was walking with a cane and hunched over in a pretty scary limping sort of way. Still, I think we could outrun them if we needed to—the chick was wearing leggings that looked a lot like the ones our Caroline from the florist shop was wearing."

"Really? Let me see." Amanda crawled forward and peered over the edge. They were gone. "Let's go find them." She grabbed one of the ropes and clicked into her climbing harness.

Jackson settled a hand over hers while shaking his head. "Oh, so now you're brave? No. You'll scare them even more than they scared us. Besides, if it is her, we know where to find them without making a horror film scene out of this forest."

"Are you seriously not going to at least *try*? We might lose them forever. I mean, they've already been lost for nearly fifty years."

"That girl is probably under thirty so I doubt that. If you go running down there to find her after the wild-eyed jealous rant you made at their store, she's likely to call the cops on us."

Hmmm. "Good point. What do we do?"

"We wait. Do you think that was Jacob?"

"How the hell do I know? I was plastered against the wall, remember? You saw him. Did he look eighty years old?"

The sun had disappeared and the glow of its final shards of light silhouetted Jackson. Amanda could no longer get clear expressions from his features. "Could be. He moved pretty slowly."

"Slow as in old or hurt? Or slow as in scary and dangerous?"

Jackson snickered. "Don't worry, beautiful. I won't let him hurt you."

She raised a brow. "You know, I'm sure that's probably true but if he's hurt he can't climb, right? So, maybe we should just hang out here for a while, enjoy the food—and safety."

Jackson put his thumbs under his armpits and waved his arms like a bird. "Cluck, cluck, cluck, cluck. You're chicken, aren't you? You went from ready to chase them down to hiding out in a nanosecond. Make up your mind, Amanda."

She looked at the food, then at the man across from her with his arm slung over a leg. She wasn't scared at all. Hot and bothered, yes. Frightened, nope.

"We stay."

His eyes turned hot and smoky. "I was hoping you'd say that."

• • •

When Amanda woke hours later, the scent of candlewax was the strangest of accents to pine and dirt smells. The soft rise and drop of Jackson's chest underneath her head was comforting—just as the thud, thud, thud of his heart. The moon was full and had replaced the earlier sunshine, casting a surreal glow over the landscape below. This was the closest thing to camping that Amanda had experienced.

The thought of trudging out into the wilderness and facing heat, bugs, snakes, and other wild things wasn't her cup of tea. Nor was going a day without a shower and shampoo. Nope, her idea of a vacation involved a Marriott, a beach, and a spa. The worst experience in her mind was washing sand from the crack of her ass after lying on a lounger while waves crashed nearby.

Yet here she was, camping on a ledge above the trees in the middle of nowhere—at night.

With Jackson. And there wasn't a spa on the planet that could entice her away.

Her right side was warm and toasty against him. She shifted and he pulled a blanket over her shoulders with his free hand. "Are you cold, babe?"

Babe? To her knowledge, no one in her life had ever used that term in conversation. Not about her. Sure, he'd used it at the flower shop but that was just an act. This time there was no one to hear or impress. "Nope, not a bit. Kinda toasty, in fact."

"Good, we'd better get moving, then."

Amanda felt a lot better about doing so with the sun shining down and the shadows diminished. She glanced at her phone. Crap, dead battery. One of the pitfalls of camping was obviously lack of electricity, along with running water. "What time is it?"

Jackson, ever prepared, had a watch. "Seven a.m."

"Holy crap, we have work. Oh my God, they'll fire me if I keep disappearing like this. Yes, let's go."

Amanda ditched fear for urgency and scaled down the rocks almost as skillfully as Jackson. As they tromped through the trees, sunlight hit the trunks and emphasized something neither of them had noticed before: There were more messages scrawled into the tree trunks. In fact, as Amanda took in the forest, she stopped in her tracks and gasped. "Look at the trees."

Jackson stopped with his chest to her back. "Whoa."

There were at least six more trees carved with phrases. *Find Me. Found You. Love Me. Love You.* "Do you think it's some sort of game?"

He shrugged. "I have no idea. Do you want to go see where they lead?"

Amanda took a couple of steps into the pine-laden dirt, then stopped. She had a meeting at ten. What to do? She really wanted to go back in there and see more, but—she had a job to do. She shook her head. "No, I can't. I have to go to work. There's a meeting at ten."

His fingers rested on her shoulder and squeezed. "No worries. They'll still be there Saturday. I'll pick you up in the morning and we'll check it out. Okay?"

"Sure."

"Or I could just come over Friday and we'd get an even earlier start?" He gave her a shove toward the car.

He was inviting himself to stay over? It felt kind of like a step toward—something more. "I suppose you could."

Chapter Twenty-Six

Friday night seemed like eons away but when it finally came, Amanda was nervous. She'd rushed home after work and showered, then changed into yoga pants and a loose shirt. When would he arrive? They hadn't really set a time. What would they do? Her mind went straight to the bedroom and she snickered. *Get your mind out of the gutter, woman.*

He pounded on the door at seven. Anyone else would use the doorbell. In his hands were red boxes of DVDs. "Thought we could watch a movie and order pizza if you're okay with it. It's not going to torture you to stay in and take it easy?"

She took in his jeans hung low on his hips, and the T-shirt that clung to him like he was candy. Hmmm, staying in with *that* wasn't exactly torture. How was he so good at encouraging her to do things she thought she hated? Like rock climbing, eating pizza, and—she glanced at the movie label—watching horror flicks. Those were such frivolous and dumb things.

"Sure."

• • •

They left at six thirty Saturday morning and were in the trees within an hour. Morning dew coated everything in a glistening sheen. Their feet would be soaked in minutes. Amanda ignored the way her shoes made a squishing noise with each step and trudged behind Jackson. She loved the way they rolled as he walked. She could look at that all day.

The messages on the trees repeated themselves off and on. There were also carvings of dogs and other things interspersed with the words like a kid had spent hours there.

"Look, there's a cabin." Jackson pointed toward a tuft of smoke that rose between the thicket.

It was closer to a shack than a cabin. Judging by the smoke and the fact that the ground surrounding had been manicured neatly, the place was inhabited. "This is starting to feel like a scene from some horror flick. Why the hell did we watch that movie last night?"

Jackson snickered. "Guess I didn't think that through very well. All I was thinking about was the right kind of movie to get you in my lap, not scare you to death when we came here. Sorry."

"I'm a big girl. I can handle it. Besides, I took six months of kickboxing classes a year ago so if whoever's in there goes *Deliverance* on us, I'm prepared."

Jackson shot her a quirked brow. "Seriously? You took kickboxing?"

He acted like he didn't believe her. "What? You don't think I can box? I'm stronger than—"

"No, I'm just trying to imagine those long legs reaching up to snap a man's jaw. That'd be lethal. Sexy but lethal."

She nodded smugly. "You have no idea. Keep that in mind next time you think about pissing me off. Look, someone's stepping out the door." She grabbed Jackson's bicep.

A scruffy dog with gray hair, speckled with brown, scuffed off the porch and squatted in the grass. It was followed by a man in dingy coveralls. Yep, just like one of the backwoods freaks from their movie last night. She swallowed the lump in her throat.

The man limped across the porch, his knees buckled, and he grabbed a chair, then lowered into a disjointed recline. Okay, so it was a senior citizen version of *Deliverance*. Not quite as scary

She rose and stepped toward the house. Jackson grabbed her arm. "Hey, what are doing?"

She shot a glance at his fingers, then smiled into his eyes. "I'm going to meet our neighbor. Wanna come?"

"What if he has a shotgun up there and we startle him?" Oh brother, now *he* was getting chicken?

"No shotgun that I can see…and the guy doesn't look like he moves fast enough to hurt a fly. Neither does his dog."

Rover, or whatever the animal's name, was splayed out on the grass soaking in the morning sun that splintered through the trees.

"Good point." Jackson dropped his arm and followed Amanda.

Anticipation bubbled into her chest. Could this be Jacob Rickert? Surely he hadn't been here all along, hidden right under their noses—on his own property. That would be too easy.

"I see you coming, whoever you are. Stop right there." Birds bolted into the air above the house, startled by the voice. It wasn't him. Who had called out? Where had the voice come from?

Jackson's tap on her shoulder startled Amanda almost as much as the voice. "There's your shotgun." He pointed over her shoulder to a man in jeans, T-shirt, and tennis shoes standing in the trees to their right. The shotgun wasn't aimed their way but he held it all the same just to make sure they were aware of the threat.

Amanda hesitated. The man looked to be mid-fifties or later, graying around the edges but clean-shaven and clean-dressed. The T-shirt wasn't torn or tattered and the shoes were Nikes. Bad guys didn't wear nice running shoes, did they? She smiled though her gut was fluttering. "Hi! We were just wandering around up here, doing a little rock-climbing, and saw the tree carvings. Our curiosity got the best of us. We didn't mean to intrude." She didn't mention the climbing was yesterday.

"Where's your ropes?"

Busted. "In our car. We haven't really started yet."

Jackson stood at her side. Silent. Geez, he could at least—

"Actually we climbed yesterday and saw the trees. There was a girl running around up here with a man and she screamed. It was late and my girlfriend here got spooked. We just wanted to make sure she was okay. Have you seen her? She had spiky hair and I think her name was—"

"Caroline. Her name was Caroline and she's my daughter but she's not here. She had to work."

Jackson nudged Amanda forward. "I guess if she's at work, then she's fine. You guys live here? This is really remote."

The man squinted but left the shotgun at his side. "That's why we're a little careful. Mind if I ask who you are just in case I have to ask my friend here to call the police later?"

Amanda tripped forward. "I'm Amanda Gillespie and this is Jackson Holstenar. We're—"

"Attorneys. Or at least, *he* is. Your dad's name is Robert, right?"

"Yes, sir." Jackson kept walking and Amanda had no choice but to continue or get tromped.

"How is he? We were a little worried when we hadn't heard back."

Jackson darted a glance from the paunchy middle-aged guy to the old man on the porch who eyed them with an empty glare.

Following his gaze, the man with the shotgun grinned. "Don't worry about him. He won't hurt a soul. This is his place. Well, his family's place, but the rest of them live elsewhere." The dog lifted its head, took in the group, then dropped back to slumber.

Amanda found her voice. "Jackson's dad had a stroke and he's been recuperating. What were you expecting to hear back about?"

The man stepped her way and squinted again. "Robert's in the hospital? Which one? We need to go visit."

Jackson waved. "No, he's at home now. He just can't talk very well and he has to relearn a few things, mostly motor skills. He hasn't been to work in quite a while. I've been sort of taking care of things until he's able."

"You think he will be? Able, that is. 'Cause we're going to be in a big mess if he isn't."

Amanda couldn't stand it anymore. She had to know. She pointed toward the porch. "Is that Jacob Rickert? The soldier?"

The man gasped. His eyes widened. "You know? How'd you know?"

She rolled her eyes. "We're attorneys. Part of our job is to find people. Do you have a name, mister? You know ours but we don't have yours."

"Sorry about that. My name is Bob Levy Sanders. I'm a—"

Amanda gasped. No way. She strode forward and searched the man's face. "Oh my God, you're Bob Levy."

Jackson snickered. Okay, the man had said that part but what he hadn't said was, "You're the journalist who did that big piece on war veterans in *Time Magazine* a few years ago. It was amazing, made me cry."

Bob Levy leaned the shotgun against a tree and nodded. His face broke into a smile. "Thank you. It took a few years to put together. It was my wife's passion. I can't really blame her after what happened to her dad." He hooked a thumb toward the porch.

"So he *is* Jacob? And you're his…son-in-law?"

Bob didn't acknowledge. "When she became ill, I had to force myself to finish. We'd looked for him for years and the entire process led us to so many different men who'd dealt with all sorts of hardships."

"You told the stories well. All those men who'd done so much for our country and they were practically indigent when they returned."

Bob motioned for them to follow him as he turned toward the house. "Many of them were. Jacob, here, was one of the worst. His head injury—"

Amanda threw a hand over her mouth. The article had told a story of a man with several wounds from shrapnel, the worst of which had required surgery to remove a piece of metal lodged in his skull. "Oh my God, he's patient R? The man in your story with no last name?"

Jackson had been silent, trying to understand. "Patient R? What are you talking about?"

Amanda whirled around. "There was a man who returned from Korea with a serious head injury. He has a metal plate in his head. They did four surgeries to piece his face together and two to remove shrapnel in his head, hip, and leg but he survived. Unfortunately, no one knew who he was. His dog tags were lost at the hospital and everyone knew him only as Jacob R."

Bob's eyes clouded as he listened. "You have a good memory. I wrote that article five years ago. It took my wife and me two years to find out which hospital he'd ended up in. Then there was another two months of searching to find out where he went from there. When we located the mental hospital, we were relieved. At least someone who knew something about his injury was with him."

Jackson finally put the pieces together. "But he didn't stay there. He walked out."

Bob smiled. "Yeah, he walked out without anyone even noticing. My Carol was fit to be tied. Her dad, a war hero, wandering around in the streets alone with no one to care for him. We didn't sleep for days. She called every police station within five hours of the hospital. Oklahoma. Texas. She even called a couple in Louisiana."

Amanda trudged up the steps after Bob, who placed a hand on the old man's shoulder and squeezed. She waved into the quiet eyes. "Hi." He didn't respond, just touched Bob's hand and closed his eyes.

Bob walked in the house and held the door for them to follow. They did. When the screen banged shut behind, Amanda sighed. "Where'd he end up?"

Bob pulled a coffee container from the fridge, pried off the lid, and scooped some brown grounds into a pot. "That's the amazing part. He was right here. He walked his ass all the way from that mental hospital to this damned cabin in the woods. Can you believe that? The man can't remember a damn thing about his family or the war, but he found this house. *His* house."

Amanda felt tears welling up in her eyes. "He grew up here?"

Bob filled the pot with water and placed it on the stove. When the blue flames burst up to warm the pot, he turned their way and shook his head. "No, this is where he and his wife spent their honeymoon. Of all the places he'd been in the world, this place was the only one he could remember well enough to get back to. Makes you want to cry."

Damn right. Amanda sucked in a breath and willed herself to be calm. God, she hated being such an emotional rollercoaster rider.

"How romantic," Jackson said. He clutched her shoulders and squeezed. The tears flowed.

Jacob Rickert—patient R. A man who'd saved more than half his unit by acting as a human decoy to draw troops away as they searched for a way out of an ambush. He'd been practically blown to bits before they were able to save him. Several of the men with him hadn't been so lucky but he'd managed to save more than were lost.

Then he returned home, destined to a life of mental illness with no identity and no family to care for him. Until a strange woman showed up at the hospital saying he was her lost husband. She'd given up on him and married again, only to find him alive. He'd been declared dead at home, and on the battlefield. She escorted him away and he wasn't seen again for years. He showed up at the mental hospital years later. It took months for them to realize his wife had died and he was alone and disoriented. They'd searched for family with no luck.

Then he walked out and no one bothered to attempt to find him. According to the magazine, he had simply disappeared.

"You found him."

Bob nodded. "Yep. Those carvings on the trees? It was how Carol's mom would search for him. The poor woman couldn't leave him alone for more than a few hours or he'd start walking and trying to find her. They started this game. One of them would put *Find me* on first one tree, then another in order to leave a trail. When the other would finally locate the missing spouse, she'd put *Found you*. After a while he'd stick with the trees and not run away. Eventually he carved other things into the trees. You probably saw them."

Amanda's throat had closed up but she nodded. *Love me? Love you.*

Oh God.

Jackson's breath brushed warmly against her ear. "Are you okay?"

Water streamed down her cheeks. She nodded, then changed it to a head shake. No, she wasn't okay. Her heart ached for a man who'd lost so much.

The teapot, ancient as the house, whistled. "You guys want some coffee? I don't have tea but most people prefer coffee in the morning anyway."

Jackson clutched Amanda tightly. "We'd better go, sir. Listen, with my dad ill, I need to talk to you about a contract he was working on before he went into the hospital. Do you know about it?"

Bob nodded. "Yes. The archeological study."

"That's right. We can't close on this contract until we have that cleaned up. Do you know what it's about?"

Bob nodded. "It's about Jacob. Everything is about Jacob. And Caroline, of course."

Chapter Twenty-Seven

"We have to go see my dad." Jackson was missing something. "I think he didn't want this deal to go through."

Amanda's face had dried and she looked exhausted but still beautiful as ever. She nodded.

Jackson thought he had it figured out. The archeological thing didn't make sense but stalling on the property so the family could enjoy their last days with their war hero grandfather made sense. Why force the man out of his home and uproot his stability after such a hard-fought battle to obtain said stability? The man deserved more. He deserved to live in a real home with his entire family around him. His wife, his children, his grandchildren, and a thousand pets. Unfortunately he had lost much of that so this was the next best thing.

On the porch Amanda futilely attempted to neaten herself. These past few weeks with her had intensified every miniscule bit of affection Jackson had. Before, she'd stayed at arm's length, keeping her emotions sanely intact. He liked her emotional insanity better. She tossed her head back and flapped her hands in an effort to blow-dry her tear-stained face.

So fricking cute.

"What's the big deal in waiting?" She stepped off the porch and he followed.

"According to David, the client has several contracts that are backed up until this deal is done. They stand to lose money if things don't move."

He waved at the two men and stepped over the sleeping dog. A lot of good that mutt would do if an intruder showed.

The hound lifted his head and Amanda ran her hand over the dog's ears as she passed. "Why don't they just go somewhere else? It's not like there isn't a lot of other land available."

That was what he wondered too. "I know. I don't get it. That's why I need to talk to Dad. You don't mind if we go by there on the way back?"

She tripped over a stump. "You mean to your parents' house?"

"Yeah."

"Uh, I, should probably go do some laundry or something."

Jackson laughed and turned to peer into her eyes. "You're afraid of them. Admit it. You made an ass of yourself at dinner that night and you thought you'd never have to face them again."

She shrugged. "I didn't exactly put my best foot forward. They're gonna hate me."

Wrong. He put a hand under her chin and lifted it so he could drop a kiss on her mouth. "They'll love you once they understand the backstory. Who wouldn't? Besides I really need Dad to help me understand David's angle on this. Why's he pushing so hard?"

Amanda pulled him back into another kiss that lasted a few minutes, then sighed. "Why does anyone push on big deals? Money. Go figure out where the money is, was, and will be, and you'll have your answer."

Jackson wrapped his arms around her and squeezed. "Yes, counselor. I love it when you get bossy. Can we channel that for later when we get back to your place?"

"Does that mean you'll drop me at home before you go see your parents?"

"Uh, no, but nice try."

They walked in silence to his Jeep. He still felt like he'd missed something about the Rickert land. What was there left to know?

It took less than fifteen minutes to drive to his parents' ranch house. As he pulled in the drive, Amanda shot him a puzzled look. "Are we making a pit stop?"

"No, this is home."

Her eyes swiveled toward the three-railed fence and the field of bluebonnets beyond. "I thought your parents lived in the city."

He shook his head. "Nope, they have an apartment there but this is where they live—where I grew up. Since I was about ten. Carter lives down there." He pointed toward a distant roof. "Lived, I mean. You know where he lives now. His mother's still there, a great lady."

• • •

Amanda acknowledged her misjudgment when they crunched over the gravel driveway to stop behind a sprawling ranch-style home with Austin limestone walls and a wraparound porch. She'd expected a downtown place right in the midst of the social scene, not something remote and quiet.

A burly dog with white around one ear and black on the other bound toward them. Its eyes were transparent blue. "That's Titus. He's a blue-heeler mix. Smart dog. Watch this."

Jackson held up a hand. The dog sat. He motioned to the left, the dog walked—sideways. He motioned to the right, the dog backtracked his movements. Two hand movements toward the house and the dog had put his steps in reverse.

"Wow. He's well trained."

The front door slung opened and reverberated against the wall. They both focused on the porch as Jackson's dad came out, leaning heavily on a walker. He dragged his right foot but stepped with the left, then pushed the walker forward and echoed the movement. As they approached, Jackson's mother hovered behind to make sure no mishaps occurred. "Look who dropped in, Robert."

Robert Holstenar remained focused on his feet, ignoring their approach, but grunted an acknowledgement.

Jackson's whispered over Amanda's shoulder, "Last chance to run, babe."

Amanda planted a swift elbow to his gut and smiled. "Hi there, remember me?"

Lynn Holstenar raised a brow but kept her hands firmly planted on her husband's waist until Robert lowered to a porch swing. "Sure we do. Amanda, right? Carter's gir—"

Lynn's words stopped when Jackson strung his fingers through Amanda's hand and stepped onto the porch.

"How is Carter, Mom? Have you talked to him lately?" Was Jackson enjoying his mother's confusion?

Lynn raised her eyes from their hands to Amanda then Jackson. "Last I heard, he and his *girlfriend* had made a show at the craft fair last weekend. Did she tell you about that?"

Huh, what? "What craft fair?"

"Oh, please, everyone in town saw you two. Probably more of you than him since you apparently bared your britches."

"What?" Jackson dropped Amanda's hand and stepped back

Was everyone Jackson knew crazy? "I have no idea what you're talking about. What fair?"

Robert sat hunched in his chair. "Sssss…sssss. Sssss." Was he laughing?

Lynn Holstenar plopped down on the swing beside Robert and thumped his leg. "Stop that. This isn't funny. Can't you see what's going on here?"

Robert sucked in his cheeks and Amanda felt like laughing at his exaggerated I'm-in-trouble face.

Jackson crossed his arms and leaned against the wall by the door. "Exactly what *is* going on here, Mandy?"

Gulp. How the hell do I know? She opened her mouth to speak but thought of—nothing. How can you explain something when you don't even know what the something *is?* "Maybe we should let your mother speak as she seems to know the details better than anyone."

Lynn Holstenar's eyes narrowed and Amanda felt their laser-like sternness. "I don't know what kind of game you're playing there, sweetie, but this is my *son* and that other boy may as well be. Sure they're competitive, but you can't just hop back and forth like it doesn't matter."

Jackson rolled his eyes. "Mom, ease up. I'm sure there's a logical explanation. Isn't there, Amanda?"

Sure there was. Only problem—she had no idea what the explanation would be. Apparently she'd just left East Deliverance, Texas, with the injured vet and wound up in West Deliverance. There was only one way to handle her situation. Amanda kept her mouth shut.

Lynn huffed. "Just go grab the paper off the table and take a look. The fair's all over the community section with a real nice picture starring the two of them. Apparently they decided to get dressed up and take snapshots but ended up on the ground with her butt hanging out. Becky said it was the most hysterical thing she'd seen in a decade. Apparently you have some very pretty panties." More laser-beam eyes.

Jackson darted *his* eyes between Amanda and his mother, then shoved off the wall and disappeared into the house. His bellowing laughter preceded his return.

"Oh, my God. That is hysterical—and it's definitely *not* Amanda. Look, Mom."

Lynn peered at the paper where his finger pointed out—a dark ponytail at the edge. "She's wearing a wig?"

Jackson rolled his eyes. "No. She's not wearing a wig. That's Carter's girlfriend all right, but it's *not* Amanda."

His mother sagged her shoulders and Robert lifted a hand and patted her leg. "I'm confused," Lynn whispered.

"So am I." Amanda searched the picture where a giant green ape-like creature sprawled under what appeared to be a nineteeth-century saloon girl. Her hooped skirt was over her head and yep, her panties were vividly displayed in full color. "Wow, your paper's in color? All we get is black and white. Of course I never buy it because I can just read it on my tablet."

Jackson laughed. "Mom, don't worry. That's not Amanda. We came here to talk about the BookMyss deal. Amanda and I have been—"

"Amanda and you were holding hands when you walked up."

"Yes, what I need to know is—"

"You've never brought a woman here before."

"No, but that's not important. Let's talk about the deal."

"Yes, it *is* important. Why would you bring one of Carter's girls here if she's—"

Jackson growled and raised his voice. "I brought her here because she's helping with the BookMyss thing and, and she's *not* one of Carter's girls."

Lynn still didn't get it. "But when we met, you introduced her as Carter's girlfriend."

Jackson strung a hand in his hair and Amanda wondered where this was going. His patience was wearing out and obviously he wasn't ready to explain her to his parents. How could he? It wasn't like they'd really ever put a name to their relationship anyway. "I did, but that was before she dumped him."

Lynn focused on Amanda again. "You dumped Carter? Why? He's a great guy."

Amanda sighed. "Yes, he's a great guy. Everyone says that. I *know* he's a great guy."

"Then why'd you dump him?"

Jackson coughed. "Because she's in love with me, Mom. Now leave her alone."

Amanda's jaw dropped. "I am?"

Lynn echoed her expression. "She is?"

Robert twisted his fingers into his pant leg. "Ssss…sssss…ssss."

Jackson knelt down in front of Amanda and pulled her face to his. Amanda's stomach knotted. Was she?

"Look at me, Mandy. You know it's true. We've been trying for years to pretend it's not there but you know this is right."

Amanda wanted to believe it, but—"You set me up with Carter."

"That was the stupidest idea I've ever had."

He was right. She *was* in love with him but he'd never really admitted the same. He'd recognized her feelings, but what about his? Had he set her up with Carter to try to get rid of her?

"No, I supposed it was a nice thing to do. Set your friends up with each other. I mean how else would you handle it? What an awkward situation."

Jackson put a hand under her chin. "The only awkward part was seeing my best friend trying to kiss and make out with my girl. I wanted to kill him. I probably would have if you hadn't dumped him first."

Was he saying what she thought he was? "So, what does that mean exactly?"

Lynn Holstenar interrupted. "Yeah, Jackson, what does that mean?"

Both Jackson and Amanda turned to his mom and spoke in unison. "Shut up."

Amanda would have to apologize for that later but this was *her* moment and she'd have it even if there was an audience. She pulled Jackson's hair until he was staring into her eyes. "Focus here, Jax. What are you telling me? I need to know because I can't keep doing this weekend investigator routine with you if you're not—"

"I'm telling you I love you, Amanda. I've loved you since our senior year in college—it just took you running away for me to realize it. Thank God I found you."

Her insides did a somersault. Then his words registered. "You found me."

He nodded, not realizing what he'd said.

"Jackson, that's it! Didn't David say something about family meaning everything? Maybe he *knew* about Rickert."

Chapter Twenty-Eight

Amanda had to write it all down. She always thought better with a piece of paper and a pen. "Mrs. Holstenar, do you have a pad of paper I can borrow?"

Jackson's mother glanced at her son, then to Amanda. "What on earth do you need a pad of paper for?"

Amanda smiled. "I'm sorry I snapped earlier, but, well, Jackson was—"

Lynn raised a brow. "Baring his heart to you and now you want a pad of paper. Why?"

Jackson's mother was a tad bit on the caustic side. Amanda would need to get used to her comments. "I need to make a list, write everything down." Obviously she didn't get it. Amanda needed to piece it all together. "Jackson said it took me running away for him to realize, then he said he was glad he found me, right?"

Jackson stepped into his mother's kitchen and returned with a yellow pad of paper. He handed it to Amanda. She met his eyes, full of love, and nodded. Did he know where she was going?

Lynn coughed. "So far, you haven't exactly answered him either. For all he knows, you're going to write down the pros and cons of Jackson over Carter."

Amanda looked at the woman as if she'd lost her mind. Why would she say that? That was the dumbest thing ever.

Jackson laughed. "Mom, this is how Amanda works. Just stay with her and let her finish and you'll see what she means."

Lynn growled but Robert pinched his wife's leg so she kept silent.

Amanda turned to the paper and started writing. "Remember when we first talked about the contract? None of the stuff about the archeological find was in there. I wish I had a copy of that one because this would be over and done with."

Jackson smiled. "You and me both."

Amanda nodded. He *got it.* She leaned over and kissed him. "Yes, you and me. So. What else do we know? We know that BookMyss has a ton of pre-paid invoices from your company for deliveries of…what, exactly? I didn't really get that part."

Jackson shrugged. "You'd have to ask David."

Her eyes were wide and excited. "Right. And they're in a rush to get this property so they can build out a manufacturing plant. But that's the strange thing about this. BookMyss is a warehouse company. They don't actually *make* anything. They simply order, store, and ship products. They don't need that land and, to be honest, why would they want it? It's out in the middle of nowhere and not even close to a major freeway or airport. It would cost a fortune to build there, not to mention utilities and expenses would be cost-prohibitive."

Jackson moved closer and watched as she wrote down her thoughts. The scent of his cologne infused her with energy. She could feel his warmth and the words he'd just spoken fired her to keep going.

He tapped the paper. "You said, where's the money in the deal, right?"

"Yep. But I was wrong. This isn't just about the money. It never was."

Confusion crossed his face and she wanted to kiss it away because he just didn't get his part in this. "Come on, honey, string it all together. I left in the early part of spring. David took over the contract. Before that, who was working on it?"

She met his eyes and he held steady. He smiled. "You called me honey."

Oh, she did. "Um, yeah."

"You hate nicknames."

She rolled her eyes. "That's all you got out of everything I just said?"

He took the pen out of her hand and dropped it on the pad. "Nope, I'm with you…maybe even a little ahead now. Babe. You and I were working on the contract together before you left. David took it over. Then it got shelved for some reason."

Jackson nodded. "The girl at the flower shop. What was her last name?"

Yes! "Sanders."

"Liquor!" Robert Holstenar shouted, startling all of them.

Jackson frowned. "Not now, Dad."

"Yessss. Is bow liquor." He slammed a hand on the walker and it crashed over on its side.

Lynn Holstenar opened her mouth and gasped. "Oh my God, he's right. Jackson, he's not saying liquor…he's saying Rickert. It's about Rickert. And David. And that girl. Where's that damn picture?"

Jackson and Amanda both stared at Robert. Amanda had no idea what Lynn meant. Apparently neither did Jackson. "What picture, Mom?"

Lynn's voice took on a steely tone. "David's dad died in Korea. His mom struggled badly to raise four boys and he's always had a chip on his shoulder as a result. There had to be a connection. He was bitter. It was odd that he clung to something for so long. Said his dad had died a hero—but someone else took all the glory."

Jackson and Amanda spoke in unison. "Jacob Rickert?"

Jackson's mother shook her head. "I don't know. He has a picture in his office that was taken about a month before his dad died. It showed four of them. He said only one came out alive."

Jackson sighed. "I thought I understood but now I'm lost. Why would this have anything to do with David's dad? It's business, a real-estate deal. That has nothing to do with family."

Amanda scrunched her nose. "That land belongs to the man whom he believes killed his father. You're doing a deal with them. People will do just about anything for family."

"That's a stretch. The only reason he'd want to do that deal would be if he was trying to exact some sick sort of revenge. It doesn't make sense. Besides, if that's what he wanted, he could just go out to Rickert's cabin and wreak havoc in person."

Lynn gasped. "What cabin?"

Jackson stopped moving. "You didn't know? He's living on the property with Caroline's dad. The guy carries a shotgun and runs off anyone that comes around."

Lynn was still clueless. "Who's Caroline?"

Out of the corner of Amanda's eye, she noticed Robert moving his hands in agitation. How awful to want to speak but your body betrays you such that words can't be understood. "I think your dad wants to tell you something."

Robert mumbled something to Lynn and she nodded. "We need to go to the office. All of us."

Family is all that counts. Those were David's words. Amanda realized that in all the months of working together, she'd never learned a thing about him—nothing about his family. Nor about him.

She'd never asked. How self-involved was that?

It took an agonizing half hour or more to get Robert cleaned, dressed, and into the car. Impatient as Amanda was, she knew the time was well spent.

The walker would be an impediment as would the speech issue but she glanced at the elder Holstenar and knew he'd handle things well. This was what he did best. She may have never spent much time around him but she'd observed a few of his speeches at company functions. Enough to know she was about to see an event that she'd never forget.

Traffic was almost as slow as Robert's walker but once at the office, they all piled out. Jackson retrieved the walker from the trunk and lifted his dad to a stand. They both stared at each other for a brief second and nodded.

Lynn had filled them in briefly in the car but Amanda was still confused. She cast a glance toward Jackson who returned her gaze. His eyes still held a small cloud of confusion as well. Good to know she wasn't the only lost one.

Amanda was right about Mr. Holstenar. He strode into the lobby of their building with as much panache as possible. Hard to do with a walker that had tennis balls on the feet but somehow he managed. He sagged in the elevator but only briefly—once they reached the right floor, the man led the entire group to an office at the end of the hall.

Jackson rushed to clear the desk and hold the chair for his dad. So this was the executive office of the company president. Fifteen-foot ceilings, hardwood beams, floor-to-ceiling glass. She turned toward the window—and the most amazing view of downtown imaginable.

A strange beep brought her back to the new world. She hadn't heard that sound in a while—almost two years. They still used an older-style pbx system for their phones. "Glad to have you back, Mr. Holstenar," a voice greeted. "How can I help you?"

Jackson lifted a brow as if waiting for his dad to respond. The elder Holstenar pointed to his son and Jackson responded. "Please find David and send him into my office as soon as possible. Thank you."

"Yes, sir."

Chapter Twenty-Nine

It took thirty-four minutes for David to slink through the doors of the Holstenar's executive office. Amanda hid her smug feeling of satisfaction that he was finally about to pay for firing her—or "encouraging her to leave"—and misleading them all. Sure, it was mean to wish him ill but hey, what he had done was mean too.

In the meantime, Lynn called security and asked for something to be retrieved from the company vault. While they waited, Amanda's phone buzzed a message. She glanced at the screen, then looked up. Jackson?

This bastard's going down.

"Helloooo, David." Lynn Holstenar spoke first. Amanda suspected she chose to do so for multiple reasons. Because she seemed a tad on the controlling side *and* she wanted him to believe her husband fully recovered. That would put the fear of God in David, right?

David drew a long sip of coffee from the Starbucks cup in his hand. He'd stopped for coffee on the way? Not good. He kicked one foot up on their expensive-looking coffee table, then crossed it with the other.

Amanda bugged her eyes. "Hey. Have some manners."

David snapped his eyes her way, and narrowed them to slits. "What are you doing here?"

Jackson stepped forward and shoved David's feet to the floor. "She's with me."

David showed a split-second flash of panic but recovered quickly. Sliding up tall, he smiled and nodded at Robert. "Good to see you, sir. You look well."

Robert nodded and smiled but Lynn spoke. "Well enough to give you what's needed. Or required. David, it has come to our attention that you took on a contract last year that had been assigned to Amanda before she hastily left our company. This particular contract was to build a warehouse/production facility for BookMyss."

"Yes, that's correct. We split up the cases among the remaining staff and I ended up with that one."

Lynn pulled a pair of abalone-rimmed glasses from her handbag and perused a stack of paper in her lap. "How convenient. Tell me, didn't you think that would be considered a conflict of interest?"

David's eyes widened. Amanda forced her face somber but inwardly she was clapping. *Go get the asshole, Lynn.* "Why would I think that?"

"Because your mother has a vested interest in the company that has been contracted for the work. In fact, that company has already submitted three invoices and been paid for preliminary groundwork. Haven't they?"

David's mouth popped open. He darted a glance between Jackson's parents then to Amanda and Jackson. "I wasn't aware, I—"

Lynn tossed the stack of paper on Robert's desk and it slid a few inches on the shiny wood surface. "You seriously want us to believe that? Look, David, we already *knew* about your mother. We also knew about your father. Do you really think we wouldn't check these things out before we started working on a new project that has this sort of financial impact on our company? We can't afford to deal with deadbeats."

David readjusted in his chair then raised his chin. "Seems to me you can't afford *not* to. I've seen your financials for the past few years. You need this deal. Desperately."

Amanda darted a look at Jackson but he stayed focused on David. Was their company in trouble? Had she judged right in the beginning? It *was* about money?

Lynn sighed. "David, why do you think we hired you years ago?"

David blinked. "Because I'm good at what I do. I have a long-standing—"

Lynn held up a hand to silence him. "We hired you because we know who you are—who your parents are. Your father served bravely with a friend of ours. He was an honorable man and had it not been for his efforts, our friend would not have made it home."

That got his attention. David leaned forward. "Why didn't you say something?"

"We promised we wouldn't. Your mother said you had a chip on your shoulder the size of Mount Everest. She said if we gave you enough time, you'd come around. That you'd eventually see us as friends and perhaps even see our friend as family."

Amanda watched as a confused look slid across his features. "What friend would that be?"

Lynn tapped the pages. "The very friend that you're trying to kick off his land in order to make your mother a rich woman."

David's features stilled, except for his eyes. He blinked, Amanda could see the glassy look of his eyes. Was he close to tears? No way. "My mother has worked her ass off to take care of us without Dad around to help. She deserves better. She deserves to retire like all the other women and men her age. She works at BookMyss as a damn cleaning lady during the day and at the hospital nights. That's no place for a woman that old. The only good thing is the fact she was smart enough to buy into their stock."

Amanda gained a whole new level of respect for Lynn Holstenar when she rose from beside her husband's desk and grasped David's shoulder. "Do you really think she wants to be at home doing crossword puzzles and watching soap operas? She loves helping people, and you might want a better life for her, but I'd bet my socks she'd tell you to piss off."

David looked at Lynn's feet, then shot her a look.

Lynn huffed. "Okay, I'm not wearing socks so that was a bad metaphor but you know what I mean. The only person who's unhappy with our current situation is, well, you."

A tiny droplet ran down his cheek. "The one thing I remember about my dad before he left was what he said to my brothers and me. 'Family is everything. Take care of your mom, boys.' I was just—"

Lynn nodded. "We know. That's why we're going to go against your mother's request to keep this to ourselves and show you something that was found during the archeological study."

David swiped his cheek and stared. "There was really something there? I thought that was all just a ruse to stall the project."

Lynn laughed. "Well, you're right about that. What we found wasn't any big thousand-year-old Indian burial ground or something equally magnificent. Instead, we found things left behind by a soldier who honored the men he'd served with. According to his son, these men asked to be buried by the river and just happened to know someone who could get the job done."

Lynn hit a button on the phone. "Bring those boxes in now, please."

The door burst open and a squeaky dolly rolled forward with two aluminum boxes. There was a man behind pushing, but he was barely visible.

David ran a hand across his face. "What's that?"

Amanda wanted to ask the same question but stayed silent. She realized she wasn't even supposed to *be* here, but since she was a witness, she'd stay in the background.

Lynn snapped some latches on the top box. "This, David, is your past. Your father's belongings. You see, once we located Jacob Rickert, we also found these. They had been sent back with him to disperse to the families. Unfortunately that never happened. I'm not sure why."

David's voice was deadpan. "We moved a lot—it's hard to find a place for rent that's cheap and can handle four boys."

Lynn nodded. "I'm sorry that was so hard. But we found you and when Rickert *couldn't* be found—because he has an affinity for traipsing off and looking for his dead wife—we thought you'd be the right guy to manage that contract so that the Rickert family doesn't lose their legacy."

Amanda noticed that David could no longer meet their gazes. He stared at his hands, working them one against the other. "You should have told me. I tried to demolish him."

Lynn kept going. "Yes, but we wouldn't have let you. Like you said, David. Family is everything."

He did look up at those words and another droplet trickled down his cheek. "Your company *needs* that deal—you'll lose a fortune. My mother—"

Robert Holstenar chose that moment to slam his hand on the table. "No. F-f-f-famlee f-f-first."

The entire group jolted. Amanda was amazed at how well he'd articulated the words. His eyes looked fatigued but he'd sat through the entire conversation without interruption. Until now.

Lynn walked to her husband and squeezed his hand. "That's right. David, look in the boxes. Read the things your dad wrote to your mother. Jacob Rickert was his friend, and while he died and Jacob didn't, he would never have wanted you to ruin the man."

David shrugged. "The man's a vagrant who walks the streets and goes in and out of mental institutions. You think he really cares?"

"Not anymore. Not now that his son-in-law and granddaughter found him—he stays at the cabin."

"My mother could have *used* the money. Still can. If her company doesn't get this contract, she'll get laid off."

Lynn stood and squared her shoulders. "That's not going to happen because you are going to help us make this deal."

David's eyes looked hopeful. "Rickert's going to sell?"

Lynn shook her head. "Nope. We're going to revise the contract to encompass the tracts of land surrounding theirs and leave Rickert alone."

David shook his head. "They wanted the whole thing."

Lynn smiled. "I've already spoken to them and we've created a three-phase plan that will ensure that the last part of the construction, conveniently on Rickert's property, won't occur until Rickert leaves. In the interim, he will be paid a lease rate that allows him to continue living on the property but signs the property over to BookMyss upon his death."

David looked like he'd just been released from prison. "They're willing to do that?"

Robert smiled. "We all have family."

Robert Holstenar beckoned David to come forward as he pulled a frame from his bottom desk drawer. "For you, son." He pushed the frame toward David.

Lynn smiled. "We had it framed when you first started working here but realized it wasn't the best of gifts at the time."

David looked at a picture of four soldiers with arms crossed over each other standing in a field of dirt. They smiled. Amanda felt her stomach clench. Behind their lithe frames was a field of destruction and they had shovels at their feet. Holy shit. Were they digging graves?

• • •

Amanda and Jackson walked out of the executive suite an hour later. They held hands but said nothing. Amanda felt exhausted and it wasn't even *her* story. Inside the elevator, Jackson braced his hands on either side of her head and stared into her eyes.

She looked at him, embarrassed. "I shouldn't have been there for that. I had no idea what it was all about. I thought I knew but—that—was awful."

Jackson smiled. "No, it wasn't. It was beautiful. That man just learned that his dad really was a great guy. He learned there was a soldier still walking this earth who knew so and wanted his family cared for even if he couldn't do it himself. Do you have any idea how much that means to a son? We all want our dads to be good guys, good fathers, good husbands. We want to grow up to be those things ourselves."

Amanda blinked. "Not everyone wants that."

He sighed. "Okay, not everyone, but most."

Amanda leveled her gaze on Jackson. The elevator door dinged and opened. A man in a suit saw them and waved. "I'll take the next one."

Jackson nodded at the guy and returned his attention to Amanda. "Amanda, you need to tell me something. I know you feel it but I want to hear the words. I want to know that you're ready to be a part of everything we just saw. A part of me."

Gulp. Could she do that? Was she ready?

"On one condition." She definitely could. She loved the guy.

He raised a brow. "Nope, no conditions. Either you love me or you don't."

Amanda wrapped her arms around his head and melded against the body she knew could make her the happiest woman on earth. "I love you. Always have…but you have to get your family in order."

He stared at her dumbfounded. "My family *is* in order. We were just there, remember?"

She shook her head. He didn't get it—that was only part of his crew. "You have to talk to Carter. He's like a brother to you. You'll hate me someday if you don't make that right."

Jackson wrapped his arms around her and squeezed until she thought she'd faint. "Babe, I'll make it right, don't you worry. Family really *is* everything—and he's part of mine. So are you now. So get ready."

She cast him an evil glance, then pulled him back into one of his mind-spinning kisses. "No problem. I've got this."

More from This Author
(From *Text Me* by Shelley K. Wall)

Carter Coben arrived home after a grueling day at work and dropped his keys on the counter. He reached for a beer, then remembered his neighbor's dog, and grabbed a bottle of water instead. A quick glance at his watch showed enough time to get Ruckus to the park before dinner. Carter had no idea why he'd volunteered to help walk the dog while Maddie recovered from surgery. Maybe because there wasn't another tenant nearby who'd think to offer?

He retrieved the keys, stepped back out of his apartment, and trudged to Maddie's place. He rapped the keys against the door and announced himself before turning one of them in the lock, knowing she wouldn't—couldn't—answer.

"Hey, Maddie, it's me."

Crash. The tinkle of glass breaking surprised him only mildly. Without much exercise, the beast was bound to break something.

Drool flew from the massive boxer/mastiff mix's mouth and plastered the hallway as he surged toward Carter.

"Jesus, Carter, watch out! He's wound tighter than a drum today," Maddie called from the next room. Her high-pitched squeak of a voice always startled Carter, mainly because the voice didn't match her appearance. She wasn't a small woman. Her German ancestry shone through in the tall and equally hefty stature. Which probably explained the size of the dog.

"Hey, Ruckus." The dog pinned him to the wall, and he rubbed between his floppy ears, staggering under the weight of his paws on his chest. "You ready to go outside, boy?"

Another string of drool threatened to land on his pants. Pushing the animal away, he peeked in on Maddie briefly before leashing Ruckus and heading to the park.

Half an hour later, Carter's patience was shot. If Ruckus didn't hurry up and get busy, he was giving up. The mutt had already watered every piece of grass in the park and only needed to take a dump. Normally the digestive reluctance wouldn't bother Carter, but he was *not* skipping his dinner plans with his girlfriend, Amanda. He sat on a rock and flipped his smartphone open to the message onscreen.

App installed, do you want to open now?

It had been a crazy idea to try Justchat now. It was a crazy idea suggested by his friend Roger, which should have been reason enough to trash it, but the idea of chatting with someone anonymously sounded—easy. God knows he needed easy at the moment.

"Sure, why not?" He clicked and made up a login and password. The lengthy questionnaire that followed almost drove him to exit. Why should they need his life history for anonymous chatting? When he finally received a "Congratulations and happy chatting!" message, there was a tiny disclaimer at the bottom of the screen that probably should have been attached to the first question.

We try to pair our members with people of similar interests and locale. Feel free to skip any questions you wish but answering helps us find better chatting friendships for you.

He stared at the open dialogue box. What would be a good way to start? Should he quote someone? Hell, no. The only quotes in his head were too obscene to get a response from anyone worth talking with. Politics or religion? Nah, that could get ugly. He shrugged and began clicking away on the letters.

For years, I've wondered if there's really anyone out there worth meeting. I mean, I see people once in a while...and I think they're

It was a little dumb but fit his mood. He really should think hard about what he'd written since he planned to jump into a long-term commitment in a couple hours. Sure, most people wouldn't consider season tickets a commitment, but for him, it meant consistency. Going to the same event with the same person regularly. Over and over again. Hmmm.

He dragged his fingers through his hair and caught a quick glimpse of *the running chick*. He laughed.

Now he remembered why he'd volunteered to walk Ruckus. Her. He'd seen her run in the park every night after work. Sometimes he'd been out for a few miles himself. Others he had just been with Maddie as she focused on her struggles with Ruckus and the boot on her foot. The girl always smiled and waved, even said "hi" to Maddie, and petted the mutt. Never a word his way, though.

He had wanted to meet her ages ago—before Amanda. And he wasn't above using the damn dog to do so. She passed and the air stirred. Maybe he wasn't all that wrapped up in Amanda after all. He couldn't decide. Most runners bounced or plodded. Not this girl. In her running pants and tight jacket, the only description that came to mind was *glide*. Yeah, she glided across the ground in an effortless stride that was so smooth it mesmerized. She giggled at her phone as she passed.

Carter's phone dinged a response and he glanced at the screen. A message from *She Hearts Dogs*. How appropriate considering his legs were almost completely wrapped in a leash at the moment.

yourself for not coming up with something really witty or interesting and not completely moronic.

Yes, that's exactly what it felt like. Ruckus yanked on the end of the leash and charged after the runner. Carter lifted his legs just as the leather tore loose from his fingers. "Shit." He'd been busy reading the message and hadn't bothered to grip the leash. The dog was bounding straight toward—

The bloodcurdling scream surprised everyone in the park except him. He saw it coming. That was what happened when you wore earphones, turned your music up high while texting, and got attacked by an overly-friendly beast from behind.

When he'd noticed her before, this wasn't exactly the type of meeting Carter had intended. She lay on the ground, blinking at the sky and Ruckus, while struggling to right herself.

The drool didn't help. What the hell was he thinking when he let go of the leash? Oh, right. He wasn't. He himself was drooling. Only Ruckus's slobber was close to landing right on her face. The tendril of spit strung lower and lower.

"Ruckus! Come." The dog turned his way just as Carter lunged and grabbed his collar. *Whew.* The slime dripped to the grass and he yanked him off. "I'm so sorry. He pulled the leash from my fingers before I could stop him. Are you all right? Did he hurt you?"

Running Chick sat up and squinted, blinded by the setting sun at his back. She gulped in air and opened her mouth to speak but said nothing. She sucked in air again and held up a finger.

Carter thrust his bottle of water down. "Here. Drink. It'll help you get your wind back. Can you stand?"

When she took the bottle, he opened his fingers to assist her. She remained silent. Hmmm. He'd never been within fifteen feet of Running Chick before. He and Jackson had made jokes she was probably ugly up close. Actually, Jackson made all the jokes. Missing teeth. Hairy moles. Cross-eyed.

Wrong. Wrong. Wrong.

Seriously wrong, in fact, and somehow that was a surprise. It was hard not to notice when she sucked in another gulp of air, forced a smile, and handed back the water. She was better than he'd thought. Sooo much better. Carter blinked and averted his eyes to the dog. *You have a girlfriend, remember?*

"I'm fine. Just got the wind knocked out of me. Don't worry about it." Great. Even her voice was nice. Unlike Maddie's, it sort of rolled out of her mouth. Nothing obnoxious about it. "You wanted to play, didn't you, Ruckus? Ol' Maddie knew what she was doing when she named you, huh? You sure know how to cause one." She leaned down and patted the dog then brushed leaves from her back. Should he tell her about the two mud spots on her butt?

Probably not.

"Isn't that the truth. You sure you don't need some help?" Should he be totally embarrassed or thrilled? It had taken four months to get this intro. Since before Amanda—the girlfriend he was about to take to dinner to celebrate their three months together. Maybe he should have thought of the dog before.

He glanced at the time. "Oh crap. I need to get going, sorry. Can I help you get anywhere? Walk you home, bandage your knee, uh, strangle the dog?" *Check for broken bones?* He shook that thought out of his head.

She laughed. "No. Seriously. I'm okay. Go. Get to your date." She waved him off and jogged away before he could say another word.

. . .

Two hours later, Carter pulled at the collar of his shirt and tried to ignore the jitters in his fingers. He was about to make the first long-term commitment of his life and it scared the shit out of him. Was it normal to be concerned? He thumbed a quick text while he waited for Amanda to show.

Hope ur right about tickets.

Between Carter's workload and his friend Jackson's busy travel schedule, he hadn't seen the man in a couple weeks and texting was their only communication. Hell, he hardly had time to see Amanda. Work always intruded, and he was damn good at his job. Industrial Project Management hadn't been the path he intended but it worked out fine and he was a kick-ass professional. His new boss apparently agreed because he was scheduled to go on four trips to Thailand over the course of the following year. Four trips for what amounted to a four million dollar project. A good feather in his cap, and hopefully a big bonus in his bank account. Thank God the job change had worked out. Getting fired over a crazy woman's temper tantrum wasn't easy to digest, especially when he'd never had a chance to resolve her mistaken assumption.

He needed the money sorely. When his dad died, he'd taken over much of the finances for his mom. Based on what he'd seen the past months, she was in dire straits, not to mention bad health. He'd tried to convince her to sell the house and stay with him for a while, but she refused.

He dropped his phone face up on the table and peered out the Starbucks window at the people walking by, none of whom were Amanda. It had been a dreary day, but meeting her was sure to brighten it. Actually, the entire week had been dismal, for March in Texas.

Ding.

He glanced down as a message appeared.

> If she not like, u can take me.

He smirked and keyed a response as the door flew open and Amanda breezed in. She was beautiful, and it always caught him off guard. Too beautiful for him, if he were honest. He never quite understood what caught her eye, and he hardly blamed her when she often seemed disinterested. Which was happening more often lately—maybe that was the way things went in a committed relationship. Everything was going well for the moment, and he was simply glad to be with her. It was hard to believe he'd lasted more than a few dates. He'd come a long way on the trust scale and he was proud that he'd given it a chance.

He stood, pecked her cheek—mainly because she turned just before he reached her lips—and smiled. "Happy three month anniversary."

Amanda smiled and went through the order line before dropping into her seat. The gift sat on the table between them in a white envelope tied with a red ribbon. He had never been much for wrapping things but added the dash of color as a last minute whim. He was proud of the results of his effort.

Her eyes twinkled as she stared at the slim package. In fact, he was pretty sure there was a drop of water gathering in the corner of her eyelid. *Aw, she's getting all sentimental.*

Good, he was on a roll. Wait until she saw them.

"You bought a gift?" Her eyebrows dipped and her voice was stark, entirely void of the elation he'd expected…the first indication something didn't fit.

"Of course. We're going to celebrate. I made reservations for dinner at Sotby's down the street." Carter kept his voice cheerful but, deep down, his gut had started to turn. She seemed .. apprehensive.

The crowds clip-clopped past on the sidewalk, but at his table, time stood still. Music blared overhead, crooning at them to "cha-a-ange the world." Ironic, if he thought about it too much.

Her face solemn, Amanda slipped a finger under the ribbon and drew it off before opening the gift. She didn't pull the tickets out; she just slid the envelope open and peered inside. A shiver went down Carter's spine.

Someone behind the counter announced the arrival of a cinnamon mocha latte. Amanda dropped the envelope, rose from the booth, and retrieved her drink. She slowly doused the beverage with condiments before stirring it with a stick and returning. Coffee steam wafted toward him.

Ding.

Carter glanced at the phone.

She seen them yet? What she say?

"You bought me baseball tickets?" She plopped back in her seat. Across from him. He should have noticed that earlier. Not next to him in the booth.

"Yeah, season tickets. We can go to all the games. It'll be fun."

"Season baseball tickets together." There was no smile, no gazing in his eyes in response to his incredible thoughtfulness and commitment. Yes, commitment. Season tickets meant he intended to take her to *all* the games. That was commitment, right?

Ding.

This time her eyes also went to his phone and the message.

Well?

"To the Astros," Carter explained.

"Yeah, I saw that." She took a sip of the latte.

"You don't like them. I thought you said you love baseball. You watched all those games like a true fan," Carter said as she pushed the envelope toward him and shook her head. Had he really misread her that badly? Should he have listened to his idiot friend?

"It's not that. It's just—I can't do this, Carter. I mean, I like you—"

Ding.

She frowned at his phone display.

Come on, tell me.

Carter chose not to respond to the message. "But…" There was a *but* phrase coming next so he offered the word. Silently he cursed Jackson for the stupid ticket idea.

"This just isn't working for me. I'm sorry."

Ding.

Before he could see the screen, she plucked the phone from the table and flung it to the floor, where the screen shattered like a broken mirror. He didn't even get a chance to read the message. Then she rose and left. That was it?

His mouth dropped open and he stared after her. *Why?*

Carter scraped the pieces of his phone from the floor and dropped them in his pocket. He snatched up the envelope and ran behind her.

"You're breaking up with me because of the tickets?" The light turned and she stepped into the street.

She walked faster and flung an answer over her shoulder. "No, I'm breaking up with you because I met someone else."

Oh. Carter stopped and stared. She raced away then turned the next corner and disappeared. He pulled the mass of electronic debris from his pocket and cursed. His phone agreement still had six months left, and the only way he'd be able to replace it was—if it were destroyed. Now *that* was a commitment, a long-term phone agreement. Which he hadn't been all that satisfied with anyway.

"I was kind of hoping I could get an upgrade." He stuck his hands in his pockets and headed down the street to the phone store. An odd calmness settled across his shoulders. Why was he numb to the rejection? He had no idea. Maybe Jackson was right—commitment just wasn't his thing.

For more books by Shelley K. Wall, check out: *Numbers Never Lie*

Praise for *Numbers Never Lie:*

"Shelley K. Wall calculates a successfully suspenseful romantic tale with this digital page-turner. I loved the supporting characters as they added a fantastic depth to the story. I'm looking forward to seeing what else this author has to offer, and if it is half as interesting as this story it will be well worth picking up."——-Night Owl Reviews

"This was one of those reads that had it all: a heavy dose of suspense that kept me glued to the edge of my seat, enough action to make me want to scream out loud, and a lovely touch of mystery and romance.…Think John Grisham meets romance with a twist, with a touch of *Mission Impossible!*"—Harlequin Junkie

"Corporate shenanigans, betrayal and a happy-ever-after are all highlighted in this exciting thriller by Wall. Additionally, there's enough technical jargon to give credence to the story without overwhelming the reader."—RT Book Reviews

Bring It On

Praise for *Bring It On*

"*Bring It On* by Shelley K. Wall is a romance full of excitement and intrigue that will keep you turning the pages. If you want a fun, sexy, and intriguing read, then this book is for you."—Harlequin Junkie

"Wall's writing has the ability to grasp readers' attention . . . Hang on till the end—it's quite a surprise."—RT Book Reviews

The Designated Drivers' Club

Praise for The Designated Drivers' Club:

"Wall's latest will tug at your heartstrings with an emotional story of coping with death, managing family, and accepting love when it's being freely given. With situations that every reader can identify with—especially the difficulties of handling new love—this is easily read in one sitting."—RT Book Reviews

In the mood for more Crimson Romance?
Check out *Christmas Clash* by Dana Volney
at *CrimsonRomance.com*.